倍斯特出版事業有限公司
Best Publishing Ltd.

新制多益
聽力題庫

短獨白(附詳盡解析)

TOEIC

Amanda
Chou ◎ 著

四大特色

1 **影子跟讀設計：補強聽力專注力和聽力理解力**
獨家「影子跟讀」搭配填空題設計，雙軌修補聽力學習盲點，確實達到學習成效。

2 **獨立短獨白演練：搭配詳盡解析，迅速理解所有出題考點**
了解問題癥結和出題者思維，面對各種題型均能觸類旁通、穩拿高分。

3 **獨立短獨白模擬試題練習：精煉短獨白試題**
短獨白模擬試題規劃輔以解析學習，應考時實收學以致用的功效，考取金色證書。

4 **道地用語強化：提升各式新制題型的答題能力**
掌握更多道地慣用語語彙，臨危不亂地應對新制題「慣用語」和
「暗示性」題型，並一舉優化口語表達。

MP3

作者序

在一份最近的研究和官方統計中揭露了一項訊息，大多數的考生在考到各個分數段時，均花費了相對應的時數。這也證明出在語言學習上確實是需要一定時間的累積才會達到某個欲達到的成果。

這次書籍規劃包含最基礎的字彙填空、和反覆演練的影子跟讀學習，能確實提升聽力專注力和聽力理解力，而非本末倒置的學習，讓考生在面對獨白題，不論考試如何變化，均能受益於聽力專注力的提升，確實回想出問題點，不是憑記憶臆測胡亂答題，在考場中亂了腳步或忐忑地猜答案。

書籍中第二部分則設計了更進階的部分：了解問題癥結點，讓考生迅速掌握考題脈絡，靈活應對各個陷阱考點。最後則是短獨白模擬試題，考生在適應這樣長度的練習後，再搭配一定題目的練習即能攻略新制多益聽力考試，事半功倍達到考試成效。

正如荀子在勸學中提到「蹞步千里」的概念，學習是需要日經月累的。儘管市面上充斥著許多解題秘方或是鄉民版上遍布的一次就考到滿分，都沒辦法代表著在非英語系國家大多數學習者的學習路徑。也因為這些想法，接續了：能夠讓大多數考生都打好根基的學習規劃，使考生都能腳踏實地、一步一腳印的漸進式累積聽力實力，達到理想成績。

Amanda Chou 敬上

使用說明
INSTRUCTIONS

UNIT ❷

洞穴和國家公園

▶ 影子跟讀「短獨白」練習　🎧 MP3 002

此篇為「**影子跟讀短獨白練習**」，規劃了由聽「**短獨白**」的shadowing練習，強化聽力專注力和掌握各個考點，現在就一起動身，開始聽「**短獨白**」！

Caves have been explored throughout the history. In the prehistory time, they were used for shelter, burial, or religious sites. Today researchers study caves because they can reveal stories and details of the past lives. Cavers explore them for the enjoyment of the activity or for physical exercise, such as rock climbing. For people who are less adventurous, a lot of the most beautiful underground caves have been changed into display caves, where lighting, floors, and other aids are installed to allow the tourists to experience the caves. Caves are way more than just holes in the ground. Some of them are quite fantastic.

一直以來洞穴就一直被人們探索著。在史前時代，洞穴是被用來當作是庇護所、掩埋場，或是宗教場地。現在研究學者們研究洞穴是因為洞穴可以透漏出以前生活的故事或是小細節。洞穴探索者喜歡洞穴是因為他們喜歡關於洞穴的運動，例如攀岩等等。對於沒有那麼熱

022

愛冒險的人，也有很多地底下的美麗的洞穴被改為展示用的洞穴。在裡面會安裝燈光、地板，還有其他的輔助來幫助遊客體驗洞穴。洞穴並不是只是地底下的一個洞，它們有些是真的很棒的！

Few scenes on Earth are as awe-inspiring as gazing over the vast mountains, and the colors of the National Parks. Yet it is only small parts of the National Parks. There is so much magnificence to be found across the countries. Parks offer everything from wonderful hiking trails, photography and wildlife viewing opportunities, to stargazing or even boating. There is so much to do at any one of the parks, and it's a fantastic way to spend time with the family. National Parks are great for all ages. It's educational and most of all, and the serenity of parks makes for a very relaxing experience. Ready or not, the adventure is out there and within the National Park!

在地球上很少地方可以像國家公園裡那廣闊的山峽和美麗的顏色一樣令人驚艷。但是這只是國家公園的一小部份。在每個國家都有很多的美景。國家公園提供了從健行步道，攝影和野生動物觀賞景點到觀星還有航行的機會。在國家公園裡面可以做的事情很多，而在那也是和家人共渡美好時光的地方。每個年齡層都很適合去國家公園，國家公園十分具教育性，而且最重要的是國家公園裡的寧靜可以提供一個十分令人放鬆的經驗。不管你準備好了沒有，冒險都是在戶外，或是在國家公園裡！

023

「影子跟讀」練習規劃
反覆演練，潛移默化中強化聽力專注力！
· Part 1 規劃「影子跟讀」練習，練就反射動作，於聽力專注力提升後，能全數回想剛才聽到的內容和考點，分數自然狂飆。

段落「填空」聽力演練，猛提升字彙實力！

· 藉由填空練習，同步提升聽力、字彙和拼字能力，一次掌握所有必考常見主題字彙，一舉獲取高分。

UNIT ❷

洞穴和國家公園

▶ 影子跟讀「短獨白填空」練習 🎧 MP3 002

除了前面的「影子跟讀短獨白練習」，現在試著在聽完對話後，完成下列填空練習，從中強化生活場景中常見的字彙以及拼字能力，答案的話請參照前面的獨白！

Caves have been _____ throughout the history. In the _____ time, they were used __ shelter, burial, or _____ sites. Today _____ study caves because they can reveal stories and details __ the past lives. Cavers explore them ___ the _____ of the activity or for _____ exercise, such as rock climbing. For people who are less _____, a lot of the most _____ caves have been changed __ display caves, where lighting, floors, and other aids are _____ __ allow the to _____ the caves. Caves are way more than just holes in the ground. Some of them are quite _____.

一直以來洞穴就一直被人們探索著。在史前時代，洞穴是被用來當作是庇護所、掩埋場，或是宗教場地。現在研究學者們研究洞穴是因為洞穴可以透露出以前生活的故事或是小細節。洞穴探索者喜歡洞穴是因為他們喜歡關於洞穴的運動，例如攀岩等等。對於沒有那麼熱

愛冒險的人，也有很多地下的美麗的洞穴被改為展示用的洞穴。在裡面會安裝燈光、地板，還有其他的輔助來幫助遊客體驗洞穴。洞穴並不是只是地底下的一個洞，它們有些是真的很棒的！

Few _____ on Earth are as _____ _____ gazing ___ the vast mountains, and the _____ ___ of the National Parks. Yet it is only small parts of the National Parks. There is so much _____ to be found across the _____. Parks offer everything from _____, hiking trails, _____ and wildlife viewing opportunities, _____ or even boating. There is so much to do ___ any one of the parks, and it's a fantastic way __ spend time with the family. National Parks are great ___ all ages. It's _____ and most of all, and the _____ of parks makes for a very relaxing experience. Ready or not, the _____ is out there and __ __ the National Park!

在地球上很少地方可以像國家公園裡那廣闊的山峽和美麗的顏色一樣令人驚艷。但是這只是國家公園的一小部份。在每個國家都有很多的美景。國家公園提供了從健行步道，攝影和野生動物觀賞景點到觀星還有航行的機會。在國家公園裡面可以做的事情很多，而在那也是和家人共渡美好時光的地方。每個年齡層都適合去國家公園，國家公園十分具教育性，而且最重要的是國家公園裡的寧靜可以提供一個十分令人放鬆的經驗。不管你準備好了沒有，冒險都是在戶外，或是在國家公園裡！

1 短獨白「影子跟讀」和填空練習

2 短獨白情境對話和解析

3 短獨白填空對照

迅速提升口說、翻譯（英翻中、中翻英）等實力，練聽力也同步提升其他語言技能！

· 涵蓋各豐富主題，包含歷史、美食等話題，練聽力也無形中掌握各類句型表達，猛提升口說、口譯和翻譯能力。

UNIT ⑬

台南－蝦米飯

▶影子跟讀「短獨白」練習 🎧 MP3 013

此篇為「影子跟讀短獨白練習」，規劃了由聽「短獨白」的shadowing練習，強化聽力專注力和掌握各個考點，現在就一起動身，開始聽「短獨白」！

Tainan Shrimp fried rice
台南－蝦米飯

Some say that Tainan is the cultural and export center of the island. The city specializes in preserving Taiwanese culture, but was also once host to Fort Zeelandia – the Dutch port that was the primary city from which that country traded with E. Asia. Beginning in the early 1600s, the Dutch East India Company at what is now Tainan was trying to get a piece of the successful spice trade that Spain operated from Manila and the Portugese operated on Macau. The Dutch also recognized the fertile soils in the area and established European style agricultural ventures, growing and exporting wheat, ginger, and tobacco. From Tainan, the Dutch not only brought much spice and porcelain back to the west, but also untold riches to the profit of their Eu-

Unit 13 台南－蝦米飯

ropean investors. Today, Tainan is the second largest city of Taiwan. Inexpensive stir fry restaurants are found everywhere. A typical family meal – whether eaten at home or while dining out – might consist of three or four such dishes to share, plus soup. It's the classic Taiwanese alternative to the British fish and chips or the American burger and fries. Inexpensive, quickly prepared, and broadly enjoyed.

有人說，台南是這個島上的文化和出口中心。這個城市保有很棒的閩南文化，這裡也有安平古堡，這個港口是當時荷蘭定為主要可以與亞洲各國交易的城市。始於 17 世紀初，荷蘭東印度公司當時為了成功與占領馬尼拉的西班牙，據有澳門的葡萄牙爭奪香料貿易，而在現在的台南據點。荷蘭人知道台南地區有肥沃的土壤，建立了歐洲風格的農業企業，種植和出口小麥、生薑和煙草。荷蘭人從台南不僅把很多的香料和瓷器運回西方，同時讓他們的歐洲投資者得到很高的利潤。在台南簡單的小吃到處都有。便宜的快炒店隨處可見。一般家庭無論是在家裡吃或外出用餐，大概會有三道或四道菜一起分享，再加上一碗湯。這種典型的台灣菜就好像是英國的炸魚排和薯條或是美國的漢堡薯條。

1 短獨白－影子跟讀和填空練習

2 短獨白－聽選填和填充

3 短獨白聽寫訓練

(B) 因為沙灘被政府關閉。

(C) 因為颱風正逼近沙灘。

(D) 因為如果人待在沙地上，對身體有害。

32. 談話者說「我想我有理由可以買新的了」，下列那個選項是最有可能的原因？

(A) 她想買件新的泳衣。

(B) 她的雨傘壞了。

(C) 她忘了帶傘。

(D) 她的雨衣破了。

33. 下列選項何者最有可能發生在談話者發言時？

(A) 他們遭受暴雨侵襲。

(B) 很多人在海裡游泳。

(C) 雨傘正在特價。

(D) 雨衣需求量很大。

31.

· 聽到對話，馬上鎖定**As you can see, with typhoon coming soon, it's pretty windy out there.** …。根據typhoon is coming（颱風來了），以及風很大，推知不適合戶外運動，會有危險性，故推知you probably need to leave是因為颱風接近的關係。

· 此題屬於推測題，題目會透過暗示，讓考生推測出答案。題目：For those who are at this sandy beach, you probably need to leave? who是關係代名詞，those是指在沙灘的那些人。前面提到，with typhoon coming soon（隨著颱風逼近），因此希望那些人離開沙灘。

32.

· 從**My umbrella is…oops**，短短幾個字，可以推測出答案。**oops**有糟糕之意，因此推測出雨傘負面的結果。從第三句My umbrella is…oops，後面接I guess I've got another excuse to buy a new one（我想我有理由可以買把新的了）這句話推知雨傘可能無法使用，壞掉機率比較大。

· 讀題時先定位關鍵字詞是重要的解題技巧，因為關鍵字後常有解題線索，如oops就是解題重點。選項中(B) Her umbrella was broken.(D) Her raincoat was broken. 兩個類似考法，不過由於提到umbrella，因此得知答案是(B) Her umbrella was broken. broken在此是壞了，不是破掉。

33.

· 首先判斷此題屬於細節及推測題，發言者說颱風逼近，風很大，希望大家遠離海灘，根據此段話推測，大雨最有可能，再找出選項中表達大雨的單字或片語。It's really pouring here.是下大雨之意。torrential rain是類似詞，故正確選項是**(A)**。

· 推測題的答案，通常不會重複短講內一樣的單字，常以同義字替換短講的關鍵字。「下列最有可能發生」的題目，通常須要先理解細節，再以換句話說的技巧，找出選項中最接近對話細節的詞彙。另外也可用「刪去法」將可能是正確選項的範圍縮小。如：(B) Many people are swimming in the ocean.已經通知大家離開，沒人游泳。(C) Umbrellas are on sale.只提到雨傘壞了，沒提到是否特價。(D) Raincoats are in high demand.雨衣需求量沒提到。

聽力理解力到位，任何提問都迎刃而解！

· 詳盡解析、確實理解各類型的**短獨白**提問，靈活應對各個出題考點！

· 釐清所有**陷阱**或**干擾選項**、掌握關鍵**轉折詞**等，聽力答題實力迅速飆升！

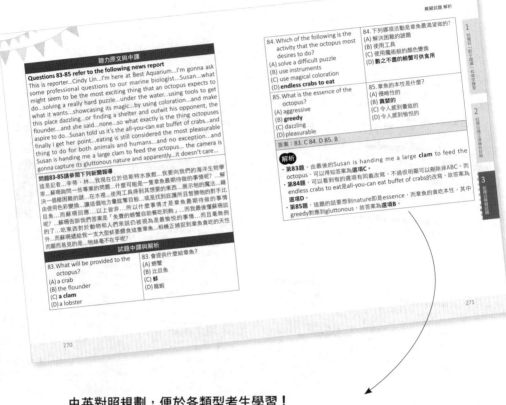

聽力原文與中譯

Questions 83-85 refer to the following news report
This is reporter...Cindy Lin...I'm here at Best Aquarium...Susan...what might seem to be the most exciting thing that an octopus expects to do...solving a really hard puzzle...under the water...using tools to get what it wants...showcasing its magic...by using coloration...and make this place dazzling...or finding a shelter and outwit his opponent, the flounder...and she said...none...so what exactly is the thing octopuses aspire to do...Susan told us it's the all-you-can eat buffet of crabs...and finally I get her point...eating is still considered the most pleasurable thing to do for both animals and humans...and no exception...and Susan is handing me a large clam to feed the octopus... the camera is gonna capture its gluttonous nature and apparently...it doesn't care...

問題83-85請參閱下列新聞報導
這是記者...辛蒂，林...我現在位於倍斯特水族館...我要向我們的海洋生物學家...蘇珊詢問一些專業的問題...什麼可能是一隻章魚最期待做的事情呢？...解決一個艱困難的謎...在水裡...使用工具得到其想要的東西...展示牠的魔法...藉由使用色彩變換...讓這個地方變眩奪目起...或是找到庇護所且智勝牠的對手比目魚...而蘇珊回應...以上皆非...所以什麼事情才是章魚最想待的事情說呢？...蘇珊告訴我們答案是「免費的螃蟹自助餐吃到飽」...而我最後懂蘇珊說的了...吃東西對於動物和人們來說仍被視為是最愉悅的事情...而且毫無例外...而蘇珊遞給我一支大型蚌要餵食這隻章魚...相機正捕捉到章魚貪吃的天性...而顯而易見的是...牠絲毫不在乎呢？

試題中譯與解析

83. What will be provided to the octopus?
(A) a crab
(B) the flounder
(C) a clam
(D) a lobster

83. 會提供什麼給章魚？
(A) 螃蟹
(B) 比目魚
(C) 蚌
(D) 龍蝦

84. Which of the following is the activity that the octopus most desires to do?
(A) solve a difficult puzzle
(B) use instruments
(C) use magical coloration
(D) endless crabs to eat

84. 下列哪項活動是章魚最渴望做的？
(A) 解決困難的謎題
(B) 使用工具
(C) 使用魔術般的顏色變換
(D) 數之不盡的螃蟹可供食用

85. What is the essence of the octopus?
(A) aggressive
(B) greedy
(C) dazzling
(D) pleasurable

85. 章魚的本性是什麼？
(A) 侵略性的
(B) 貪婪的
(C) 令人感到暈眩的
(D) 令人感到愉悅的

答案：83. C 84. D 85. B

解析
- 第**83題**，由最後的Susan is handing me a large **clam** to feed the octopus，可以得知答案為**選項C**，不過很明顯可以刪除掉ABC，而
- 第**84題**，可以看到有的選項有同義改寫，不過很明顯可以刪除掉ABC，而endless crabs to eat是all-you-can eat buffet of crabs的改寫，故答案為**選項D**。
- 第**85題**，這題的話要想到nature即是essence，而章魚的貪吃本性，其中greedy對應到gluttonous，故答案為**選項B**。

中英對照規劃，便於各類型考生學習！

· 聽力原文和試題均規劃了中英對照介面，方便所有考生觀看或對照學習，省了翻找等的時間。

多軌強化聽力，學習一次到位！

· 試題演練後，隨即對照解析觀看，並反覆利用聽力原文進行「影子跟讀」演練，多重強化聽力練習。

Unit **25**

電影工作室公告：解壓有道，讓員工玩玩水晶球、算個塔羅牌也無妨

🗨 Instructions

❶ 請播放錄音檔聽下列對話，並完成試題。🎧 MP3 057

73. According to the speaker, which of the following topics are the sessions about?
(A) astronomy
(B) making crystal balls
(C) fortune telling
(D) health problems

74. Why does the speaker say, "I benefited from that"?
(A) Studying astrology allowed him to find out his health problems.
(B) The palm reading gave him a chance to find out his health problems.
(C) He made some money from palm reading.
(D) Reading tarot cards has many benefits.

75. Which of the following is the closest in meaning to the phrase, "drag you down there", as in "It's really not my business to tell you to come to afternoon's sessions, and drag you down there"?
(A) make you come down to the basement
(B) The sessions really drag.
(C) drag something out of you
(D) make you go somewhere you might not want to go

聽力原文和對話

Questions 73-75 refer to the following talk
I know you probably work overtime lately, rewriting stories. It's really not my business to tell you to come to the afternoon's sessions, and drag you down there. They include knowing astrology, crystal ball learning, palm reading, and tarot cards. Definitely, don't get so obsessed with those things, but it won't cause a harm to get to know them. Last year, I did the palm reading and I found out my health problems. I benefited from that. Reading tarot cards allows you to get to know your career path or your relationship problems, and it's free.

問題73-75請參閱下列談話
我知道你們近期都加班，改寫故事。告知你們要來下午的會議和把你們拖到這來不在我的職權範圍。他們包括了了解星相、讀水晶球、看手相和塔羅牌。沒有必要那麼沉迷那些東西，但了解下其實也無傷大雅。去年我透過讀手相發現自己的健康問題。我從中獲益。解讀塔羅牌能讓你了解你的職涯走向或感情問題，而且是免費的。

答案：73. C 74. B 75. D

244

模擬試題規劃，「短獨白」聽力一次就上手！
· 漸進式掌握完整一回的短獨白練習，並隨即養成
  獨力完成新多益聽力試題的答題能力。

聽力模擬試題

▶ PART 4 ⓐ MP3 059

Directions: In this part, you will listen to several talks by one or two speakers. These talks will not be printed and will only be spoken one time. for each talk, you will be asked to answer three questions. Select the best response and mark the corresponding letter (A), (B), (C), (D) on your answer sheet.

71. Who most likely are the listeners?
(A) policemen
(B) photographers
(C) department employees
(D) audiences

72. According to the reporter, which cannot be found on the ground?
(A) unfinished burgers
(B) French fries
(C) precious metal
(D) coke

73. Why does the woman say, "not so tough are you"?
(A) to demonstrate the spirit of the reporter
(B) to get the applause for tackling down the criminal
(C) to respond in a mocking, humorous way
(D) to show other criminals that they need to be tougher

74. What is the purpose of this camp?
(A) tackle rattlers in the wild
(B) get the water by traveling long distance
(C) appreciate things and know about environmental conservation
(D) prepare more cotton candy

75. Why does the woman say, "I really shouldn't have fallen on deaf ears"?
(A) because it is the lesson she now learns
(B) because she has a hearing problem and she doesn't want to admit it
(C) because she never thought knowledge could be useful and someone told her before
(D) because her phone doesn't work

76. Which of the following can be the cure for dealing with the rattler?
(A) cotton candy
(B) raccoons
(C) rats
(D) rabbits

77. Which of the following items was received by the monkey?
(A) bagels
(B) banana
(C) cookies
(D) peach

78. Which of the following is not what the reporter jokes to throw at the python?
(A) bananas
(B) cookies
(C) sandwiches

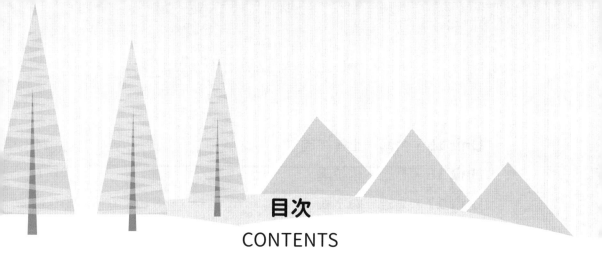

目次
CONTENTS

Part 3 短獨白模擬試題

- 【倍斯特商場】購物中心搶案，歹徒也沒多強啊！
- 【沙漠露營】沙漠環境保育營，不是蓋你，浣熊又派上用場了！
- 【叢林探險1】或許該丟些三明治和貝果啊！...或是我的餅乾（誤）
- 【叢林探險2】那些鱷魚以及巨蟒...牠們會對於我的鮪魚三明治有興趣嗎...？
- 【倍斯特水族館1】章魚到底最渴望的事情是什麼呢？有請專家告訴我們吧！
- 【倍斯特水族館2】章魚善良到讓我避開了目睹這血腥的狩獵場景
- 【晨間新聞 1】居民暗諷飛簷走壁博點閱，又不是黑雁！
- 【倍斯特航空2】在空服訓練學校的日子還頗悶呢！瞌睡蟲都找上門了
- 【倍斯特藝廊】不太好評論的藝廊四幅畫評析，有幅可能是老師繪的（暈）
- 【倍斯特慈善會】「父–子」的慈善會活動，好多大咖都要來訪

● 收錄包羅萬象的主題，從最基礎的段落「填空」演練到中階的「影子跟讀」練習，穩紮穩打練就基礎聽力專注力，並從中累積道地慣用語和必考字彙，最後演練口說、口譯和翻譯能力，一次搞定所有大小考試。

Part

1

短獨白「影子跟讀」
和填空練習

瀑布和湖泊

▶▶ 影子跟讀「短獨白」練習 🎧 MP3 001

此篇為「**影子跟讀短獨白練習**」，規劃了由聽「**短獨白**」的shadowing練習，強化聽力專注力和掌握各個考點，現在就一起動身，開始聽「**短獨白**」！

It always makes people's face light up when they come upon a waterfall at the end of the hike. It is like a special treat of nature, the icing on the cake of a good walk in the woods. It doesn't matter if it is a trickle or a torrent. People are drawn to either one for different reasons. Maybe it's the variety that's the real lure. And a single waterfall can be very different throughout the year and from year to year. On a hot summer day, they're a blast to play in. Nothing seems better when the running fresh, chilly water pour upon you from the waterfall on a hot day. Creek walking also allows you to get intimate with the waterfalls.

每當大家在健行的終點看見瀑布時，眼睛都會瞬間發亮。那就像是大自然給我們的特別的禮物，或是蛋糕上面的糖霜一樣好上加好的美好。不論是一個細流或是狂奔的流水，大家都還是因為不一樣的原因而被瀑布吸引著。或許變化才是真正的誘餌。而一個瀑布在一年之

間會有很多變化，每年也都會變得不一樣。在一個炎熱的夏日，在瀑布裡也可以玩得十分開心。好像沒有什麼是比在很熱的一天，被清新、冰涼的瀑布水沖倒到你的頭上還要美好。在小溪間行走也可以讓你和瀑布變得更親密。

A lake is surrounded by lands, and usually separated from the ocean and other rivers. There are all sorts of activities you can do on a lake, such as standing up paddling, fishing, tubing, wakeboarding, jet skiing, or taking a nap by the lake on a sleepy afternoon. You just have to be creative, and you will find out there is so much a lake can offer; even the mystery of Nessie, also known as the Loch Ness Monster. A lake also symbolizes calmness. Perhaps it's the glassy, mirror-like water, or the scenery you see in the reflection of the lake, the intangible tranquility you feel just in the presence of a lake is incredibly soothing.

湖泊是被陸地包圍，而且通常和海洋還有其他的河流分開。在湖上你可以做各式各樣的活動，例如SUP（站立式划槳）、釣魚、玩拖曳圈、滑水和騎水上摩托車，或是在慵懶的午後在湖邊睡個午覺。只要你夠有創意，在湖邊真的有很多可以玩的；甚至還有流傳出Nessie，或是大家所知道的尼斯湖水怪的傳說。湖也同時象徵著平靜。可能是因為像玻璃和鏡面般的湖水，或是湖水倒影裡的美麗風景，只要在湖泊面前就會感受到無形的寧靜，那是非常療癒的。

UNIT ❶

瀑布和湖泊

▶▶ **影子跟讀「短獨白填空」練習** 🎧 MP3 001

　　除了前面的**「影子跟讀短獨白練習」**，現在試著在聽完對話後，完成下列填空練習，從中強化生活場景中常見的字彙以及拼字能力，答案的話請參照前面的獨白！

It always makes people's face light ___ when they come ___ a _____ ___ the end of the hike. It is like a _____ treat of nature, the icing ___ the cake of a good walk ___ the woods. It doesn't matter if it is a trickle or a _____. People are drawn ___ either one ___ _____ reasons. Maybe it's the variety that's the real lure. And a _____ waterfall can be very different throughout the year and from year ___ year. ___ a hot _____ day, they're a blast ___ play in. Nothing seems better when the running _____, chilly water pour ___ you from the wa-terfall ___ a hot day. Creek walking also allows you to get _____ ___ the waterfalls.

　　每當大家在健行的終點看見瀑布時，眼睛都會瞬間發亮。那就像是大自然給我們的特別的禮物，或是蛋糕上面的糖霜一樣好上加好的美好。不論是一個細流或是狂奔的流水，大家都還是因為不一樣的原

因而被瀑布吸引著。或許變化才是真正的誘餌。而一個瀑布在一年之間會有很多變化，每年也都會變得不一樣。在一個炎熱的夏日，在瀑布裡也可以玩得十分開心。好像沒有什麼是比在很熱的一天，被清新、冰涼的瀑布水沖倒到你的頭上還要美好。在小溪間行走也可以讓你和瀑布變得更親密。

A lake is _____ ____ lands, and usually _____ ____ the ocean and other rivers. There are all sorts of _____ you can do ___ a lake, such as standing up _____, fishing, tubing, _____, jet skiing, or taking a nap ___ the lake ___ a sleepy _____. You just have to be _____, and you will find out there is so much a lake can offer; even the _____ of Nessie, also known ___ the Loch Ness Monster. A lake also _____ _____. Perhaps it's the glassy, mirror-like water, or the _____ you see ___ the _____ of the lake, the _____ _____ you feel just ___ the _____ of a lake is _____ soothing.

湖泊是被陸地包圍，而且通常和海洋還有其他的河流分開。在湖上你可以做各式各樣的活動，例如SUP（站立式划槳）、釣魚、玩拖曳圈、滑水和騎水上摩托車，或是在慵懶的午後在湖邊睡個午覺。只要你夠有創意，在湖邊真的有很多可以玩的；甚至還有流傳出Nessie，或是大家所知道的尼斯湖水怪的傳說。湖也同時象徵著平靜。可能是因為像玻璃和鏡面般的湖水，或是湖水倒影裡的美麗風景，只要在湖泊面前就會感受到無形的寧靜，那是非常療癒的。

UNIT ❷

洞穴和國家公園

▶▶ 影子跟讀「短獨白」練習　🎧 MP3 002

此篇為「**影子跟讀短獨白練習**」，規劃了由聽「**短獨白**」的shadowing練習，強化聽力專注力和掌握各個考點，現在就一起動身，開始聽「**短獨白**」！

Caves have been explored throughout the history. In the prehistory time, they were used for shelter, burial, or religious sites. Today researchers study caves because they can reveal stories and details of the past lives. Cavers explore them for the enjoyment of the activity or for physical exercise, such as rock climbing. For people who are less adventurous, a lot of the most beautiful underground caves have been changed into display caves, where lighting, floors, and other aids are installed to allow the tourists to experience the caves. Caves are way more than just holes in the ground. Some of them are quite fantastic.

　　一直以來洞穴就一直被人們探索著。在史前時代，洞穴是被用來當作是庇護所、掩埋場，或是宗教場地。現在研究學者們研究洞穴是因為洞穴可以透漏出以前生活的故事或是小細節。洞穴探索者喜歡洞穴是因為他們喜歡關於洞穴的運動，例如攀岩等等。對於沒有那麼熱

愛冒險的人，也有很多地底下的美麗的洞穴被改為展示用的洞穴。在裡面會安裝燈光、地板，還有其他的輔助來幫助遊客體驗洞穴。洞穴並不是只是地底下的一個洞，它們有些是真的很棒的！

Few scenes on Earth are as awe-inspiring as gazing over the vast mountains, and the colors of the National Parks. Yet it is only small parts of the National Parks. There is so much magnificence to be found across the countries. Parks offer everything from wonderful hiking trails, photography and wildlife viewing opportunities, to stargazing or even boating. There is so much to do at any one of the parks, and it's a fantastic way to spend time with the family. National Parks are for all ages. It's educational and most of all, and the serenity of parks makes for a very relaxing experience. Ready or not, the adventure is out there and within the National Park!

在地球上很少地方可以像國家公園裡那廣闊的山峽和美麗的顏色一樣令人驚艷。但是這只是國家公園的一小部份。在每個國家都有很多的美景。國家公園提供了從健行步道，攝影和野生動物觀賞景點到觀星還有航行的機會。在國家公園裡面可以做的事情很多，而在那也是和家人共渡美好時光的地方。每個年齡層都適合去國家公園，國家公園十分具教育性，而且最重要的是國家公園裡的寧靜可以提供一個十分令人放鬆的經驗。不管你準備好了沒有，冒險都是在戶外，或是在國家公園裡！

1 短獨白「影子跟讀」和填空練習

2 短獨白獨立演練和詳解

3 短獨白模擬試題

洞穴和國家公園

▶ 影子跟讀「短獨白填空」練習　🎧 MP3 002

　　除了前面的**「影子跟讀短獨白練習」**，現在試著在聽完對話後，完成下列填空練習，從中強化生活場景中常見的字彙以及拼字能力，答案的話請參照前面的獨白！

　　Caves have been ＿＿＿＿＿ throughout the history. In the ＿＿＿＿＿ time, they were used ＿＿＿ shelter, burial, or ＿＿＿＿＿ sites. Today ＿＿＿＿＿ study caves because they can reveal stories and details ＿＿＿ the past lives. Cavers explore them ＿＿＿ the ＿＿＿＿＿ of the activity or for ＿＿＿＿＿ exercise, such as rock climbing. For people who are less ＿＿＿＿＿, a lot of the most ＿＿＿＿＿ ＿＿＿＿＿ caves have been changed ＿＿＿ display caves, where lighting, floors, and other aids are ＿＿＿＿＿ ＿＿＿ allow the ＿＿＿＿＿ to ＿＿＿＿＿ the caves. Caves are way more than just holes in the ground. Some of them are quite ＿＿＿＿＿.

　　一直以來洞穴就一直被人們探索著。在史前時代，洞穴是被用來當作是庇護所、掩埋場，或是宗教場地。現在研究學者們研究洞穴是因為洞穴可以透漏出以前生活的故事或是小細節。洞穴探索者喜歡洞穴是因為他們喜歡關於洞穴的運動，例如攀岩等等。對於沒有那麼熱

愛冒險的人，也有很多地底下的美麗的洞穴被改為展示用的洞穴。在裡面會安裝燈光、地板，還有其他的輔助來幫助遊客體驗洞穴。洞穴並不是只是地底下的一個洞，它們有些是真的很棒的！

Few _____ on Earth are as _____ ___ gazing ___ the vast mountains, and the _____ of the National Parks. Yet it is only small parts of the National Parks. There is so much _____ to be found across the _____. Parks offer everything from _____ hiking trails, _____ and wildlife viewing opportunities, ___ _____ or even boating. There is so much to do ___ any one of the parks, and it's a fantastic way ___ spend time with the family. National Parks are ___ all ages. It's _____ and most of all, and the _____ of parks makes for a very relaxing experience. Ready or not, the _____ is out there and ___ the National Park!

在地球上很少地方可以像國家公園裡那廣闊的山峽和美麗的顏色一樣令人驚艷。但是這只是國家公園的一小部份。在每個國家都有很多的美景。國家公園提供了從健行步道，攝影和野生動物觀賞景點到觀星還有航行的機會。在國家公園裡面可以做的事情很多，而在那也是和家人共渡美好時光的地方。每個年齡層都適合去國家公園，國家公園十分具教育性，而且最重要的是國家公園裡的寧靜可以提供一個十分令人放鬆的經驗。不管你準備好了沒有，冒險都是在戶外，或是在國家公園裡！

大峽谷和日出

▶ 影子跟讀「短獨白」練習 🎧 MP3 003

此篇為「影子跟讀短獨白練習」，規劃了由聽「短獨白」的shadowing練習，強化聽力專注力和掌握各個考點，現在就一起動身，開始聽「短獨白」！

One of the best ways to peek at nature's wonders is to pay a visit to the canyons. Although there is just one that was named as such, the earth is home to many grand canyons. From very steep cliffs to extremely narrow valleys, each reveals a sense of wonder and magnificence while documenting thousands of years of geological history. Although each is unique in its own way, there are still must sees for any nature lover. But be aware, if you have a fear of heights, you may feel uncomfortable just gazing down at the canyon, or if you don't have enough gigabytes for your memory cards, you might be taking a lot of pictures. Canyon is a scenic wonder that attracts travelers with its numerous trails both the experienced and inexperienced hikers.

要窺視大自然奇景最棒的方法之一就是去看一些峽谷！雖然只有

一個峽谷是命名為大峽谷，地球上還有很多其他的大峽谷！從很陡峭的懸崖到很窄的峽谷，每一個都透露出自然的奇景和雄偉，同一時候它也為幾千年的地質歷史做下了紀錄。雖然每一個峽谷都有它特別的地方，還是有很多是大自然愛好者必去的地方。但小心！如果你怕高的話，你可能從狹谷看下去的時候會很害怕，或是你的記憶卡可能會因為你可能會拍很多照片而容量不足。峽谷是一個用很多步道吸引遊客的美麗景點。步道有適合比較有經驗的登山客，也有給比較沒有經驗的人。

Kicking back on the beach, a cold beer in hand while watching the sun go down is one of the many travelers' pleasures. But there's something way more rewarding about dragging yourself from bed in the pitch black and half sleepingly hiking to the top of a mountain or the edge of a cliff to see the sun rise in all its glory on a good day. You'll have the whole day stretching out ahead of you, and full of amazing adventures to be had. Or, if you are feeling snoozy, you can always go back to bed to take a well-deserved nap afterwards. Head to one of these amazing spots and be ready to be dazzled!

放鬆地坐在海邊，一邊享受著手中的冰啤酒，一邊看著夕陽西下是很多旅行者最享受的事情之一。但是在一個好日子，當天還是黑漆漆的時候，就把你自己從床上拖起來，然後在半睡半醒間健行到山頂，或是懸崖的一角，看太陽榮耀的升起，是比看夕陽還要更有價值的。你看完之後還有一整天在你眼前，以及很多冒險等著你。或者是如果你覺得想睡覺，你可以回去睡一個你應得的午覺。去最棒的地方看日出，然後你可能會因為日出的美而覺得眼花撩亂！

1 短獨白「影子跟讀」和填空練習

2 短獨白獨立演練和詳解

3 短獨白模擬試題

大峽谷和日出

▶ 影子跟讀「短獨白填空」練習　🎧 MP3 003

除了前面的**「影子跟讀短獨白練習」**，現在試著在聽完對話後，完成下列填空練習，從中強化生活場景中常見的字彙以及拼字能力，答案的話請參照前面的獨白！

One of the best ways ___ peek at nature's _____ is to pay a visit ___ the _____. Although there is just one that was named as such, the earth is home ___ many grand canyons. From very _____ cliffs ___ _____ _____ valleys, each _____ a sense ___ wonder and _____ while _____ thousands of years of _____ history. Although each is _____ ___ its own way, there are still must sees ___ any nature lover. But be aware, if you have a fear ___ _____, you may feel _____ just gazing down at the canyon, or if you don't have enough _____ ___ your _____ cards, you might be taking a lot of pictures. Canyon is a _____ _____ that attracts _____ ___ its _____ trails ___ the experienced and _____ hikers.

要窺視大自然奇景最棒的方法之一就是去看一些峽谷！雖然只有

一個峽谷是命名為大峽谷，地球上還有很多其他的大峽谷！從很陡峭的懸崖到很窄的峽谷，每一個都透露出自然的奇景和雄偉，同一時候它也為幾千年的地質歷史做下了紀錄。雖然每一個峽谷都有它特別的地方，還是有很多是大自然愛好者必去的地方。但小心！如果你怕高的話，你可能從狹谷看下去的時候會很害怕，或是你的記憶卡可能會因為你可能會拍很多照片而容量不足。峽谷是一個用很多步道吸引遊客的美麗景點。步道有適合比較有經驗的登山客，也有給比較沒有經驗的人。

1 短獨白「影子跟讀」和填空練習

Kicking back ___ the beach, a cold beer ___ hand while watching the sun go down is one of the many travelers' _____. But there's something way more _____ about dragging yourself ___ bed in the pitch black and half sleepingly hiking ___ the top of a mountain or the edge of a cliff ___ see the sun rise in all its glory ___ a good day. You'll have the whole day _____ out ahead ___ you, and full ___ _____ adventures to be had. Or, if you are feeling snoozy, you can always go back to bed to take a _____ nap afterwards. Head to one of these amazing _____ and be ready ___ be _____!

2 短獨白獨立演練和詳解

3 短獨白模擬試題

　　放鬆地坐在海邊，一邊享受著手中的冰啤酒，一邊看著夕陽西下是很多旅行者最享受的事情之一。但是在一個好日子，當天還是黑漆漆的時候，就把你自己從床上拖起來，然後在半睡半醒間健行到山頂，或是懸崖的一角，看太陽榮耀的升起，是比看夕陽還要更有價值的。你看完之後還有一整天在你眼前，以及很多冒險等著你。或者是如果你覺得想睡覺，你可以回去睡一個你應得的午覺。去最棒的地方看日出，然後你可能會因為日出的美而覺得眼花撩亂！

露營和健行

此篇為「**影子跟讀短獨白練習**」，規劃了由聽「**短獨白**」的shadowing練習，強化聽力專注力和掌握各個考點，現在就一起動身，開始聽「**短獨白**」！

Have you ever fancied waking up surrounded by nothing but nature and falling asleep under a blanket of stars? It is perhaps one of the best ways to enjoy some quality time with nature. Camping has started to grow on many people through time. Not only do the outdoorsy peeps enjoy this activity, but also folks who are not a big fan of outdoor activities. It has evolved into a more complex system where you may find luxurious camping styles to very down to earth ones. Whatever fits your needs, it will for sure be a memorable experience and a great opportunity to touch base with nature and your inner adventurous self. As romantic as it sounds, don't forget to check out the rules and possible dangers at your campsite.

你有曾經幻想過在大自然的包圍下醒來，在一片星空下睡著嗎？這或許是和大自然分享親密時光最棒的方法。隨著時間，越來越多人

喜歡露營。不只是喜好戶外活動的人，不喜歡戶外的人也漸漸開始喜歡露營。露營已經進化為一個複雜的系統。你可以找到奢華的露營風格，還有非常腳踏實地的，不管哪一種比較符合你的需求，露營都一定會給你一個難忘的回憶，而那也是跟大自然以及內在那個冒險的你再次聯繫的好機會。儘管聽起來很浪漫，別忘了查詢相關的露營規則以及營地有可能的危險。

Walking among forests, trees, lakes, rivers, waterfalls, jungles... with only a bag of necessities on you, you don't feel more down to earth than this. Sweats are dripping down, legs are getting sore, but you feel more aware and focused at the present nevertheless. Hiking is also a very popular activity to do, and there are groups of people who would identify themselves as the "hikers". What is so fascinating about this activity is that it doesn't require too much for you to do it. Almost everyone can do it, and there are a variety of trails for everyone to enjoy. Perhaps it's time to step away from our electronic devices and get in touch with your friends and your true self in the simplest form.

走在森林、樹、湖、小河、瀑布、叢林...等等之中，而身上只帶了一個背包大小的必需品，沒有什麼比這樣還要腳踏實地了。你的汗在滴，腳也越來越痠，但是你卻越來越察覺到周遭以及專注在現在。健行是一個很受歡迎的活動，而且也有一些人自稱他們為「登山客」。這個活動這麼吸引人是因為它沒有太多的門檻。幾乎每個人都可以健行，而且也有很多種步道供大家選擇。也許是時候放下你的電子產品並且用最簡單的方式來和你的朋友和自己聯絡感情了。

露營和健行

▶ 影子跟讀「短獨白填空」練習　🎧 MP3 004

除了前面的**「影子跟讀短獨白練習」**，現在試著在聽完對話後，完成下列填空練習，從中強化生活場景中常見的字彙以及拼字能力，答案的話請參照前面的獨白！

Have you ever fancied waking ___ _____ ___ nothing but nature and falling asleep ___ a _____ of stars? It is perhaps one of the best ways to enjoy some _____ time with nature. Camping has started to grow ___ many people through time. Not only do the _____ peeps enjoy this activity, but also folks who are not a big fan ___ outdoor activities. It has evolved ___ a more _____ system where you may find _____ camping styles ___ very down ___ earth ones. Whatever fits your needs, it will ___ sure be a _____ experience and a great opportunity ___ touch base with nature and your inner _____ self. As romantic ___ it sounds, don't forget to check out the rules and _____ dangers ___ your campsite.

你有曾經幻想過在大自然的包圍下醒來，在一片星空下睡著嗎？這或許是和大自然分享親密時光最棒的方法。隨著時間，越來越多人

喜歡露營。不只是喜好戶外活動的人，不喜歡戶外的人也漸漸開始喜歡露營。露營已經進化為一個複雜的系統。你可以找到奢華的露營風格，還有非常腳踏實地的不管哪一種比較符合你的需求，露營都一定會給你一個難忘的回憶，而那也是跟大自然以及內在那個冒險的你再次聯繫的好機會。儘管聽起來很浪漫，別忘了查詢相關的露營規則以及營地有可能的危險。

Walking _____ forests, trees, lakes, rivers, waterfalls, _____... with only a bag of _____ on you, you don't feel more down ___ earth than this. _____ are dripping down, legs are getting sore, but you feel more aware and focused at the _____ nevertheless. Hiking is also a very _____ activity to do, and there are groups of people who would _____ themselves as the "hikers". What is so _____ about this activity is that it doesn't _____ too much ___ you to do it. Almost everyone can do it, and there are a variety of _____ for everyone to enjoy. Perhaps it's time to step away ___ our _____ devices and get in touch with your _____ and your true self in the _____ form.

走在森林、樹、湖、小河、瀑布、叢林...等等之中，而身上只帶了一個背包大小的必需品，沒有什麼比這樣還要腳踏實地了。你的汗在滴，腳也越來越痠，但是你卻越來越察覺到周遭以及專注在現在。健行是一個很受歡迎的活動，而且也有一些人自稱他們為「登山客」。這個活動這麼吸引人是因為它沒有太多的門檻。幾乎每個人都可以健行，而且也有很多種步道供大家選擇。也許是時候放下你的電子產品並且用最簡單的方式來和你的朋友和自己聯絡感情了。

釣魚和瑜珈

▶ 影子跟讀「短獨白」練習 🎧 MP3 005

　　此篇為「影子跟讀短獨白練習」，規劃了由聽「短獨白」的shadowing練習，強化聽力專注力和掌握各個考點，現在就一起動身，開始聽「短獨白」！

　　Fishing is an ancient practice that can be dated back to 40, 000 years ago. Catching fish was necessary back then for the food source. However, in this era, not all people fished for food. There were also people who were just into the thrills of catching fish. It's the suspense of not knowing what you might catch, and the effort you put into while fighting the fish that get many people addicted. It feels like Christmas sometimes. You never know what presents you might get! The little taps you feel from the fishing poles and the patience it takes for the big fish to knock on your door are all part of the fun. Who says fishing is always relaxing? Back then, the fishermen would never understand why people caught fish and released them.

　　釣魚是一個可以追溯回四萬年前人們就會做的古老的事。在過去，人們抓魚是為了食物的來源，可是在現在這個時代，並不是所有

的人釣魚都是為了要吃。也有很多人釣魚是為了抓到魚的刺激感。也就是那不知道會抓到什麼魚的懸疑，還有你跟魚大戰的時候讓很多人迷上釣魚。其實有時後釣魚就好像是聖誕節一樣，你永遠都不知道你會拿到什麼禮物！釣魚桿上你感覺到的輕敲，還有要等候大魚來敲門的耐心也都是釣魚好玩的一部分。誰說釣魚一定是很輕鬆的？在以前的時候，漁夫一定不會瞭解怎麼現在會有人抓到魚又釋放掉魚。

It is said that when yoga was first invented, it was designed as a warm up for the long-hour meditation to come. However, to many people, yoga is more than that. After twisting and turning your body and mind as much as you can, you learned to be more focused and flexible. It's an exercise not only for your body, but also for your mind and soul. Somewhere between inhaling and exhaling, the loads of the worries on your mind quietly unload and instead peace sneaks in your heart gently. Also, focusing in the present is something that is literally practiced within such exercise.

據說一開始發明瑜珈的時候，它是為了接下來長時間的靜坐所設計出的暖身運動。但是對很多人來說瑜伽不只是那樣而已。在你盡力地扭轉你的身心之後，你會變得更專注和更柔軟。這個練習不止是針對身體而已，還有你的頭腦和心靈。大約在吸氣吐氣之間的某處，你心裡沈重的煩惱都默默地在那裡卸貨，而平靜則悄悄的湧上心頭。還有就是，專注在當下也是瑜珈確實在練習的一件事。

釣魚和瑜珈

▶ 影子跟讀「短獨白填空」練習 🎧 MP3 005

　　除了前面的**「影子跟讀短獨白練習」**，現在試著在聽完對話後，完成下列填空練習，從中強化生活場景中常見的字彙以及拼字能力，答案的話請參照前面的獨白！

　　_____ is an _____ practice that can be dated back ___ 40, 000 years ago. Catching fish was _____ back then ___ the food source. However, in this era, not all people fished for food. There were also people who were just ___ the_____ of catching fish. It's the _____ ___ not knowing what you might catch, and the effort you put ___ while fighting the fish that get many people _____. It feels like _____ sometimes. You never know what _____ you might get! The little taps you feel from the fishing poles and the _____ it takes for the big fish to knock ___ your door are all part ___ the fun. Who says fishing is always relaxing? Back then, the _____ would never _____ why people caught fish and _____ them.

　　釣魚是一個可以追溯回四萬年前人們就會做的古老的事。在過

去，人們抓魚是為了食物的來源，可是在現在這個時代，並不是所有的人釣魚都是為了要吃。也有很多人釣魚是為了抓到魚的刺激感。也就是那不知道會抓到什麼魚的懸疑，還有你跟魚大戰的時候讓很多人迷上釣魚。其實有時後釣魚就好像是聖誕節一樣，你永遠都不知道你會拿到什麼禮物！釣魚桿上你感覺到的輕敲，還有要等候大魚來敲門的耐心也都是釣魚好玩的一部分。誰說釣魚一定是很輕鬆的？在以前的時候，漁夫一定不會瞭解怎麼現在會有人抓到魚又釋放掉魚。

It is said that when yoga was first _____, it was _____ ___ a warm up ___ the long-hour _____ to come. However, to many people, yoga is more than that. After _____ and turning your body and mind as much as you can, you learned ___ be more focused and _____. It's an exercise not only for your body, but also for your mind and soul. Somewhere between _____ and exhaling, the loads of the _____ on your mind quietly unload and instead _____ sneaks ___ your heart gently. Also, _____ in the present is something that is _____ practiced _____ such exercise.

據說一開始發明瑜珈的時候，它是為了接下來長時間的靜坐所設計出的暖身運動。但是對很多人來說瑜伽不只是那樣而已。在你盡力地扭轉你的身心之後，你會變得更專注和更柔軟。這個練習不止是針對身體而已，還有你的頭腦和心靈。大約在吸氣吐氣之間的某處，你心裡沈重的煩惱都默默地在那裡卸貨，而平靜則悄悄的湧上心頭。還有就是，專注在當下也是瑜珈確實在練習的一件事。

UNIT ❻

運動和水上運動

　　此篇為**「影子跟讀短獨白練習」**，規劃了由聽**「短獨白」**的shadowing練習，強化聽力專注力和掌握各個考點，現在就一起動身，開始聽**「短獨白」**！

　　Sports are very popular worldwide. Can you imagine while you grow up playing basketball, other kids on the other side of the world grow up surfing or skiing? It may sound bizarre when you meet people that have never heard of your favorite sport before, but likewise, they cannot believe you don't know their sports, either. It usually results from the natural settings of the country. Nevertheless, it is fun to keep the varieties in the world. When you go traveling, sports games are something that you can either enjoy watching or playing. Who says a smile is the only universal language? Sports can serve the same purpose as well. You just might meet your best friend playing a sport together somewhere far away from home.

　　全世界都很喜歡運動。你可以想像當你從小打籃球長大的時候，在世界的另一邊，其他小孩是衝浪長大或是滑雪長大的嗎？你可能會

覺得很奇怪當你遇到有人沒聽過你最喜歡的運動是什麼，可是一樣的，他們可能也不敢相信你不知道怎麼玩他們的運動。這有可能是因為地域自然場景的不同。但是讓世界各地有不一樣的運動也很好玩啊。當你旅行的時候就可以看不一樣的運動比賽或是玩不一樣的運動。誰說只有微笑是世界共通的語言？我覺得運動也是一樣的。你可能會在離家很遠的地方遇到你最好的朋友！

Did you know that there is about 71 percent of the earth's surface is water and only 29 percent is land-covered? With around 7.3 billion people living on earth, we started to expand our playground towards the water. There are all sorts of activities we can do in the water, and with some practice, many more people are introduced to such sports. Almost all of us have wonderful memories playing in the water. Be it swimming, snorkeling, or sailing, people are always drawn to the ocean. However, when you are in the water, make sure you know your limit and risks before you enter the water.

你知道地球表面有百分之七十　都是水嗎？只有百分之二十九是陸地。而陸地上有大約七十三億人口，所以我們就開始朝著水源開闊我們可以玩耍的地方。在水裡我們可以做很多不一樣的活動，而在多家練習之後，越來越多人開始了水上活動。我們幾乎在水上玩耍都有很好的回憶，不管是游泳、浮潛，還是風帆，大家總是被水吸引。但是當你在水裡的時候，要知道自己的極限在那裡，還有在下水前知道潛在的風險是什麼。

運動和水上運動

▶▶ 影子跟讀「短獨白填空」練習　🎧 MP3 006

除了前面的**「影子跟讀短獨白練習」**，現在試著在聽完對話後，完成下列填空練習，從中強化生活場景中常見的字彙以及拼字能力，答案的話請參照前面的獨白！

Sports are very _____ worldwide. Can you imagine while you grow ____ playing _____, other kids ____ the other side of the world grow up surfing or skiing? It may sound _____ when you meet people that have never heard ____ your _____ sport before, but likewise, they cannot believe you don't know their sports, either. It usually results ____ the _____ settings of the country. Nevertheless, it is fun to keep the _____ in the world. When you go _____, sports games are something that you can either enjoy _____ or playing. Who says a smile is the only _____ language? Sports can serve the _____ purpose ____ well. You just might _____ your best friend playing a sport _____ somewhere far away ____ home.

全世界都很喜歡運動。你可以想像當你從小打籃球長大的時候，在世界的另一邊，其他小孩是衝浪長大或是滑雪長大的嗎？你可能會

覺得很奇怪當你遇到有人沒聽過你最喜歡的運動是什麼，可是一樣的，他們可能也不敢相信你不知道怎麼玩他們的運動。這有可能是因為地域自然場景的不同。但是讓世界各地有不一樣的運動也很好玩啊。當你旅行的時候就可以看不一樣的運動比賽或是玩不一樣的運動。誰說只有微笑是世界共通的語言？我覺得運動也是一樣的。你可能會在離家很遠的地方遇到你最好的朋友！

Did you know that there is about 71 percent of the earth's _____ is water and only 29 percent is land-covered? ___ around 7.3 billion people living ___ earth, we started to _____ our _____ towards the water. There are all sorts of activities we can do ___ the water, and with some _____, many more people are _____ ___ such sports. Almost all of us have _____ _____ playing in the water. Be it swimming, snorkeling, or sailing, people are always drawn ___ the ocean. However, when you are in the water, make sure you know your _____ and _____ before you enter the water.

你知道地球表面有百分之七十一都是水嗎？只有百分之二十九是陸地。而陸地上有大約七十三億人口，所以我們就開始朝著水源開闊我們可以玩耍的地方。在水裡我們可以做很多不一樣的活動，而在多家練習之後，越來越多人開始了水上活動。我們幾乎在水上玩耍都有很好的回憶，不管是游泳、浮潛，還是風帆，大家總是被水吸引。但是當你在水裡的時候，要知道自己的極限在那裡，還有在下水前知道潛在的風險是什麼。

音樂和節慶

▶▶ 影子跟讀「短獨白」練習　🎧 MP3 007

　　此篇為「影子跟讀短獨白練習」，規劃了由聽「短獨白」的shadowing練習，強化聽力專注力和掌握各個考點，現在就一起動身，開始聽「短獨白」！

　　Music is one of those magical things that can bring you to an entirely different place instantly. Sounds bizarre and wild, but we all have the experience when you put on your earphones and certain songs take you down memory lane. The reason is because music is such a unique creation and no two songs are exactly the same (also with the great help of copyright). When you are traveling, you come across different types of music, and different melodies. It is the music that connects you and the memories you have when you travel. The lyrics, the rhythm, and the tone of a song say a lot about the place. In a way, it is a great way to travel around the world within an hour. Start collecting the music you encounter on the road, just in case you want to go back from time to time.

　　音樂是那些可以瞬間帶你到別的空間的神奇事物之一，聽起來很

詭異又很狂野，可是我們都有在戴上耳機之後，某首歌曲帶我們回到某個回憶的經驗。原因是因為音樂是一個很獨特的創作，而且世界上沒有兩首歌是完全一模一樣的（加上還有智慧財產權的幫忙）。你在旅行的時候可能會遇到不一樣種類的音樂，和不一樣的旋律。就是那些音樂連結了你和你旅行的時候的回憶。歌詞、節奏，還有曲調都跟我們說了很多關於這個地方的事情。在某方面來說，這是一個在一個小時內環遊世界很好的辦法。開始搜集你旅行的時候遇到的音樂吧，以免有的時候你想要再回到那個地方。

The smell of the candy shop, the cheering words people wish upon each other and just the joyful spirits everyone is showing in the festival are enough to make a festival fun. Festivals are usually celebrations with specific purposes. It could be religious or used as commemoration; the purposes vary in each case. Nevertheless, they could just be the excuses people made up to have fun since what these festivals hold in common is the fact that festivals are always fun-guaranteed. Big feasts, breathtaking fireworks, festive music and dance, and the fun atmosphere are just all over the place.

糖果店裡的味道，大家互相祝福的話語，還有大家高興的精神就已經足夠讓一個節日好玩了！節日通常都是因為慶祝某個原因而誕生，可能是宗教的因素，又或者是用來紀念某一件事；每個節日背後的原因都不大一樣。但是也有可能是大家為了要玩樂所編出來的藉口啦。因為所有節日的共同點就是他們都幾乎是保證好玩的。大餐、令人驚嘆的煙火、節慶的音樂和舞蹈，到處都是的歡樂氣氛。

音樂和節慶

▶▶ 影子跟讀「短獨白填空」練習　🎧 MP3 007

　　除了前面的「**影子跟讀短獨白練習**」，現在試著在聽完對話後，完成下列填空練習，從中強化生活場景中常見的字彙以及拼字能力，答案的話請參照前面的獨白！

　　Music is one of those _____ things that can bring you ____ an entirely different place _____. Sounds bizarre and wild, but we all have the experience when you put ____ your _____ and certain songs take you down _____ lane. The reason is because music is such a unique _____ and no two songs are _____ the same (also with the great help ____ copyright). When you are _____, you come ____ different types of music, and different _____. It is the music that _____ you and the memories you have when you _____. The _____, the rhythm, and the _____ of a song say a lot ____ the place. In a way, it is a great way ____ travel around the world within an hour. Start _____ the music you _____ ____ the road, just in case you want to go back ____ time to time.

　　音樂是那些可以瞬間帶你到別的空間的神奇事物之一，聽起來很詭異又很狂野，可是我們都有在戴上耳機之後，某首歌曲帶我們回到某個回憶的經驗。原因是因為音樂是一個很獨特的創作，而且世界上沒有兩首歌是完全一模一樣的（加上還有智慧財產權的幫忙）。你在旅行的時候可能會遇到不一樣種類的音樂，和不一樣的旋律。就是那些音樂連結了你和你旅行的時候的回憶。歌詞、節奏，還有曲調都跟我們說了很多關於這個地方的事情。在某方面來說，這是一個在一個小時內環遊世界很好的辦法。開始搜集你旅行的時候遇到的音樂吧，以免有的時候你想要再回到那個地方。

The _____ of the candy shop, the _____ words people wish ___ each other and just the _____ spirits everyone is showing ___ the _____ are enough ___ make a festival fun. Festivals are usually _____ ___ specific _____. It could be _____ or used ___ _____; the _____ vary ___ each case. Nevertheless, they could just be the _____ people made up ___ have fun since what these _____ hold ___ _____ is the fact that festivals are always _____. Big _____, breathtaking fireworks, festive music and dance, and the fun _____ are just all ___ the place.

　　糖果店裡的味道，大家互相祝福的話語，還有大家高興的精神就已經足夠讓一個節日好玩了！節日通常都是因為慶祝某個原因而誕生，可能是宗教的因素，又或者是用來紀念某一件事；每個節日背後的原因都不大一樣。但是也有可能是大家為了要玩樂所編出來的藉口啦。因為所有節日的共同點就是他們都幾乎是保證好玩的。大餐、令人驚嘆的煙火、節慶的音樂和舞蹈，到處都是的歡樂氣氛。

表演和遊樂園

　　此篇為**「影子跟讀短獨白練習」**，規劃了由聽「**短獨白**」的shadowing練習，強化聽力專注力和掌握各個考點，現在就一起動身，開始聽「**短獨白**」！

　　When you are traveling, you come across many different forms of performances or shows and then you realize quickly that different cultures enjoy different types of entertainment. Some performances can only be seen at certain places, such as traditional dances or sports games whereas some performances are shown all over the world. From the most iconic performances to a random show you step upon, while walking back to your hotel. They all make some differences for your journey. Remember to learn about different cultures and the stories behind the performances and to enjoy the shows with an open mind.

　　你在旅行的時候會遇到很多不同形式的表演或是秀，然後你很快就會發現原來不一樣的文化喜歡不一樣的娛樂方式。有的表演是只有在某些地方才看得見，例如傳統的舞蹈或是球賽，但有的表演是在世界各地都看得見的。從最具代表性的表演到你走回飯店不小心看到的

表演都會使你的旅程有點不同。記得要試著學習在每個表演背後的文化和故事，還有以開闊的心胸來看表演喔！

Amusement parks always hold a very special place in our hearts. It's a place filled with joy, laughter, excitement, ice creams and slurpees. Just like its name, you go there to get amused and entertained. There are all sorts of rides and facilities in the park for people to enjoy. This is the place where your wildest imagination comes true and so do your worst nightmares sometimes. This is the place where Harry Potter meets Roller Coasters and Mickey Mouse comes to shake your hands in the heat-stroke prone outfit. It sounds dreamy, but another feature of the amusement parks is the long lines. Expect to wait in lines, and stay hydrated! Buckle up and have fun!

遊樂園在我們的心中都有一個很特別的地位。那是一個充滿了快樂、歡笑、刺激、冰淇淋還有思樂冰的地方。就像它的名字一樣，你就是去那裡遊樂，還有被娛樂的。那裡有各種不同的遊樂和園區設施你可以使用。這是一個你最狂野的想像或是有的時候最恐怖的惡夢成真的地方。這裡也是哈利波特遇到雲霄飛車，還有米奇老鼠穿著可能會中暑的衣服來跟你握手的地方。聽起來很夢幻，可是遊樂園另一個特色就是排隊。所以預期要排隊，然後要多喝水！繫好安全帶玩得愉快！

UNIT ❽

表演和遊樂園

▶▶ 影子跟讀「短獨白填空」練習 🎧 MP3 008

除了前面的**「影子跟讀短獨白練習」**，現在試著在聽完對話後，完成下列填空練習，從中強化生活場景中常見的字彙以及拼字能力，答案的話請參照前面的獨白！

When you are _____, you come ___ many different forms of _____ or shows and then you realize quickly that different cultures enjoy different types of _____. Some performances can only be seen ___ _____ places, such ___ _____ dances or sports games whereas some performances are shown all ___ the world. From the most _____ performances to a _____ show you step ___, while walking back ___ your hotel. They all make some differences ___ your _____. Remember to learn ___ different cultures and the _____ ___ the _____ and to enjoy the shows ___ an open mind.

你在旅行的時候會遇到很多不同形式的表演或是秀，然後你很快就會發現原來不一樣的文化喜歡不一樣的娛樂方式。有的表演是只有在某些地方才看得見，例如傳統的舞蹈或是球賽，但有的表演是在世界各地都看得見的。從最具代表性的表演到你走回飯店不小心看到的

表演都會使你的旅程有點不同。記得要試著學習在每個表演背後的文化和故事，還有以開闊的心胸來看表演喔！

_____ parks always hold a very _____ place ___ our hearts. It's a place filled ___ joy, laughter, _____, ice creams and slurpees. Just like its name, you go there to get _____ and entertained. There are all sorts ___ rides and facilities ___ the park for people to enjoy. This is the place where your _____ _____ comes true and so do your worst _____ sometimes. This is the place where Harry Potter meets Roller Coasters and Mickey Mouse comes to shake your hands ___ the heat-stroke prone _____. It sounds _____, but another _____ of the _____ parks is the long lines. Expect to wait in lines, and stay _____! Buckle ___ and have fun!

　　遊樂園在我們的心中都有一個很特別的地位。那是一個充滿了快樂、歡笑、刺激、冰淇淋還有思樂冰的地方。就像它的名字一樣，你就是去那裡遊樂，還有被娛樂的。那裡有各種不同的遊樂和園區設施你可以使用。這是一個你最狂野的想像或是有的時候最恐怖的噩夢成真的地方。這裡也是哈利波特遇到雲霄飛車，還有米奇老鼠穿著可能會中暑的衣服來跟你握手的地方。聽起來很夢幻，可是遊樂園另一個特色就是排隊。所以預期要排隊，然後要多喝水！繫好安全帶玩得愉快！

航遊和配備

　　此篇為「**影子跟讀短獨白練習**」，規劃了由聽「**短獨白**」的shadowing練習，強化聽力專注力和掌握各個考點，現在就一起動身，開始聽「**短獨白**」！

　　Imagine there is a way of travel with which you can travel to different countries but stay in the same room. All the visas are taken care of, and the meals are all included. There are all kinds of entertainment for you to enjoy when you are on board. What am I referring to? Cruises of course! Being on a cruise is many people's dream. They can live on a boat comfortably and travel to different countries this way. It's vacation all the way. There is no waste of your vacation time. Picking your own route and favorite destinations are possible nowadays. However, make sure you wash your hands and look out for stomach flu. You don't want to be a killjoy of everyone's trip!

　　想像看看有一種旅遊方式是可以讓你到很多個國家旅行，但是你都是住同一個房間。所有的簽證都處理好了，而且餐點也都有包括。你在船上的時候有各種娛樂供你選擇。我是在說什麼呢？當然是遊輪

囉！去坐遊輪一直都是很多人的夢想。他們可以在一個船上舒服的旅行到不一樣的國家。全程都是度假。完全不浪費你的假期。現在你也可以選擇你自己的路線還有最喜歡的目的地。但是，要確保你洗手，並且小心腸病毒。你不想要掃大家的興的！

It is very interesting to do people watching when you are in a different country. The way people dress represents their identity or who they are as a part of that city. We all know there are roughly two kinds of outfits in every country; formal ones and the casual ones. However, each country has their own definition of what "formal" is. What might be acceptable in one country might not be appropriate in another. Also, each country has their own styles. It's very easy to tell people apart once you get the hang of it. In addition, there are also traditional costumes. In most cases, traditional costumes are used for festivals or as everyday wear.

當你在國外時觀察周遭的人其實很有趣。人們穿著的方式代表了他們的身份，或是在這個城市的一份子。我們都知道其實每個國家的服裝都可以大略的歸為兩種：正式和休閒。但是每個國家對於正式的定義也很不同。在這個國家可以接受的服裝，在別的國家可能會很不適當。還有就是，每個國家也都有他們自己的風格。其實你抓到訣竅之後，很好分別大家從哪裡來的。除此之外，還有傳統服飾。大部分來說傳統服飾可以分為在慶典或是每天生活中穿的兩種。

UNIT 9

航遊和配備

▶ 影子跟讀「短獨白填空」練習 🎧 MP3 009

除了前面的**「影子跟讀短獨白練習」**，現在試著在聽完對話後，完成下列填空練習，從中強化生活場景中常見的字彙以及拼字能力，答案的話請參照前面的獨白！

_____ there is a way of travel with which you can travel ___ different countries but stay ___ the same room. All the _____ are taken care ___, and the meals are all included. There are all kinds ___ entertainment for you to enjoy when you are on board. What am I referring to? _____ of course! Being ___ a cruise is many people's _____. They can live ___ a boat _____ and travel ___ different countries this way. It's vacation all the way. There is no waste ___ your vacation time. Picking your own _____ and favorite _____ are _____ nowadays. However, make sure you wash your hands and look out ___ _____ flu. You don't want to be a _____ of everyone's trip!

想像看看有一種旅遊方式是可以讓你到很多個國家旅行，但是你都是住同一個房間。所有的簽證都處理好了，而且餐點也都有包括。

你在船上的時候有各種娛樂供你選擇。我是在説什麼呢？當然是遊輪囉！去坐遊輪一直都是很多人的夢想。他們可以在一個船上舒服的旅行到不一樣的國家。全程都是度假。完全不浪費你的假期。現在你也可以選擇你自己的路線還有最喜歡的目的地。但是，要確保你洗手，並且小心腸病毒。你不想要掃大家的興的！

It is very interesting ___ do people watching when you are ___ a different country. The way people dress _____ their _____ or who they are as a part ___ that city. We all know there are roughly two kinds of outfits in every country; formal ones and the _____ ones. However, each country has their own definition ___ what "formal" is. What might be _____ ___ one country might not be _____ ___ another. Also, each country has their own styles. It's very easy to tell people apart once you get the hang ___ it. In addition, there are also traditional _____. In most cases, traditional costumes are used ___ _____ or as everyday wear.

　　當你在國外時觀察周遭的人其實很有趣。人們穿著的方式代表了他們的身份，或是在這個城市的一份子。我們都知道其實每個國家的服裝都可以大略的歸為兩種：正式和休閒。但是每個國家對於正式的定義也很不同。在這個國家可以接受的服裝，在別的國家可能會很不適當。還有就是，每個國家也都有他們自己的風格。其實你抓到訣竅之後，很好分別大家從哪裡來的。除此之外，還有傳統服飾。大部分來説傳統服飾可以分為在慶典或是每天生活中穿的兩種。

UNIT ⑩

名產和美酒

▶ **影子跟讀「短獨白」練習** 🎧 MP3 010

　　此篇為**「影子跟讀短獨白練習」**，規劃了由聽**「短獨白」**的shadowing練習，強化聽力專注力和掌握各個考點，現在就一起動身，開始聽「短獨白」！

　　We all have had some truly sensational meals in some once-in-a-life time restaurants and in some distant locations. We learned how to say "delicious" in every possible language from those truly blessed moments. However, sometimes it's the simple dishes that have been executed in the most authentic way stand out; a bowl of Pho by the street in Vietnam or a slice of Margarita pizza in Italy for instance. To add on an exotic note, it only exists in those places. The specialty food we tasted not only brought us a happy belly, but also stories and great memories about the place.

　　我們都有過在某個遙遠的地方，然後某個一輩子難得去一次的餐廳吃到令我們驚為天人的美食。因為那些幸運的時刻，我們學會了怎麼用各種可能的語言說「好好吃！」但是我們最喜歡的通常都是那些很簡單但是卻很道地的食物。例如在越南路邊吃到一碗牛肉河粉，或

是一片在義大利吃到的瑪格麗特披薩。而且那些都只有在當地才吃的到，因為這樣，那些食物又更有異國風情一些。這些美食不只讓我們吃得開心，也讓我們得知一些關於這個地方的故事並留下關於這個地方美好的回憶。

Going wine tasting in your vacation is like the icing on the cake. It makes the whole trip that much better. Besides, sometimes you get to try wines that can only be found in those specific regions. I often find myself being introduced to wines like they are people. This is Chardonnay and that is Merlot. Very nice to meet you guys. They each have their own personalities, appearances and their own friends. This one goes very well with chicken and that one pairs perfectly with chocolate. It is indeed a sensory experiment and examination. Among all the glasses of wine you taste, there are going to be a few of them you find yourself in love with, and if you have enough budget, you can bring them home with you.

在你的假期中去品酒就像在蛋糕上面放上糖霜一樣，讓整個旅程更加的美好。除此之外，你有的時候還可以試喝只有在那個地區才有出產的酒。我常常發現當別人在跟我介紹酒的時候，好像在介紹人一樣。這是夏多內，那是梅洛。很高興認識你們。他們都有自己的個性和外表，也有自己的朋友。這瓶和雞肉很搭，那瓶跟巧克力是絕配！品酒真的是感官的實驗也是檢驗。在這麼多杯酒之中，你可能會愛上其中幾個，而如果這時候你也還有足夠的預算的話，你還可以帶它們回家。

UNIT ⑩

名產和美酒

除了前面的**「影子跟讀短獨白練習」**，現在試著在聽完對話後，完成下列填空練習，從中強化生活場景中常見的字彙以及拼字能力，答案的話請參照前面的獨白！

We all have had some truly _____ meals in some once-in-a-life time _____ and ___ some _____ locations. We learned how to say "delicious" ___ every _____ language from those truly _____ _____. However, sometimes it's the simple dishes that have been _____ ___ the most _____ way stand ___; a bowl of Pho by the street in Vietnam or a slice of Margarita pizza ___ Italy for instance. To add ___ an exotic note, it only _____ in those places. The _____ food we tasted not only _____ us a happy belly, but also _____ and great memories ___ the place.

我們都有過在某個遙遠的地方，然後某個一輩子難得去一次的餐廳吃到令我們驚為天人的美食。因為那些幸運的時刻，我們學會了怎麼用各種可能的語言說「好好吃！」但是我們最喜歡的通常都是那些很簡單但是卻很道地的食物。例如在越南路邊吃到一碗牛肉河粉，或

是一片在義大利吃到的瑪格麗特披薩。而且那些都只有在當地才吃的到，因為這樣，那些食物又更有異國風情一些。這些美食不只讓我們吃得開心，也讓我們得知一些關於這個地方的故事並留下關於這個地方美好的回憶。

Going wine tasting in your _____ is like the icing ___ the cake. It makes the whole trip that much better. Besides, sometimes you get to try wines that can only be found ___ those _____ regions. I often find myself being _____ ___ wines like they are people. This is Chardonnay and that is Merlot. Very nice to meet you guys. They each have their own _____, _____ and their own friends. This one goes very well ___ chicken and that one pairs perfectly with _____. It is indeed a _____ _____ and examination. Among all the _____ of wine you taste, there are going to be a few ___ them you find yourself ___ love with, and if you have enough _____, you can bring them home ___ you.

在你的假期中去品酒就像在蛋糕上面放上糖霜一樣，讓整個旅程更加的美好。除此之外，你有的時候還可以試喝只有在那個地區才有出產的酒。我常常發現當別人在跟我介紹酒的時候，好像在介紹人一樣。這是夏多內，那是梅洛。很高興認識你們。他們都有自己的個性和外表，也有自己的朋友。這瓶和雞肉很搭，那瓶跟巧克力是絕配！品酒真的是感官的實驗也是檢驗。在這麼多杯酒之中，你可能會愛上其中幾個，而如果這時候你也還有足夠的預算的話，你還可以帶它們回家。

購物中心和餐廳

▶▶ **影子跟讀「短獨白」練習** 🎧 **MP3 011**

此篇為「**影子跟讀短獨白練習**」，規劃了由聽「**短獨白**」的shadowing練習，強化聽力專注力和掌握各個考點，現在就一起動身，開始聽「**短獨白**」！

Some travelers get to know a place through its historical museums and monuments, while others through its scenic landscapes and traditional cuisine, but for globetrotters who love to shop, there are no truer ways to experience a place than by bargaining with merchants in a bazaar, browsing the handcrafts of local artisans or trying on designer clothes at the boutique in town. Shopping in a foreign country can be both exciting and rewarding, but it's not without its downfalls. The art of bargaining is often a challenge for visitors that are used to fixed prices at their mall at home, and the sea of cheap knock-offs and tacky souvenirs in just about any major tourist destination makes it difficult to tell when you've found a true local gem.

有一些遊客喜歡從具歷史性的博物館或是紀念碑來認識一個地方，其他人則是從美麗的風景和傳統的美食切入。但是對於熱愛購物

的世界旅行者來說，沒有什麼比在市集裡跟店家殺價，在當地的工匠店裡瀏覽手工藝品，或是在鎮上的精品店裡試穿設計師服飾更直接認識這個地方的辦法。在國外購物可以是很刺激也很值回票價的，但是它還是有它的缺點。對於在自己國家時習慣於固定價格的遊客們來說，殺價是很具挑戰性的。在每個觀光景點都有賣的眾多便宜的盜版，和廉價的紀念品之中，很難說你是不是真的找到了當地的好貨。

Let's look through your past dining experiences in restaurants when you are on the road. If they are only mediocre, then they don't stand out in your trips at all, but if they are rather great experiences, you talk about it till all of your friends are very jealous. If the experiences are bad though, sometimes we get a little bit dramatic and say something like "I'll never go back!" What is this that we are doing? It seems more than what we think it is. Restaurant reservations to table service, entertainment to engagement—every aspect of the customer experience in a restaurant adds up to the diner's overall satisfaction.

我們來回想看看你過去旅行去過的餐廳好了。如果他們很平庸的話，他們就完全不會出現在你旅行的回憶裡，但是如果是蠻好的經驗，你會一直跟你的朋友說，直到你確定他們都非常的忌妒。如果是不好的經驗的話，我們有的時候會有點誇張然後說了這類的話：「我永遠都不會回去吃了！」我們這樣到底是在幹嘛呢？餐廳的經驗好像比我們想的還要重要一點。從餐廳訂位，到桌邊服務，娛樂到參與，每一個顧客在餐廳的經驗都會影響到顧客整體的體驗。

1 短獨白「影子跟讀」和填空練習

2 短獨白獨立演練和詳解

3 短獨白模擬試題

UNIT ⑪

購物中心和餐廳

▶▶ 影子跟讀「短獨白填空」練習 🎧 MP3 011

除了前面的**「影子跟讀短獨白練習」**，現在試著在聽完對話後，完成下列填空練習，從中強化生活場景中常見的字彙以及拼字能力，答案的話請參照前面的獨白！

Some travelers get to know a place through its _____ museums and _____, while others through its scenic _____ and traditional _____, but ___ globetrotters who love to shop, there are no truer ways ___ experience a place than by bargaining ___ _____ in a bazaar, browsing the _____ of local _____ or trying ___ designer clothes at the _____ ___ town. Shopping ___ a _____ country can be both exciting and rewarding, but it's not without its _____. The art of _____ is often a challenge ___ visitors that are used ___ fixed _____ at their mall ___ home, and the sea of cheap _____ and tacky _____ ___ just about any major tourist _____ makes it _____ to tell when you've found a true _____ gem.

有一些遊客喜歡從具歷史性的博物館或是紀念碑來認識一個地

方，其他人則是從美麗的風景和傳統的美食切入。但是對於熱愛購物的世界旅行者來說，沒有什麼比在市集裡跟店家殺價，在當地的工匠店裡瀏覽手工藝品，或是在鎮上的精品店裡試穿設計師服飾更直接認識這個地方的辦法。在國外購物可以是很刺激也很值回票價的，但是它還是有它的缺點。對於在自己國家時習慣於固定價格的遊客們來說，殺價是很具挑戰性的。在每個觀光景點都有賣的眾多便宜的盜版，和廉價的紀念品之中，很難說你是不是真的找到了當地的好貨。

Let's look through your past dining experiences in _____ when you are ___ the road. If they are only _____, then they don't stand out ___ your trips at all, but if they are rather great experiences, you talk about it till all of your friends are very _____. If the experiences are bad though, sometimes we get a little bit _____ and say something like "I'll never go back!" What is this that we are doing? It seems more than what we think it is. Restaurant _____ to table service, _____ to engagement—every aspect ___ the customer experience ___ a restaurant adds ___ to the diner's overall satisfaction.

我們來回想看看你過去旅行去過的餐廳好了。如果他們很平庸的話，他們就完全不會出現在你旅行的回憶裡，但是如果是蠻好的經驗，你會一直跟你的朋友說，直到你確定他們都非常的忌妒。如果是不好的經驗的話，我們有的時候會有點誇張然後說了這類的話：「我永遠都不會回去吃了！」我們這樣到底是在幹嘛呢？餐廳的經驗好像比我們想的還要重要一點。從餐廳訂位，到桌邊服務，娛樂到參與，每一個顧客在餐廳的經驗都會影響到顧客整體的體驗。

博物館和建築物

此篇為「影子跟讀短獨白練習」，規劃了由聽「短獨白」的shadowing練習，強化聽力專注力和掌握各個考點，現在就一起動身，開始聽「短獨白」！

Museums are places where great collections of art or a certain subject is displayed. It is usually a great place to go if you wish to know more about the subjects. Experts who are the best in those areas collect all the best possible items for you in the museums. We are all very blessed to live in the modern era. We don't have to go through all the fuss to find the bits and pieces. All we have to do is just visit the museums and you see all of them together. Organized and with descriptions on them. What are the better ways to learn things than this?

博物館是個具有偉大藝術收藏或某個特定主題的展示場所。如果你對某個主題很有興趣的話，通常去博物館是一個很好的選擇。有很多在那些領域是頂尖的專家收集了很多關於那個主題最好的作品，然後存放在博物館裡。我們在這個摩登的時代真的很幸福。因為我們不用大費周章的去找那些零零碎碎的作品。我們只要去一趟博物館，你

就可以看到所有的收集了。而且他們還整齊地排列，並且備註介紹。還有什麼比這樣更好的方式學東西呢？

Whenever we travel to places, we are attracted to the famous buildings. It's not that most of us have a deep interest in the architecture or because the travel book tells us it's a must-see. It's more about how the designs of these buildings reflect their time and culture in which they were built. It is perhaps boring to look around the architecture surrounding our everyday lives now. However, imagine what we have now only exists in our time. These buildings would stand tall and tells stories about our everyday lives years later. A lot like photography, architecture captures details of specific moments in time and tells us stories from a long time ago.

每當我們在旅行的時候，我們總是被有名的建築物給吸引。那不是因為我們對建築有濃厚的興趣或是只是因為旅遊書跟我們說那是必去的地方。比較是因為建築設計可以反映當年建造這個建築物的時候，那時的年代和文化。或許現在看看你周遭環境中的建築物好像蠻無聊的。但是想像一下如果這些建築物只有任我們這個年代才存在。這些建築物會高高地站著，告訴好幾年後的人我們每天生活的故事。許多就像攝影、建築物也可以捕捉某個時刻的細節並且跟我們說好久好久以前的故事。

博物館和建築物

▶影子跟讀「短獨白填空」練習　🎧 MP3 012

除了前面的**「影子跟讀短獨白練習」**，現在試著在聽完對話後，完成下列填空練習，從中強化生活場景中常見的字彙以及拼字能力，答案的話請參照前面的獨白！

_____ are places where great _____ ___ art or a certain subject is _____. It is usually a great place to go if you wish ___ know more about the _____. Experts who are the best in those areas _____ all the best possible items for you ___ the museums. We are all very blessed ___ live in the modern era. We don't have to go through all the _____ to find the bits and pieces. All we have to do is just visit the _____ and you see all of them together. _____ and with _____ ___ them. What are the better ways to learn things than this?

博物館是個具有偉大藝術收藏或某個特定主題的展示場所。如果你對某個主題很有興趣的話，通常去博物館是一個很好的選擇。有很多在那些領域是頂尖的專家收集了很多關於那個主題最好的作品，然後存放在博物館裡。我們在這個摩登的時代真的很幸福。因為我們不用大費周章的去找那些零零碎碎的作品。我們只要去一趟博物館，你

就可以看到所有的收集了。而且他們還整齊地排列，並且備註介紹。還有什麼比這樣更好的方式學東西呢？

Whenever we travel to places, we are attracted ___ the _____ buildings. It's not that most of us have a deep interest ___ the _____ or because the _____ book tells us it's a must-see. It's more about how the designs ___ these buildings _____ their time and culture ___ which they were built. It is perhaps boring to look around the _____ surrounding our everyday lives now. However, imagine what we have now only exists ___ our time. These buildings would stand tall and tells stories about our everyday lives years later. A lot like _____, architecture _____ details ___ _____ moments ___ time and tells us stories ___ a long time ago.

每當我們在旅行的時候，我們總是被有名的建築物給吸引。那不是因為我們對建築有濃厚的興趣或是只是因為旅遊書跟我們說那是必去的地方。比較是因為建築設計可以反映當年建造這個建築物的時候，那時的年代和文化。或許現在看看你周遭環境中的建築物好像蠻無聊的。但是想像一下如果這些建築物只有在我們這個年代才存在。這些建築物會高高地站著，告訴好幾年後的人我們每天生活的故事。許多就像攝影、建築物也可以捕捉某個時刻的細節並且跟我們說好久好久以前的故事。

台南－蝦米飯

　　此篇為「影子跟讀短獨白練習」，規劃了由聽「短獨白」的shadowing練習，強化聽力專注力和掌握各個考點，現在就一起動身，開始聽「短獨白」！

Tainan Shrimp fried rice
台南－蝦米飯

　　Some say that Tainan is the cultural and export center of the island. The city specializes in preserving Taiwanese culture, but was also once host to Fort Zeelandia – the Dutch port that was the primary city from which that country traded with E. Asia. Beginning in the early 1600s, the Dutch East India Company at what is now Tainan was trying to get a piece of the successful spice trade that Spain operated from Manila and the Portugese operated on Macau. The Dutch also recognized the fertile soils in the area and established European style agricultural ventures, growing and exporting wheat, ginger, and tobacco. From Tainan, the Dutch not only brought much spice and porcelain back to the west, but also untold riches to the profit of their European investors. Today, Tainan is the second largest city of Taiwan. Inexpensive stir fry restaurants are found everywhere. A typical family meal – whether eaten at home or while dining out – might consist of three or four such dishes to share, plus soup. It's the classic Taiwanese alternative to the British fish and chips or the American burger and fries. Inexpensive, quickly prepared, and broadly enjoyed.

　　有人說，台南是這個島上的文化和出口中心。這個城市保有很棒的閩南文化，這裡也有安平古堡，這個港口是當時荷蘭定為主要可以與亞洲各國交易的城市。始於 17 世紀初，荷蘭東印度公司當時為了成功與占領馬尼拉的西班牙，據有澳門的葡萄牙爭奪香料貿易，而在現在的台南據點。荷蘭人知道台南地區有肥沃的土壤，建立了歐洲風格的農業企業，種植和出口小麥、生薑和煙草。荷蘭人從台南不僅把很多的香料和瓷器運回西方，同時讓他們的歐洲投資者得到很高的利潤。在台南簡單的小吃到處都有。便宜的快炒店隨處可見。一般家庭無論是在家裡吃或外出用餐，大概會有三道或四道菜一起分享，再加上一碗湯。這種典型的台灣菜就好像是英國的炸魚排和薯條或是美國的漢堡薯條。

1 短獨白「影子跟讀」和填空練習

2 短獨白獨立演練和詳解

3 短獨白模擬試題

台南－蝦米飯

▶▶ 影子跟讀「短獨白填空」練習 🎧 MP3 013

除了前面的「**影子跟讀短獨白練習**」，現在試著在聽完對話後，完成下列填空練習，從中強化生活場景中常見的字彙以及拼字能力，答案的話請參照前面的獨白！

Tainan Shrimp Fried Rice
台南－蝦米飯

Some say that Tainan is the _____ and export center ___ the _____. The city specializes ___ _____ Taiwanese culture, but was also once host ___ Fort Zeelandia – the Dutch port that was the primary city ___ which that country traded with E. Asia. Beginning ___ the early 1600s, the Dutch East India Company ___ what is now Tainan was trying to get a piece of the _____ spice trade that Spain operated ___ Manila and the Portugese operated ___ Macau. The Dutch also _____ the _____ soils ___ the area and _____ European style _____ ventures, growing and exporting wheat, ginger, and _____. From Tainan, the Dutch not only brought much spice and _____ back to the west, but also _____ riches to the

_____ of their European investors. Today, Tainan is the second largest city of Taiwan. _____ stir fry restaurants are found everywhere. A typical family meal – whether eaten at home or while dining out – might _____ three or four such dishes to share, plus soup. It's the _____ Taiwanese _____ ___ the _____ fish and chips or the American burger and fries. _____, quickly _____, and broadly enjoyed.

　　有人説，台南是這個島上的文化和出口中心。這個城市保有很棒的閩南文化，這裡也有安平古堡，這個港口是當時荷蘭定為主要可以與亞洲各國交易的城市。始於 17 世紀初，荷蘭東印度公司當時為了成功與占領馬尼拉的西班牙，據有澳門的葡萄牙爭奪香料貿易，而在現在的台南據點。荷蘭人知道台南地區有肥沃的土壤，建立了歐洲風格的農業企業，種植和出口小麥、生薑和煙草。荷蘭人從台南不僅把很多的香料和瓷器運回西方，同時讓他們的歐洲投資者得到很高的利潤。在台南簡單的小吃到處都有。便宜的快炒店隨處可見。一般家庭無論是在家裡吃或外出用餐，大概會有三道或四道菜一起分享，再加上一碗湯。這種典型的台灣菜就好像是英國的炸魚排和薯條或是美國的漢堡薯條。

台南－鹹粥

此篇為「影子跟讀短獨白練習」，規劃了由聽「短獨白」的shadowing練習，強化聽力專注力和掌握各個考點，現在就一起動身，開始聽「短獨白」！

Tainan Salty Porridge
台南－鹹粥

　　Salty porridge is a classic southern Taiwan breakfast dish, enjoyed with gusto – and a fried donut stick – in Tainan. The rice and broth for this salty porridge are prepared so that the rice remains light and firm. In the common rice congee, the rice is cooked with large amounts of water long enough to make the grains so soft that they begin to break apart. Salty porridge in Tainan is made so that the clear fish broth is added over the cooked rice, seafood and any vegetables at the end of cooking. And the main ingredient of salty porridge is milkfish – a popular, mild-tasting white fish. There are many other ways that milkfish is enjoyed in Tainan – in soup, fried, and as fish balls, for example. Most Milkfish available in Taiwan is not wild-caught, but raised through aquaculture or fish farming systems. Traditionally, the fish fingerlings are caught in the open sea, then raised in ponds or under-water cages of warm, brackish coastal water. Production of milkfish in Southeast Asia using this method has increased nearly 1,000 times since 1950. The Philippines and Indonesia join Taiwan as the top milkfish producers and consumers.

鹹粥是一種典型的台灣南部早餐，加上油條味道就很棒。做鹹粥的米要煮到軟且粒粒分明。就一般煮粥的方式，米會加大量的水煮足夠長的時間，使米粒軟到開始分解。台南鹹粥則是把清澈魚湯加在米飯上，在烹煮最後加入海鮮和蔬菜。鹹粥的主要成分是虱目魚，這是一種很受歡迎吃起來軟嫩的魚。在台南虱目魚的吃法還有許多方式，做湯、用煎的，或做成魚丸。在台灣吃的虱目魚大部分都不是野生捕撈的，而是由養殖或養魚系統。傳統上，魚苗是在大海捕獲的，然後養在池塘或靠近沿海溫度較暖和的鹹水魚塭內。自 1950 年在東南亞用這種方法養殖虱目魚產量就增加了近 1000 倍。菲律賓和印尼加入台灣成為主要的虱目魚生產者和消費者。

UNIT ⓮

台南－鹹粥

▶▶ 影子跟讀「短獨白填空」練習　🎧 MP3 014

　　除了前面的「**影子跟讀短獨白練習**」，現在試著在聽完對話後，完成下列填空練習，從中強化生活場景中常見的字彙以及拼字能力，答案的話請參照前面的獨白！

Tainan Salty Porridge
台南－鹹粥

　　Salty _____ is a classic southern Taiwan _____ dish, enjoyed with gusto – and a fried donut stick – ___ Tainan. The rice and broth ___ this salty porridge are prepared so that the rice _____ light and firm. In the common rice _____, the rice is cooked ___ large amounts of water long enough to make the grains so soft that they begin to break apart. Salty porridge in Tainan is made so that the clear fish _____ is added over the cooked rice, seafood and any vegetables ___ the end of cooking. And the main _____ of salty porridge is milkfish – a popular, mild-tasting white fish. There are many other ways that milkfish is _____ in Tainan – in soup, fried, and as fish balls, for example. Most Milkfish available in Taiwan is not

_____, but raised through _____ or fish farming systems. Traditionally, the fish fingerlings are caught in the open sea, then raised ___ ponds or under-water cages of warm, brackish _____ water. _____ of milkfish in _____ Asia using this method has increased nearly 1,000 times since 1950. The Philippines and Indonesia join Taiwan as the top milkfish _____ and _____.

鹹粥是一種典型的台灣南部早餐，加上油條味道就很棒。做鹹粥的米要煮到軟且粒粒分明。就一般煮粥的方式，米會加大量的水煮足夠長的時間，使米粒軟到開始分解。台南鹹粥則是把清澈魚湯加在米飯上，在烹煮最後加入海鮮和蔬菜。鹹粥的主要成分是虱目魚，這是一種很受歡迎吃起來軟嫩的魚。在台南虱目魚的吃法還有許多方式，做湯、用煎的，或做成魚丸。在台灣吃的虱目魚大部分都不是野生捕撈的，而是由養殖或養魚系統。傳統上，魚苗是在大海捕獲的，然後養在池塘或靠近沿海溫度較暖和的鹹水魚塭內。自 1950 年在東南亞用這種方法養殖虱目魚產量就增加了近 1000 倍。菲律賓和印尼加入台灣成為主要的虱目魚生產者和消費者。

台南－土產牛肉

▶▶ 影子跟讀「短獨白」練習　🎧 MP3 015

此篇為「影子跟讀短獨白練習」，規劃了由聽「短獨白」的shadowing練習，強化聽力專注力和掌握各個考點，現在就一起動身，開始聽「短獨白」！

Tainan Local Beef
台南－土產牛肉

Tainan's famous beef soup a clear beef broth with Chinese herbs, poured boiling hot over raw pieces of thinly sliced beef. The heat of the soup cooks the beef as the vendor serves it. The best beef soup to be found on Tainan's streets uses local beef that comes fresh daily from the beef cattle farms near Tainan. Butchering occurs twice a day, once in the morning and once at night, in Shan Hua Tainan. This allows for the freshly butchered beef to be delivered directly to soup shops in the heart of the city and served as fresh as possible. Unlike western beef that is frozen right after butchering, Shan Hua Cattle Market provides "body temperature beef" which is cut beef that involves no freezing process and the meat structural integrity is not de-

1 短獨白「影子跟讀」和填空練習

2 短獨白獨立演練和詳解

3 短獨白模擬試題

stroyed. Beef is cut and soon delivered to the market. It is said that only "body temperature beef" can be used for the best result for Tainan beef soup. Beef farming is not a large industry in Taiwan and the domestic beef is exclusively for local restaurants. Beef is becoming more available for household cooking with French retailer Carefour and American retailer Costco selling their beef imported from Australia or the US.

台南著名的牛肉湯湯頭是中藥熬煮的清湯，滾燙的清湯，再倒入切得超薄的牛肉就可以上桌了。湯頭的熱度在上桌的同時會把牛肉幾乎燙熟。在台南最好的牛肉湯，是用每天來自台南附近養殖場的本地牛肉。台南善化牛墟，一天屠宰牛隻兩次，分別在上午和晚上，這樣可以讓新鮮屠宰的牛肉被直接送至各城市的小吃店，小吃店所提供的牛肉也就越新鮮越好。不像西方牛肉通常是在屠宰後立即冷凍，善化牛墟提供的是「溫體牛」，就是現殺，沒經過冷藏，肉質結構完整沒被破壞的，溫體牛在屠宰後很快就被供應到市場。有人說，只有「體溫牛」才能做出最棒的台南牛肉湯。牛肉養殖在台灣不是一個大產業，國內的牛肉是專門賣給小吃店。來自法國大賣場的家樂福和美國大賣場的好市多所賣的牛肉是澳大利亞和美國進口的，這樣一般家庭就比較容易買到牛肉。

台南－土產牛肉

▶▶ 影子跟讀「短獨白填空」練習 🎧 MP3 015

除了前面的「**影子跟讀短獨白練習**」，現在試著在聽完對話後，完成下列填空練習，從中強化生活場景中常見的字彙以及拼字能力，答案的話請參照前面的獨白！

Tainan Local Beef
台南－土產牛肉

　　Tainan's _____ beef soup a clear beef broth ___ Chinese herbs, poured boiling hot over raw pieces ___ _____ sliced beef. The heat of the soup cooks the beef ___ the _____ serves it. The best beef soup ___ be found on Tainan's streets uses local beef that comes fresh daily ___ the beef cattle farms near Tainan. Butchering occurs twice a day, once in the morning and once at night, in Shan Hua Tainan. This allows for the _____ butchered beef to be delivered directly ___ soup shops in the heart of the city and served as fresh ___ possible. Unlike _____ beef that is frozen right ___ butchering, Shan Hua Cattle Market provides "body temperature beef" which is cut beef that involves no _____ process and the meat _____ integrity is not _____. Beef is cut and soon _____ ___ the market. It is said that only "body _____ beef" can be used ___ the best result for Tainan beef soup. Beef farming is not a large industry in Taiwan and the _____ beef is _____ ___ local restaurants. Beef is becoming more available for _____ cooking with French retailer Carefour and American _____ Costco selling their beef _____ ___ Australia or the US.

台南著名的牛肉湯湯頭是中藥熬煮的清湯，滾燙的清湯，再倒入切得超薄的牛肉就可以上桌了。湯頭的熱度在上桌的同時會把牛肉幾乎燙熟。在台南最好的牛肉湯，是用每天來自台南附近養殖場的本地牛肉。台南善化牛墟，一天屠宰牛隻兩次，分別在上午和晚上，這樣可以讓新鮮屠宰的牛肉被直接送至各城市的小吃店，小吃店所提供的牛肉也就越新鮮越好。不像西方牛肉通常是在屠宰後立即冷凍，善化牛墟提供的是「溫體牛」，就是現殺，沒經過冷藏，肉質結構完整沒被破壞的，溫體牛在屠宰後很快就被供應到市場。有人說，只有「體溫牛」才能做出最棒的台南牛肉湯。牛肉養殖在台灣不是一個大產業，國內的牛肉是專門賣給小吃店。來自法國大賣場的家樂福和美國大賣場的好市多所賣的牛肉是澳大利亞和美國進口的，這樣一般家庭就比較容易買到牛肉。

高雄－楊桃湯

▶▶ 影子跟讀「短獨白」練習 🎧 MP3 016

此篇為「影子跟讀短獨白練習」，規劃了由聽「短獨白」的shadowing練習，強化聽力專注力和掌握各個考點，現在就一起動身，開始聽「短獨白」！

Kaohsiung Star Fruit Drink
高雄－楊桃湯

Star fruit – also known as carambola – is a sweet and juicy tropical fruit with five distinct ridges running its length. Carambola's roots, branches, leaves, flowers, and fruits all can be used for medicinal purposes. Carambola contains sucrose, fructose, glucose, malic acid, citric acid, oxalic acid and vitamins B1, B2, C and protein. In ancient times, it was used for its antibiotic effect to fight malaria. Star fruit in Taiwan is commonly used for sore throat. Turning the fruit into fermented juice is as simple as combining equal parts sliced fruit and sugar in a large jar, covering it to keep the insects out, and setting the jar in the sun for a few days.

楊桃是一種五角形、甜美多汁的熱帶水果。楊桃的根、枝、葉、花、果都有藥用性質。楊桃含有蔗糖、果糖、葡萄糖、蘋果酸、檸檬酸、草酸、維生素 B1、B2、C 及蛋白質。在古代，楊桃的抗生素效果被用來對抗瘧疾。在台灣楊桃常用於治咽喉腫痛。楊桃汁是由發酵過的楊桃所做的，發酵的楊桃做法很簡單，楊桃切片後每一層撒上糖放入一個大罐子，蓋起來防止害蟲入侵，放在太陽下幾天就完成了。

Alcohol content would increase to the level of a fruit wine if the jar was left for a full three weeks. Vendors serve up the fermented drink ice cold in plastic to-go cups with straws. Fermented star fruit drink can also be served hot. In addition to ready to serve cold star fruit drink, vendors also sell concentrated star fruit drink in bottles. In winter people like to add hot water to the concentrated star fruit drink.

如果放滿三星期，楊桃發酵後的酒精含量就能釀成水果酒。攤販賣的楊桃湯通常會把冰冷的楊桃湯倒入塑料外帶杯裝的吸管。楊桃湯也可以做熱飲。一般攤販除了賣馬上可以喝的冰楊桃湯，他們也會賣瓶裝的濃縮楊桃湯。冬天很多人喜歡買濃縮的楊桃湯回家自己加熱水。

高雄－楊桃湯

▶▶ 影子跟讀「短獨白填空」練習 🎧 MP3 016

　　除了前面的**「影子跟讀短獨白練習」**，現在試著在聽完對話後，完成下列填空練習，從中強化生活場景中常見的字彙以及拼字能力，答案的話請參照前面的獨白！

Kaohsiung Star Fruit Drink
高雄－楊桃湯

　　Star fruit – also known ____ carambola – is a sweet and _____ fruit ____ five _____ _____ running its _____. Carambola's roots, _____, _____, flowers, and fruits all can be used ____ _____ purposes. Carambola _____ sucrose, fructose, _____, malic acid, citric acid, oxalic acid and _____ B1, B2, C and protein. In ancient times, it was used for its _____ effect ____ fight _____. Star fruit in Taiwan is _____ used for sore _____. Turning the fruit into _____ juice is as simple ____ combining _____ parts sliced fruit and sugar ____ a large jar, covering it to keep the insects out, and setting the jar ____ the sun ____ a few days.

楊桃是一種五角形、甜美多汁的熱帶水果。楊桃的根、枝、葉、花、果都有藥用性質。楊桃含有蔗糖、果糖、葡萄糖、蘋果酸、檸檬酸、草酸、維生素 B1、B2、C 及蛋白質。在古代，楊桃的抗生素效果被用來對抗瘧疾。在台灣楊桃常用於治咽喉腫痛。楊桃汁是由發酵過的楊桃所做的，發酵的楊桃做法很簡單，楊桃切片後每一層撒上糖放入一個大罐子，蓋起來防止害蟲入侵，放在太陽下幾天就完成了。

Alcohol _____ would _____ to the level of a fruit wine if the jar was left for a full three weeks. Vendors serve ___ the fermented drink ice cold in _____ to-go cups with straws. Fermented star fruit drink can also be served _____. In addition ___ ready to serve cold star fruit drink, _____ also sell concentrated star fruit drink in _____. ___ winter people like to add hot _____ to the concentrated star fruit drink.

如果放滿三星期，楊桃發酵後的酒精含量就能釀成水果酒。攤販賣的楊桃湯通常會把冰冷的楊桃湯倒入塑料外帶杯裝的吸管。楊桃湯也可以做熱飲。一般攤販除了賣馬上可以喝的冰楊桃湯，他們也會賣瓶裝的濃縮楊桃湯。冬天很多人喜歡買濃縮的楊桃湯回家自己加熱水。

高雄－鹹水鴨

▶▶ 影子跟讀「短獨白」練習 🎧 MP3 017

此篇為**「影子跟讀短獨白練習」**，規劃了由聽**「短獨白」**的shadowing練習，強化聽力專注力和掌握各個考點，現在就一起動身，開始聽**「短獨白」**！

Kaohsiung Salted Duck
高雄－鹹水鴨

Salted duck tastes effortless and simple, though the Kaohsiung cooks who prepare it have several steps to follow in order to make it well. Its ingredients are simply duck, salt, pepper, ginger, green onion, and other spices. These are not hard to come by, so it is the various steps of marinating, cooking, and cooling that give the dish its traditional texture and taste. Traditional cooks may maintain the "starter broth" from previous salted duck cooking sessions to yield an even richer experience. Salted duck is a cold dish of sliced duck. Salted duck was originally a specialty of Nanjing, China, capital of the Qing Dynasty. The Qing emperor conquered and annexed Taiwan in the mid seventeenth century, ruling it for over two centuries. It's reasonable to assume that salted duck was brought to Taiwan from Chi-na. An amusing story from Nanjing attempts to explain how duck became so popular there centuries ago. Legend has it that a dispute about excess noise caused all the roosters to be killed. The result was no noisier wake-up calls, but also no more chicken to eat. This is said to be the time period when the locals turned to duck as a source of protein.

　　鹽水鴨吃起來是那麼輕鬆和簡單的味道，雖然簡單但是還是需要好幾個步驟才能做得出好吃的鹽水鴨。鹽水鴨的材料只是簡單的鴨、鹽、胡椒、薑、蔥和其他香料。這些材料都不難取得，透過醃製，烹調和冷卻的各個步驟，讓這道菜有很特別的傳統肉質和口感。有些廚師可能會保留煮過的鹽水鴨的高湯再加入煮新鹽水鴨，這樣可以讓味道更加豐富。鹽水鴨通常是切片的一道涼菜。鹽水鴨源自中國南京，是清朝首都的特產。清朝皇帝在十七世紀中期吞併台灣，統治了兩個多世紀。因此，可以合理的假設，台灣的鹽水鴨是源自中國。在南京有一個讓人莞爾一笑的說法，解釋為何鴨肉在那裡幾百年前這麼流行。傳說是過度噪音的糾紛導致所有的公雞被殺害。也因此早晨不會聽到吵醒居民的啼叫聲，但同時也沒有雞肉可以吃了。也就在那時，當地人把吃鴨肉作為蛋白質取得的來源。

高雄－鹹水鴨

▶▶ 影子跟讀「短獨白填空」練習　🎧 MP3 017

　　除了前面的「**影子跟讀短獨白練習**」，現在試著在聽完對話後，完成下列填空練習，從中強化生活場景中常見的字彙以及拼字能力，答案的話請參照前面的獨白！

Kaohsiung Salted Duck
高雄－鹹水鴨

　　Salted duck tastes _____ and _____, though the Kaohsiung cooks who prepare it have _____ steps to follow in order ___ make it well. Its _____ are simply duck, salt, pepper, ginger, green onion, and other spices. These are not hard to come by, so it is the various steps ___ marinating, cooking, and cooling that give the dish its _____ _____ and taste. Traditional cooks may _____ the "starter broth" ___ previous salted duck cooking sessions to yield an even richer experience. Salted duck is a cold dish of _____ duck. Salted duck was _____ a _____ of Nanjing, China, capital of the Qing Dynasty. The Qing _____ conquered and annexed Tai-wan ___ the mid seventeenth century, ruling it for ___ two centuries. It's _____ to _____ that salted duck was brought to Taiwan from China. An _____ story ____ Nan-jing _____ to explain how duck became so _____ there centuries ago. Legend has it that a _____ about excess noise caused all the roosters to be killed. The _____ was no noisier wake-up calls, but also no more chicken to eat. This is said to be the time _____ when the locals turned to duck as a source of _____.

鹽水鴨吃起來是那麼輕鬆和簡單的味道，雖然簡單但是還是需要好幾個步驟才能做得出好吃的鹽水鴨。鹽水鴨的材料只是簡單的鴨、鹽、胡椒、薑、蔥和其他香料。這些材料都不難取得，透過醃製，烹調和冷卻的各個步驟，讓這道菜有很特別的傳統肉質和口感。有些廚師可能會保留煮過的鹽水鴨的高湯再加入煮新鹽水鴨，這樣可以讓味道更加豐富。鹽水鴨通常是切片的一道涼菜。鹽水鴨源自中國南京，是清朝首都的特產。清朝皇帝在十七世紀中期吞併台灣，統治了兩個多世紀。因此，可以合理的假設，台灣的鹽水鴨是源自中國。在南京有一個讓人莞爾一笑的說法，解釋為何鴨肉在那裡幾百年前這麼流行。傳說是過度噪音的糾紛導致所有的公雞被殺害。也因此早晨不會聽到吵醒居民的啼叫聲，但同時也沒有雞肉可以吃了。也就在那時，當地人把吃鴨肉作為蛋白質取得的來源。

屏東－東港鮪魚

此篇為「影子跟讀短獨白練習」，規劃了由聽「短獨白」的shadowing練習，強化聽力專注力和掌握各個考點，現在就一起動身，開始聽「短獨白」！

Pingtung Dong Gang Tuna
屏東－東港鮪魚

There is no better time to go to Dong Gang port in Pingtung than during the annual Blue Fin Tuna Cultural Festival. Every year from May to July, the visitor can find a major celebration of tuna, founded securely in Pingtung's coastal Dong Gang Township in this tropical, southern area of Taiwan. Pacific blue fin tuna is much sought after, especially in Taiwan and Japan, for high quality sushi and sashimi. The Taiwanese tuna catch used to go almost exclusively to Japan, where bidders still pay top dollar for the rights to serve the biggest and best of the catch. Now, "tuna fever" captures the entire island of Taiwan during the later spring and early summer timeframe. In Taiwan, blue fin tuna is often referred to as "black tuna," but it is the same fish. Sakura shrimp and salted oilfish eggs are also popular in Dong Gang. The growth period for Sakura shrimp runs from November to June in the nearby coastal waters of Dong Gang port. Sakura shrimp has red pigment and light-emitting organs. It is usually fried or dried. Oilfish's eggs are salted, pressed and dried. It is usually thin sliced and is eaten with garlic and raw white radish.

東港黑鮪魚文化觀光季是去屏東東港的好時機。每年 5 月至 7 月，在台灣這個熱帶南部地區的屏東沿海東港鎮遊客可以看到有關黑鮪魚主要慶祝活動。太平洋黑鮪魚有很高的市場需求，特別是在台灣和日本，因為可以用來做高品質的壽司和生魚片。台灣以前捕獲的鮪魚幾乎都是賣去日本，投標人會付最高的價錢來買到最大和最好的魚。「黑鮪魚熱潮」現在則在春季和初夏時間風靡台灣。在台灣，這樣的藍鰭金槍魚常常被稱為「黑鮪魚」。東港還有櫻花蝦、油魚子。櫻花蝦產期為每年 11 至翌年 6 月就在東港溪出海口附近。櫻花蝦全身佈滿紅色素及發光器，通常會乾製或炸酥。油魚子的卵鹽醃後晾乾，吃的時候切成薄片再配上蒜苗與白蘿蔔。

屏東－東港鮪魚

▶▶ 影子跟讀「短獨白填空」練習　🎧 MP3 018

　　除了前面的「**影子跟讀短獨白練習**」，現在試著在聽完對話後，完成下列填空練習，從中強化生活場景中常見的字彙以及拼字能力，答案的話請參照前面的獨白！

Pingtung Dong Gang Tuna
屏東－東港鮪魚

　　There is no better time to go to Dong Gang _____ in Pingtung than _____ the _____ Blue Fin Tuna Cultural Festival. Every year from May to July, the visitor can find a major _____ of _____, founded securely ___ Ping-tung's _____ Dong Gang Township ___ this tropical, southern area of Taiwan. Pacific blue fin tuna is much sought after, especially in Taiwan and Japan, ___ high _____ sushi and sashimi. The Taiwanese tuna catch used to go almost _____ to Japan, where _____ still pay top dollar for the rights to serve the biggest and best ___ the catch. Now, "tuna fever" captures the entire _____ of Taiwan during the later spring and early summer _____. In Taiwan, blue fin tuna is often referred

___ as "black tuna," but it is the same fish. Sakura _____ and salted oilfish eggs are also popular in Dong Gang. The _____ period for Sakura shrimp runs ___ November to June ___ the nearby coastal waters ___ Dong Gang port. Sakura shrimp has red _____ and light-emitting _____. It is usually fried or dried. Oilfish's eggs are salted, pressed and dried. It is usually thin sliced and is eaten ___ _____ and _____ white radish.

東港黑鮪魚文化觀光季是去屏東東港的好時機。每年 5 月至 7 月，在台灣這個熱帶南部地區的屏東沿海東港鎮遊客可以看到有關黑鮪魚主要慶祝活動。太平洋黑鮪魚有很高的市場需求，特別是在台灣和日本，因為可以用來做高品質的壽司和生魚片。台灣以前捕獲的鮪魚幾乎都是賣去日本，投標人會付最高的價錢來買到最大和最好的魚。「黑鮪魚熱潮」現在則在春季和初夏時間風靡台灣。在台灣，這樣的藍鰭金槍魚常常被稱為「黑鮪魚」。東港還有櫻花蝦、油魚子。櫻花蝦產期為每年 11 至翌年 6 月就在東港溪出海口附近。櫻花蝦全身佈滿紅色素及發光器，通常會乾製或炸酥。油魚子的卵鹽醃後晾乾，吃的時候切成薄片再配上蒜苗與白蘿蔔。

屏東－潮州旗魚黑輪

▶▶ 影子跟讀「短獨白」練習　🎧 MP3 019

　　此篇為「影子跟讀短獨白練習」，規劃了由聽「短獨白」的shadowing練習，強化聽力專注力和掌握各個考點，現在就一起動身，開始聽「短獨白」！

Pintung-Oo-lián, Fishcakes, Oolen, Tian Bu La
屏東－潮州旗魚黑輪

　　Fish cake or oolen/tian bu la is a savory fried fish cake, primarily made of a paste of various types of seafood, potato starch, sugar, and pepper. The ingredients are ground and mashed into a smooth mixture, then shaped into a log for frying. The result is a springy, slightly chewy texture – that "Q" that is so important and popular in Taiwanese cuisine. Normally, the fried fish cake is served on a stick with a sweet and sour sauce. These fried fish cakes, along with fish balls and other delicacies are also available floating in a soup – inspired by the Japanese, as are fish cakes themselves. Pintung County, on the southernmost tip of Taiwan, is home to beautiful natural parks, seaports, and unique coral beaches. It is also the location where, in 1874, the

Japanese landed and won bloody victories against the local tribes. This was the beginning of a twenty-year war for the island, won ultimately by the Japanese. This early battle is memorialized at the historic site ShiMen Ancient Battle-field. Though the site's memorials are somber, the mountainous landscape is breath-taking. Beautiful temples, artist colonies, tribal grounds and many other fascinating attractions are available throughout Pintung.

黑輪是一種用魚漿做的美味油炸小吃，主要由各類海鮮、馬鈴薯澱粉、糖和胡椒粉所做。把混合均勻的麵糊做成長條狀後再油炸。這樣做出來的黑輪就是很有彈性、耐嚼感，也就是大家喜歡的台灣美食的「Q」感。黑輪的吃法是串在竹子上，加上甜酸醬。通常是煮一大鍋黑輪，搭配魚丸和其他食材，這種靈感來自於日本人的小吃。屏東縣位在台灣的最南端，這裡有美麗的自然公園、海港和獨特的珊瑚海灘。這裡也是 1874 年日本軍隊抵達後與當地部落作戰的地方。原住民在這個島嶼與日本人對抗二十多年的戰爭，最後由日本人戰勝。這個早期的戰鬥歷史的紀念遺址就是現在的石門古戰場。雖然紀念史蹟是嚴肅的，這裡的山區景觀卻是讓人驚歎。整個屏東地方都可以看到美麗的寺廟、藝術家集聚、部落地方和其他許多迷人丰采的景觀。

屏東－潮州旗魚黑輪

▶ 影子跟讀「短獨白填空」練習　🎧 MP3 019

除了前面的「影子跟讀短獨白練習」，現在試著在聽完對話後，完成下列填空練習，從中強化生活場景中常見的字彙以及拼字能力，答案的話請參照前面的獨白！

Pintung-Oo-lián, Fishcakes, Oolen, Tian Bu La
屏東－潮州旗魚黑輪

Fish cake or oolen/tian bu la is a _____ fried fish cake, _____ made ___ a paste of _____ types of seafood, potato starch, sugar, and pepper. The _____ are ground and mashed ___ a _____ mixture, then shaped into a log for frying. The result is a springy, _____ chewy texture – that "Q" that is so _____ and popular ___ Taiwanese _____. Normally, the fried fish cake is served on a stick ___ a sweet and sour sauce. These fried fish cakes, along with fish balls and other _____ are also _____ floating ___ a soup – inspired ___ the Japanese, as are fish cakes themselves. Pintung County, on the southernmost tip of Taiwan, is home ___ beautiful natural parks, seaports, and _____ coral beaches. It is also the _____ where, in 1874, the Japanese landed and won _____ victories against the _____ tribes. This was the beginning of a twenty-year war ___ the island, won ultimately ___ the Japanese. This early battle is _____ ___ the _____ site ShiMen Ancient _____. Though the site's memorials are somber, the _____ landscape is breath-taking. Beautiful _____, artist colonies, tribal grounds and many other _____ attractions are available throughout Pintung.

1 短獨白「影子跟讀」和填空練習

黑輪是一種用魚漿做的美味油炸小吃，主要由各類海鮮、馬鈴薯澱粉、糖和胡椒粉所做。把混合均勻的麵糊做成長條狀後再油炸。這樣做出來的黑輪就是很有彈性、耐嚼感，也就是大家喜歡的台灣美食的「Q」感。黑輪的吃法是串在竹子上，加上甜酸醬。通常是煮一大鍋黑輪，搭配魚丸和其他食材，這種靈感來自於日本人的小吃。屏東縣位在台灣的最南端，這裡有美麗的自然公園、海港和獨特的珊瑚海灘。這裡也是 1874 年日本軍隊抵達後與當地部落作戰的地方。原住民在這個島嶼與日本人對抗二十多年的戰爭，最後由日本人戰勝。這個早期的戰鬥歷史的紀念遺址就是現在的石門古戰場。雖然紀念史蹟是嚴肅的，這裡的山區景觀卻是讓人驚歎。整個屏東地方都可以看到美麗的寺廟、藝術家集聚、部落地方和其他許多迷人半采的景觀。

2 短獨白獨立演練和詳解

3 短獨白模擬試題

宜蘭－三星蔥油餅

▶ 影子跟讀「短獨白」練習 🎧 MP3 020

　　此篇為「影子跟讀短獨白練習」，規劃了由聽「短獨白」的shadowing練習，強化聽力專注力和掌握各個考點，現在就一起動身，開始聽「短獨白」！

Onion Scallion Flatbread
宜蘭－三星蔥油餅

　　One well-known and well-loved finger food in Taiwan is scallion flatbread. It uses such simple ingredients and preparation, though the result is so tasty! The cook prepares a basic wheat flour and water dough, rolls a large piece out to add oil, diced scallions and salt, then rolls small pieces into circles for pan-frying into flaky finger food. In Ilan and other areas of Taiwan, street vendors offer either plain or in a classic Taiwanese style with an egg. This treat arrived in Taiwan from mainland China when the imperial army and its supporters fled during the communist takeover. The origin of scallion flatbread – or sometimes called fried green onion pancake – is not specifically known. Some sources suppose that the Indian population of Beijing may have had a hand in developing this Chinese treat, since it is similar to a flatbread they loved from their cuisine, called paratha. Ilan county in the northeast coastal area of Taiwan was home to two aboriginal groups: a mountain settlement of Atayal people and a coastal and riverbank group of settlements by the Kavalan, after which the county is named. The best scallion flatbread is from Ilan where it grows the best green onion called Sansing Green Onion.

蔥油餅是眾所皆知且深受大家喜愛的台灣小吃。雖然只是簡單的材料和做法，但就是非常好吃！做法是用基本的小麥粉和水做成麵團再桿成一大塊，在麵皮上加油、香蔥和鹽，捲成圓形狀，要煎之前再桿開好下鍋油煎，這就是有層次的蔥油餅。在宜蘭及台灣等地區，街頭攤販會賣一般或加蛋的蔥油餅。這種小吃是當時國民黨在大陸撤退逃離到台灣時所帶進來的小吃。蔥油餅或蔥花大餅並沒有考據的來源。有些來源指出在北京的印度人口對這個在中國的小吃有啟發的影響，因為這與印度人自己的印度大餅很類似。在台灣東北部沿海地區的宜蘭縣是兩個當地原住民：一是靠山的泰雅族人和沿海河岸而居的噶瑪蘭人，這也是宜蘭縣被命名的起源。最好的蔥油餅在宜蘭，因為這裡所生長的三星蔥是最棒的蔥。

宜蘭－三星蔥油餅

▶▶ 影子跟讀「短獨白填空」練習　🎧 MP3 020

除了前面的「**影子跟讀短獨白練習**」，現在試著在聽完對話後，完成下列填空練習，從中強化生活場景中常見的字彙以及拼字能力，答案的話請參照前面的獨白！

Onion Scallion Flatbread
宜蘭－三星蔥油餅

One well-known and well-loved finger food in Taiwan is scallion flatbread. It uses such simple ingredients and _____, though the result is so tasty! The cook prepares a _____ wheat flour and water _____, rolls a large piece out to add oil, diced scallions and salt, then rolls small pieces ___ circles for pan-frying into _____ finger food. In Ilan and other areas of Taiwan, street _____ offer either plain or ___ a classic _____ style ___ an egg. This treat arrived in Taiwan from mainland China when the imperial army and its _____ fled _____ the _____ takeover. The origin ___ scallion flatbread – or sometimes called fried green onion pancake – is not _____ known. Some sources suppose that the Indian _____ of Beijing may have had a hand ___ developing this Chinese _____, since it is similar ___ a flatbread they loved from their _____, called paratha. Ilan county in the northeast coastal area of Taiwan was home ___ two _____ groups: a mountain settlement ___ Atayal people and a _____ and riverbank group ___ settlements by the Kavalan, after which the _____ is named. The best scallion flatbread is ___ Ilan where it grows the best green onion called Sansing Green Onion.

　　蔥油餅是眾所皆知且深受大家喜愛的台灣小吃。雖然只是簡單的材料和做法，但就是非常好吃！做法是用基本的小麥粉和水做成麵團再桿成一大塊，在麵皮上加油、香蔥和鹽，捲成圓形狀，要煎之前再桿開好下鍋油煎，這就是有層次的蔥油餅。在宜蘭及台灣等地區，街頭攤販會賣一般或加蛋的蔥油餅。這種小吃是當時國民黨在大陸撤退逃離到台灣時所帶進來的小吃。蔥油餅或蔥花大餅並沒有考據的來源。有些來源指出在北京的印度人口對這個在中國的小吃有啟發的影響，因為這與印度人自己的印度大餅很類似。在台灣東北部沿海地區的宜蘭縣是兩個當地原住民：一是靠山的泰雅族人和沿海河岸而居的噶瑪蘭人，這也是宜蘭縣被命名的起源。最好的蔥油餅在宜蘭，因為這裡所生長的三星蔥是最棒的蔥。

1 短獨白「影子跟讀」和填空練習

2 短獨白獨立演練和詳解

3 短獨白模擬試題

宜蘭－魚丸米粉

　　此篇為「影子跟讀短獨白練習」，規劃了由聽「短獨白」的shadowing練習，強化聽力專注力和掌握各個考點，現在就一起動身，開始聽「短獨白」！

Ilan-Fish Ball and Rice Noodle Soup
宜蘭－魚丸米粉

　　Tofu (or Dou Fu) and other soy products like fresh or frozen green soybeans for eating, soy sauce and soy milk are important staples in Taiwanese kitchens and are plentiful in street vendors' stalls. Taiwan is within the top 10 countries in soybean consumption in the world. Almost 10 percent of Taiwan's arable land is planted to soybeans, yet 97 percent of the soy Taiwan needs is imported from other countries. In fact, US soybeans account for 55 percent of what Taiwan imports of this high protein snack, condiment or main dish. Small scale manufacturers still make bean curd by hand and deliver it to markets and restaurants every morning. The process for making bean curd involves soaking soy beans, grinding them, straining off the soy milk, then coagulating what is left before placing the semi-solid remainder into a mold so that it can "set." Once tofu is made, it is eatable. It can also be made into different products. Oily tofu is fried tofu, which is popularly added in soups or hot pot in Taiwan. Fried tofu is a key ingredient in making an authentic bowl of fish and noodle soup in Ilan.

　　豆腐或其他豆製品如用來吃的新鮮或冷凍毛豆、醬油和豆漿都是在台灣的家庭或路邊攤烹煮的重要食材。台灣是全世界消費黃豆排名前 10 名的國家。台灣的耕地有近 10%是種植黃豆，而台灣所需要的黃豆有 97%是從其他國家進口的。事實上，美國的黃豆佔台灣進口量的 55%，黃豆是高蛋白的來源，也可做調味品或主菜。小規模的豆腐生產廠家還是有人用手工做豆腐，每天早晨提供給市場和餐館。豆腐的製作方法包括浸泡大豆，研磨，過濾豆漿，凝固後把半成品放入模型「成型」。一旦豆腐做好了，可以馬上食用，也可以做成不同產品。油豆腐可以放入湯或火鍋，在台灣這都是流行的吃法。油豆腐是宜蘭魚丸米粉的一個關鍵食材。

宜蘭－魚丸米粉

▶▶ 影子跟讀「短獨白填空」練習　🎧 MP3 021

除了前面的「影子跟讀短獨白練習」，現在試著在聽完對話後，完成下列填空練習，從中強化生活場景中常見的字彙以及拼字能力，答案的話請參照前面的獨白！

Ilan-Fish Ball and Rice Noodle Soup
宜蘭－魚丸米粉

Tofu (or Dou Fu) and other soy _____ like fresh or frozen green soybeans ____ eating, soy sauce and soy milk are important staples ____ Taiwanese _____ and are _____ ____ street vendors' stalls. Taiwan is within the top 10 countries in soybean consumption in the world. Almost 10 percent of Taiwan's _____ land is _____ ____ soybeans, yet 97 percent of the soy Taiwan needs is _____ ____ other countries. In fact, US soybeans account ____ 55 percent of what Taiwan imports ____ this high _____ snack, _____ or main dish. Small scale _____ still make bean curd ____ hand and deliver it to _____ and restaurants every morning. The process for making bean curd involves soaking soy beans, grinding them, straining ____ the soy milk, then _____ what is left before placing the semi-solid _____ into a mold so that it can "set." Once tofu is made, it is _____. It can also be made ____ different _____. Oily tofu is fried tofu, which is popularly added ____ soups or hot pot in Taiwan. Fried tofu is a key _____ ____ making an _____ bowl of fish and noodle soup in Ilan.

豆腐或其他豆製品如用來吃的新鮮或冷凍毛豆、醬油和豆漿都是在台灣的家庭或路邊攤烹煮的重要食材。台灣是全世界消費黃豆排名前 10 名的國家。台灣的耕地有近 10%是種植黃豆，而台灣所需要的黃豆有 97%是從其他國家進口的。事實上，美國的黃豆佔台灣進口量的 55%，黃豆是高蛋白的來源，也可做調味品或主菜。小規模的豆腐生產廠家還是有人用手工做豆腐，每天早晨提供給市場和餐館。豆腐的製作方法包括浸泡大豆，研磨，過濾豆漿，凝固後把半成品放入模型「成型」。一旦豆腐做好了，可以馬上食用，也可以做成不同產品。油豆腐可以放入湯或火鍋，在台灣這都是流行的吃法。油豆腐是宜蘭魚丸米粉的一個關鍵食材。

嘉義－豆花

▶▶ 影子跟讀「短獨白」練習　🎧 MP3 022

此篇為「影子跟讀短獨白練習」，規劃了由聽「短獨白」的shadowing練習，強化聽力專注力和掌握各個考點，現在就一起動身，開始聽「短獨白」！

Chiayi Tofu Pudding, Doufu Hua, Douhua
嘉義－豆花

Tofu pudding, doufu hua, douhua, or translated directly "tofu flower" is a simple, traditional dessert, forms of which you can find around East Asia. The Taiwan form can be cold in summer or warm in winter, but always refreshing. Rolling carts of soy milk vendors were common in earlier days, bringing their product into neighborhoods and making all the kids beg their mothers for a little money to buy this treat. It is simply soy milk made fresh daily into a gelatin-like form, floating in a thin brown sugar syrup and topped with sweetened black beans, red beans, or peanuts. In other parts of Asia, there might be ginger or almond in the syrup, or it may also be savory and served for breakfast. It is possible to find these forms of tofu pudding also in Taiwan, but the most traditional is simply topped with sugar syrup. Chiayi county has a strong, diverse economy with lumber from the Ali mountains in the west, central location for strong transportation and communication sectors, plus strong industry and educational institutions. Chiayi hosts a famous international music festival during the last two weeks of December, providing performance and learning opportunities for participants from across the globe.

豆腐布丁、豆腐花、豆花，或直接翻譯成「豆花」其實就是一個簡單的、傳統的甜點，這在東南亞很普遍。台灣的豆花在夏天是吃冷的，在冬天是吃溫的，兩種吃法都會讓人很驚喜。在早期流動豆漿攤販是很常見的，他們在社區裡賣豆花，很多孩子就會向媽媽討一點錢來買這種甜點。這其實是豆漿做成有膠狀的甜點，在上面淋上黑糖漿加上甜黑豆、紅豆或花生。在亞洲其他地區，有些地方會加薑或杏仁的糖漿，或是做成鹹的，或者也有人當早餐吃。在台灣這種口味的豆花也很普遍，但真正傳統的口味只是淋上糖漿。嘉義縣因為有阿里山山脈生產木材而有強大也多樣化的經濟與運輸和通信行業，也有很不錯的產業和教育機構。嘉義在 12 月的最後兩個星期會舉辦來自世界各地的國際著名音樂節，提供參加者表演和學習的機會。

嘉義－豆花

▶▶ 影子跟讀「短獨白填空」練習　🎧 MP3 022

除了前面的**「影子跟讀短獨白練習」**，現在試著在聽完對話後，完成下列填空練習，從中強化生活場景中常見的字彙以及拼字能力，答案的話請參照前面的獨白！

Chiayi Tofu Pudding, Doufu Hua, Douhua
嘉義－豆花

Tofu pudding, doufu hua, douhua, or _____ directly "tofu flower" is a simple, traditional _____, forms ___ which you can find around East Asia. The Taiwan form can be cold ___ summer or warm in winter, but always _____. Rolling carts of soy milk _____ were common ___ earlier days, bringing their product ___ neighborhoods and making all the kids _____ their mothers ___ a little _____ to buy this treat. It is simply soy milk made fresh daily ___ a gelatin-like form, floating ___ a thin brown sugar _____ and topped ___ _____ black beans, red beans, or _____. In other parts of Asia, there might be _____ or almond ___ the syrup, or it may also be savory and served for _____. It is _____ to find these forms of tofu pudding also in Taiwan, but the most _____ is simply topped ___ sugar syrup. Chiayi county has a strong, _____ economy ___ _____ from the Ali mountains ___ the west, _____ location ___ strong _____ and _____ sectors, plus strong industry and _____ institutions. Chiayi hosts a famous _____ music festival during the last two weeks ___ December, providing _____ and learning _____ ___ participants from across the globe.

豆腐布丁、豆腐花、豆花，或直接翻譯成「豆花」其實就是一個簡單的、傳統的甜點，這在東南亞很普遍。台灣的豆花在夏天是吃冷的，在冬天是吃溫的，兩種吃法都會讓人很驚喜。在早期流動豆漿攤販是很常見的，他們在社區裡賣豆花，很多孩子就會向媽媽討一點錢來買這種甜點。這其實是豆漿做成有膠狀的甜點，在上面淋上黑糖漿加上甜黑豆、紅豆或花生。在亞洲其他地區，有些地方會加薑或杏仁的糖漿，或是做成鹹的，或者也有人當早餐吃。在台灣這種口味的豆花也很普遍，但真正傳統的口味只是淋上糖漿。嘉義縣因為有阿里山山脈生產木材而有強大也多樣化的經濟與運輸和通信行業，也有很不錯的產業和教育機構。嘉義在 12 月的最後兩個星期會舉辦來自世界各地的國際著名音樂節，提供參加者表演和學習的機會。

UNIT ㉓

雲林－炊仔飯

▶▶ 影子跟讀「短獨白」練習　🎧 MP3 023

此篇為「**影子跟讀短獨白練習**」，規劃了由聽「**短獨白**」的shad-owing練習，強化聽力專注力和掌握各個考點，現在就一起動身，開始聽「**短獨白**」！

Yunlin Steamed Stuffed Rice
雲林－炊仔飯

Tube rice, zhu tong fan, or bamboo rice is a traditional food of indigenous Taiwanese people. This savory dish is made from sticky rice and numerous local ingredients, all cooked but then stuffed into about a 20 cm (8 inch) long mature, green bamboo stalk, then sealed and steamed. Because of the steaming, the rice and ingredients are melded together in a sticky, delicious tower or served in an opened bamboo stalk. The bamboo stalk was an excellent container not only to cook this light meal, but also for early hunters and gatherers to carry some nourishment on their expeditions. Primary ingredients are pork – or wild boar – shitake mushrooms, shallots and shrimp. Street vendors serve it with a delicious sauce and may top it with peanuts, pork thread or cilantro. Steamed stuffed rice is a similar dish using small bowls rather than bamboo stalks. Steamed stuffed rice originated in Yunlin and only can be found in Yunlin. Different from sticky rice used in tube rice, steamed stuffed rice uses regular cooked rice, stuffed with meat sauce and green peas into a small bowl then steamed. Tube rice can be found all over the island but steamed stuffed rice can only be found in Yunlin.

　　竹筒飯是台灣原住民的傳統食品。這種美味的菜餚是由糯米和當地食材煮熟後，放入約 20 公分（八吋）的綠竹筒密封好後再蒸熟。因為有蒸過，因此所有的材料會混合在一起，煮好時切開來就可直接食用。竹筒是一種很棒的食材容器，不但能用來煮輕食，早期獵人打獵時也用來盛裝他們的食物。竹筒飯主要成分是野豬肉、香菇、紅蔥和蝦。有些小販會加上美味的醬料和花生、肉鬆或香菜。炊仔飯也是一種類似竹筒飯的美食，是用碗當蒸具而不是竹筒。炊仔飯起源於雲林，也只有在雲林才有。不同於竹筒飯裡所用的糯米，炊仔飯是用一般的米飯，將肉燥、青豆等配料都放到碗裡後再蒸熟。竹筒飯在台灣全島都可以吃的到，但是炊仔飯只有在雲林才有。

雲林－炊仔飯

▶▶ 影子跟讀「短獨白填空」練習　🎧 MP3 023

除了前面的「影子跟讀短獨白練習」，現在試著在聽完對話後，完成下列填空練習，從中強化生活場景中常見的字彙以及拼字能力，答案的話請參照前面的獨白！

Yunlin Steamed Stuffed Rice
雲林－炊仔飯

Tube rice, zhu tong fan, or bamboo rice is a traditional food of _____ Taiwanese people. This savory dish is made ____ sticky rice and _____ local ingredients, all cooked but then stuffed ____ about a 20 cm (8 inch) long mature, green _____ stalk, then sealed and _____. Because ____ the steaming, the rice and ingredients are _____ together ____ a sticky, delicious tower or served ____ an opened _____ stalk. The bamboo stalk was an excellent _____ not only to cook this light meal, but also for early _____ and gatherers to carry some _____ on their _____. Primary ingredients are pork – or wild boar – shitake mushrooms, shallots and shrimp. Street vendors serve it ____ a _____ sauce and may top it ___ peanuts, pork thread or cilantro. Steamed stuffed rice is a similar dish using small bowls rather than bamboo stalks. Steamed stuffed rice _____ ___ Yunlin and only can be found ___ Yunlin. Different ___ sticky rice used ___ tube rice, steamed stuffed rice uses _____ cooked rice, stuffed ___ meat sauce and green peas ___ a small bowl then steamed. Tube rice can be found all over the _____ but steamed stuffed rice can only be found ___ Yunlin.

竹筒飯是台灣原住民的傳統食品。這種美味的菜餚是由糯米和當地食材煮熟後，放入約 20 公分（八吋）的綠竹筒密封好後再蒸熟。因為有蒸過，因此所有的材料會混合在一起，煮好時切開來就可直接食用。竹筒是一種很棒的食材容器，不但能用來煮輕食，早期獵人打獵時也用來盛裝他們的食物。竹筒飯主要成分是野豬肉、香菇、紅蔥和蝦。有些小販會加上美味的醬料和花生、肉鬆或香菜。炊仔飯也是一種類似竹筒飯的美食，是用碗當蒸具而不是竹筒。炊仔飯起源於雲林，也只有在雲林才有。不同於竹筒飯裡所用的糯米，炊仔飯是用一般的米飯，將肉燥、青豆等配料都放到碗裡後再蒸熟。竹筒飯在台灣全島都可以吃的到，但是炊仔飯只有在雲林才有。

東海－雞腳凍

▶▶ 影子跟讀「短獨白」練習　🎧 MP3 024

　　此篇為「影子跟讀短獨白練習」，規劃了由聽「短獨白」的shadowing練習，強化聽力專注力和掌握各個考點，現在就一起動身，開始聽「短獨白」！

Taichung Cold Chicken Feet
東海－雞腳凍

　　Cold chicken feet. While the name may not be appealing to some western tastes, chicken feet are an important part of traditional cuisines all over the world. Nowhere are chicken feet more popular than Taiwan, Hong Kong, and China. In fact, poultry producers in the United States make significant profits exporting chicken feet to Asia. Over the past 20 years, occasional poultry import bans due to faltering trade agreement negotiations or fears of avian flu have restricted the flow of US chicken to Asia. Typically, when added together, Taiwan, Hong Kong, and China are the destination of almost 25 percent of the US' poultry exports – an indication of how important chicken feet really are in the culture. Chicken feet are a traditional dim sum treat, originating in the Cantonese region of China, making them a perfect dish to enjoy from a street vendor in Taiwan. In night markets in Taiwan, especially the most famous place to buy them in Taichung City, they are served cold. It's not normally a hot and spicy dish, instead relying on the richness of the gelatinous texture of the feet, the skin, and the cooking process.

雞腳凍。雖然這個名字可能不會吸引西方人的胃口，雞爪其實是世界各地傳統美食一個重要的食材。沒有其他地方的雞爪比台灣、香港和中國更受歡迎。事實上，美國家禽生產商出口到亞洲雞爪有獲得顯著的利潤。在過去的 20 年裡，有時因為搖擺不定的貿易協定談判或對禽流感的憂慮禁止家禽進口，而制約了美國雞肉在亞洲的流動。一般情況下，台灣、香港和中國的市場需求加起來占有美國禽肉出口 24% 的量，這也顯示雞爪在這些文化裡的重要性。雞爪是廣式飲茶的小吃，源自於中國的廣東地區，後來成為台灣流行的美食。在台灣的夜市，最有名的雞腳凍是在台中的夜市，這是冷食的。雞腳凍通常不是辛辣的小吃，雞腳凍好吃的地方是在雞腳的凝膠質，這是雞腳的皮所滷出來的口感。

東海一雞腳凍

▶▶ 影子跟讀「短獨白填空」練習　🎧 MP3 024

　　除了前面的**「影子跟讀短獨白練習」**，現在試著在聽完對話後，完成下列填空練習，從中強化生活場景中常見的字彙以及拼字能力，答案的話請參照前面的獨白！

Taichung Cold Chicken Feet
東海一雞腳凍

　　Cold chicken feet. While the name may not be _____ ___ some western _____, chicken feet are an important part ___ traditional cuisines all over the world. Nowhere are chicken feet more _____ than Taiwan, Hong Kong, and China. In fact, _____ producers in the United States make _____ profits exporting chicken feet ___ Asia. Over the past 20 years, _____ poultry import bans due to faltering trade _____ negotiations or fears of _____ have _____ the flow ___ US chicken to Asia. Typically, when added together, Taiwan, Hong Kong, and China are the _____ of almost 25 percent of the US' poultry exports – an _____ ___ how important chicken feet really are ___ the culture. Chicken feet are a traditional dim sum treat, _____ in the _____ region of China, making them a _____ dish ___ enjoy from a street vendor ___ Taiwan. In night markets in Taiwan, especially the most _____ place to buy them in Taichung City, they are served cold. It's not normally a hot and spicy dish, instead relying ___ the richness of the _____ texture ___ the feet, the skin, and the cooking process.

雞腳凍。雖然這個名字可能不會吸引西方人的胃口，雞爪其實是世界各地傳統美食一個重要的食材。沒有其他地方的雞爪比台灣、香港和中國更受歡迎。事實上，美國家禽生產商出口到亞洲雞爪有獲得顯著的利潤。在過去的 20 年裡，有時因為搖擺不定的貿易協定談判或對禽流感的憂慮禁止家禽進口，而制約了美國雞肉在亞洲的流動。一般情況下，台灣、香港和中國的市場需求加起來占有美國禽肉出口24％的量，這也顯示雞爪在這些文化裡的重要性。雞爪是廣式飲茶的小吃，源自於中國的廣東地區，後來成為台灣流行的美食。在台灣的夜市，最有名的雞腳凍是在台中的夜市，這是冷食的。雞腳凍通常不是辛辣的小吃，雞腳凍好吃的地方是在雞腳的凝膠質，這是雞腳的皮所滷出來的口感。

台中－豬血糕

▶▶ 影子跟讀「短獨白」練習 🎧 MP3 025

　　此篇為「影子跟讀短獨白練習」，規劃了由聽「短獨白」的shadowing練習，強化聽力專注力和掌握各個考點，現在就一起動身，開始聽「短獨白」！

Taichung Pig's Blood Rice Cake
台中－豬血糕

　　Pig's blood rice cake is served on a stick in many night markets in Taiwan. The name is perhaps a little too honest for some, but the ingredients and texture are not completely unfamiliar to anyone who eats sausage, especially traditional European forms like boudin from France. Firm, yet chewy is the best way to describe the texture. This treat on a stick is made from sticky rice cooked in pork blood. Once firm, the warm cake is usually dipped in a soy-pork broth or sweet and sour sauce and rolled in cilantro and sweet peanut powder. The origins of such a dish likely date back to old days when farmers did not want to waste the blood that drained from ducks that they had slaughtered. Duck meat and blood are valuable in Chinese medicine, so making a rice cake from the duck blood was not only frugal, but also healthy. Visitors to Taichung City can enjoy the best pig's blood rice cake at Fengjia Night Market in Taichung County. This night market is the second largest in Taiwan.

1 短獨白「影子跟讀」和填空練習

串在竹籤上的豬血糕在很多台灣夜市都有賣。這個名字也許太真實了一點，但它的成分和質感對於吃香腸的人來說並不是完全陌生，特別是歐洲傳統的香腸，如來自法國的 boudin。口感紮實也有嚼勁是很多人描述吃豬血糕的感覺。豬血糕由糯米加豬血所煮成的。一旦蒸熟成型後，熱熱的豬血糕通常沾醬吃或裹上香菜和花生粉。這個小吃的起源可能要追溯到以前農民不想浪費他們宰殺的鴨子所排出的血液。鴨肉和血在中藥裡是很有價值的，所以用鴨血所做的豬血糕不僅節儉，而且還健康。隨著時間的轉換，與豬肉比起來鴨肉變得更加昂貴，所以豬血就取代鴨血來做豬血糕。遊客可以在台中的逢甲夜市吃到最好的豬血糕。逢甲夜市是台灣第二大夜市。

2 短獨白獨立演練和詳解

3 短獨白模擬試題

台中－豬血糕

▶▶ 影子跟讀「短獨白填空」練習 🎧 MP3 025

除了前面的「**影子跟讀短獨白練習**」，現在試著在聽完對話後，完成下列填空練習，從中強化生活場景中常見的字彙以及拼字能力，答案的話請參照前面的獨白！

Taichung Pig's Blood Rice Cake
台中－豬血糕

Pig's blood rice cake is served ____ a _____ in many night markets in Taiwan. The name is perhaps a little too _____ for some, but the ingredients and texture are not _____ unfamiliar ____ anyone who eats sausage, especially traditional European forms like boudin from France. Firm, yet chewy is the best way ____ describe the texture. This treat ____ a stick is made ____ sticky rice cooked ____ pork blood. Once firm, the warm cake is usually dipped ___ a soy-pork broth or sweet and sour sauce and rolled ____ cilantro and sweet peanut powder. The _____ of such a dish likely date back to old days when farmers did not want to waste the blood that _____ ____ ducks that they had _____. Duck meat and blood are _____ ____ Chinese medicine, so making a rice cake ___ the duck blood was not only frugal, but also healthy. Visitors to Taichung City can enjoy the best pig's blood rice cake at Fengjia Night Market ___ Taichung County. This night market is the second largest in Taiwan.

串在竹籤上的豬血糕在很多台灣夜市都有賣。這個名字也許太真實了一點，但它的成分和質感對於吃香腸的人來說並不是完全陌生，特別是歐洲傳統的香腸，如來自法國的 boudin。口感紮實也有嚼勁是很多人描述吃豬血糕的感覺。豬血糕由糯米加豬血所煮成的。一旦蒸熟成型後，熱熱的豬血糕通常沾醬吃或裹上香菜和花生粉。這個小吃的起源可能要追溯到以前農民不想浪費他們宰殺的鴨子所排出的血液。鴨肉和血在中藥裡是很有價值的，所以用鴨血所做的豬血糕不僅節儉，而且還健康。隨著時間的轉換，與豬肉比起來鴨肉變得更加昂貴，所以豬血就取代鴨血來做豬血糕。遊客可以在台中的逢甲夜市吃到最好的豬血糕。逢甲夜市是台灣第二大夜市。

1 短獨白「影子跟讀」和填空練習

2 短獨白獨立演練和詳解

3 短獨白模擬試題

新竹－紅豆餅

▶▶ 影子跟讀「短獨白」練習　🎧 MP3 026

　　此篇為「**影子跟讀短獨白練習**」，規劃了由聽「**短獨白**」的shadowing練習，強化聽力專注力和掌握各個考點，現在就一起動身，開始聽「**短獨白**」！

Hsinchu city Imagawayaki
新竹－紅豆餅

　　Japanese's rule over Taiwan from 1895 to 1945 influenced the island's appearance as well as its cuisine. Japan sought to make Taiwan a model colony and produced an economy that would further aid its expansionist plans. So, Japan poured many resources into the island, modernizing roads, rail, energy, and helping to boost Taiwan into the industrial powerhouse it is today. Imagawayaki (red bean pastry) is a traditional dessert dating from Japan's 18th century that is still a welcome by-product of Japan's colonization of Taiwan. It is essentially pancake batter, cooked in a special griddle that looks like a giant western muffin tin or open waffle iron with round holes instead of square holes. As the batter begins to cook, the vendor adds a large spoonful of filling on top of the batter. The most traditional type is red bean paste, though more street market stalls are also selling custard, peanut, Asian cabbage, dried turnip, and curry-filled imagawayaki. "Zhu Cheng Red Bean Pastry" is a famous place for red bean pastry in northern Hsinchu City. They sell red bean pastry with a variety of fillings such as red bean, cream butter, taro paste, sesame, dried radish and cabbage.

1 短獨白「影子跟讀」和填空練習

2 短獨白獨立演練和詳解

3 短獨白模擬試題

日本從 1895 年到 1945 年統治台灣也同時影響了台灣的飲食。日本有心要把台灣建立為一個模範殖民地以進一步的邁向日本擴張領土的目的。所以日本在台灣這個島嶼上投入了很多的資源，改建道路、鐵路、能源設施，這些後來都是幫助台灣走向工業轉型的重要背景。「紅豆餅」也就是車輪餅是一個傳統的甜點，其歷史可以追溯到日本的 18 世紀，這個小吃現在在台灣仍然很受歡迎。基本上是把麵糊倒入特殊的鐵鑄模烘烤，模子看起來像一個巨大的西式鬆餅烤具或是開放式有鐵圓孔的鬆餅，而不是一般的方型孔。麵糊煎熟後中央再填入餡，再取兩片餅皮夾合就完成。竹城紅豆餅在新竹市很受歡迎，賣的內餡有奶油，花生，最近幾年還有鹹味的紅豆餅，內餡高麗菜，蘿蔔乾甚至有咖哩內餡。賣的口味有：紅豆、奶油、芋頭、芝麻、菜脯和高麗菜。

新竹－紅豆餅

▶▶ 影子跟讀「短獨白填空」練習　🎧 MP3 026

除了前面的「**影子跟讀短獨白練習**」，現在試著在聽完對話後，完成下列填空練習，從中強化生活場景中常見的字彙以及拼字能力，答案的話請參照前面的獨白！

Hsinchu city Imagawayaki
新竹－紅豆餅

Japanese's rule ___ Taiwan from 1895 to 1945 _____ the island's _____ as well as its _____. Japan sought ___ make Taiwan a model colony and produced an _____ that would further aid its _____ plans. So, Japan poured many _____ ___ the island, modernizing roads, rail, energy, and helping to _____ Taiwan ___ the industrial _____ it is today. Imagawayaki (red bean pastry) is a traditional dessert dating ___ Japan's 18th century that is still a _____ by-product of Japan's _____ of Taiwan. It is _____ pancake batter, cooked ___ a special griddle that looks like a giant _____ muffin tin or open waffle iron ___ round holes instead ___ square holes. ___ the batter begins to cook, the vendor adds a large

_____ of filling ___ top of the batter. The most _____ type is red bean paste, though more street market stalls are also selling custard, peanut, Asian _____, dried turnip, and curry-filled imagawayaki. "Zhu Cheng Red Bean Pastry" is a famous place for red bean pastry ___ northern Hsinchu City. They sell red bean _____ with a variety of fillings such as red bean, cream butter, taro paste, sesame, dried radish and cabbage.

日本從 1895 年到 1945 年統治台灣也同時影響了台灣的飲食。日本有心要把台灣建立為一個模範殖民地以進一步的邁向日本擴張領土的目的。所以日本在台灣這個島嶼上投入了很多的資源，改建道路、鐵路、能源設施，這些後來都是幫助台灣走向工業轉型的重要背景。「紅豆餅」也就是車輪餅是一個傳統的甜點，其歷史可以追溯到日本的 18 世紀，這個小吃現在在台灣仍然很受歡迎。基本上是把麵糊倒入特殊的鐵鑄模烘烤，模子看起來像一個巨大的西式鬆餅烤具或是開放式有鐵圓孔的鬆餅，而不是一般的方型孔。麵糊煎熟後中央再填入餡，再取兩片餅皮夾合就完成。竹城紅豆餅在新竹市很受歡迎，賣的內餡有奶油，花生，最近幾年還有鹹味的紅豆餅，內餡高麗菜，蘿蔔乾甚至有咖哩內餡。賣的口味有：紅豆、奶油、芋頭、芝麻、菜脯和高麗菜。

桃園－刨冰山

▶▶ 影子跟讀「短獨白」練習 🎧 MP3 027

此篇為**「影子跟讀短獨白練習」**，規劃了由聽**「短獨白」**的shadowing練習，強化聽力專注力和掌握各個考點，現在就一起動身，開始聽**「短獨白」**！

Taoyuan Shaved Ice Mountain
桃園－刨冰山

Bao Bing is "a dessert made of shaved or finely crushed ice with flavoring." It is called Tsu Bing in Taiwanese. It makes sense to call it "Shaved Ice" in English. In general, shaved ice mountain consists of a big pile of tiny ice pieces, topped with sweet fruit like mango and sweetened condensed milk. The ice itself is incredibly fine and more similar to snow than crushed ice. A more traditional version is smaller and includes tapioca balls. It's quite easy to find shaved ice mountain with every variety of fruit imaginable, sweetened red beans, taro root, sweet potato and tapioca pearls. Another common and unique topping for shaved ice mountain is aiyu jelly. Aiyu jelly is made from a type of fig found in Taiwan, although the jelly has little flavor of its own. It just adds a wiggly, squishy texture to the popular dessert. Another very unique and traditional shaved ice is banana ice. There were no fancy toppings in the olden days when resources were very limited. Banana ice is just water mixed with sugar and banana flavoring. Freeze the mixture to form a big square ice then shave it finely. That is the old time favorite banana ice.

　　刨冰就是一種「削薄的冰上面加調味的甜點」，台語又稱為剉冰。用英文「Shaved Ice」來翻譯這個美食是很有道理的。一般的刨冰就是將冰切細後在冰的上面加上水果如芒果和煉乳。刨冰的冰是刨得很綿細，比冰塊還像雪片。有些更傳統的冰更是在綿細冰上面加上粉圓。刨冰的配料有各種水果、紅豆、芋頭、甜番薯、粉圓和珍珠都可以加。另一種常見和獨特的配料是愛玉凍。愛玉果凍是由一種在台灣生長的一種無花果所製成的，這種果凍有很特殊的味道。加了愛玉的冰吃起來有軟軟的口感很受歡迎。香蕉冰是另一種很傳統也很特別的味道。以前物資缺少的年代是加上這麼多料的冰，通常是用最便宜的用料作出最好吃的風味，於是在清冰裡加了食用性香蕉水拌入白砂糖，結凍後，即可刨成可口的香蕉冰。

桃園－刨冰山

▶▶影子跟讀「短獨白填空」練習　🎧 MP3 027

　　除了前面的「**影子跟讀短獨白練習**」，現在試著在聽完對話後，完成下列填空練習，從中強化生活場景中常見的字彙以及拼字能力，答案的話請參照前面的獨白！

Taoyuan Shaved Ice Mountain
桃園－刨冰山

　　Bao Bing is "a _____ made ___ shaved or finely crushed ice ___ flavoring." It is called Tsu Bing in Taiwanese. It makes sense to call it "Shaved Ice" in English. In general, shaved ice mountain consists ___ a big pile of tiny ice pieces, topped ___ sweet fruit like _____ and sweetened _____ milk. The ice itself is _____ fine and more similar to snow ___ crushed ice. A more traditional version is smaller and includes tapioca balls. It's quite easy to find shaved ice _____ ___ every variety ___ fruit _____, sweetened red beans, taro root, sweet _____ and tapioca pearls. Another _____ and unique topping for shaved ice mountain is aiyu jelly. Aiyu jelly is made ___ a type of fig found ___ Taiwan, although the jelly has little flavor ___ its own. It just adds a wiggly, squishy texture ___ the popular dessert. Another very unique and traditional shaved ice is _____ ice. There were no fancy toppings ___ the olden days when _____ were very limited. Banana ice is just water mixed ___ sugar and banana flavoring. Freeze the _____ ___ form a big square ice then shave it _____. That is the old time favorite banana ice.

　　刨冰就是一種「削薄的冰上面加調味的甜點」，台語又稱為剉冰。用英文「Shaved Ice」來翻譯這個美食是很有道理的。一般的刨冰就是將冰切細後在冰的上面加上水果如芒果和煉乳。刨冰的冰是刨得很綿細，比冰塊還像雪片。有些更傳統的冰更是在綿細冰上面加上粉圓。刨冰的配料有各種水果、紅豆、芋頭、甜番薯、粉圓和珍珠都可以加。另一種常見和獨特的配料是愛玉凍。愛玉果凍是由一種在台灣生長的一種無花果所製成的，這種果凍有很特殊的味道。加了愛玉的冰吃起來有軟軟的口感很受歡迎。香蕉冰是另一種很傳統也很特別的味道。以前物資缺少的年代是加上這麼多料的冰，通常是用最便宜的用料作出最好吃的風味，於是在清冰裡加了食用性香蕉水拌入白砂糖，結凍後，即可刨成可口的香蕉冰。

台北－鐵蛋

▶▶ 影子跟讀「短獨白」練習 🎧 MP3 028

　　此篇為「影子跟讀短獨白練習」，規劃了由聽「短獨白」的shadowing練習，強化聽力專注力和掌握各個考點，現在就一起動身，開始聽「短獨白」！

Taipei Iron Egg
台北－鐵蛋

　　Iron egg, fried fish cracker, and A-Gei (stuffed tofu) are local delicacies native to the northern fishing village of Danshui. The origins behind these foods tell stories of fish villagers' frugal way of life regarding not wasting any food. Iron egg is a way to preserve the eggs by re-cooking and reserving leftover eggs. Fried fish cracker is also a way to preserve abundant fish caught in the river of Danshui at a time when there was no refrigeration system. The story behind A-Gei is a cook's reinvention from leftover scrap food. Iron eggs are made by simmering hard-boiled eggs in soy sauce and spices, then drying and repeating the process for several days. Because of the long cooking time, iron eggs are black or brownish-black and their texture is rubbery and tough. The locals love the chewy experience of enjoying an iron egg. Quail eggs are the traditional type of egg used to make iron eggs, so the resulting snack is much smaller than a conventional chicken egg. Danshui was not always the laid-back tourist-friendly town on the northern edge of Taipei, but once a focal point of Spanish settlement in the 1600s and then a key to Japan's colony on Taiwan during the first half of the 1900s.

鐵蛋、魚酥、阿給這些美味都是原產於淡水北部的漁村。這些美食故事的背後都在訴說著早期漁村生活不想浪費任何食物的哲學。鐵蛋是一種以再煮過，或儲備剩蛋的方式來保存蛋，魚酥也是在彼時沒有冰箱的年代，為了保存從淡水河中所捕獲的漁獲而衍生的。阿給的由來是為了不想浪費賣剩下的食材所研發的獨特小吃。鐵蛋的作法是用醬油及五香配方的滷料煮過後，再風乾，此道程序要重覆幾天才算完成。因為長時間的滷煮，鐵蛋呈黑或黑褐色，口感有彈性且硬。當地人喜歡鐵蛋的嚼勁。傳統的鐵蛋是用鵪鶉蛋，這樣做出來的鐵蛋會比一般的雞蛋小很多。早期的淡水並非像現在給人的印象是台北北部的悠閒觀光小鎮，17 世紀時西班牙曾把這裡當殖民地，在 20 世紀上半葉時，日本人把這裡當成殖民台灣的一個關鍵的地方。

1 短獨白「影子跟讀」和填空練習

2 短獨白獨立演練和詳解

3 短獨白模擬試題

台北－鐵蛋

▶▶ 影子跟讀「短獨白填空」練習 🎧 MP3 028

除了前面的「**影子跟讀短獨白練習**」，現在試著在聽完對話後，完成下列填空練習，從中強化生活場景中常見的字彙以及拼字能力，答案的話請參照前面的獨白！

Taipei Iron Egg
台北－鐵蛋

Iron egg, fried fish cracker, and A-Gei (stuffed tofu) are local _____ native ____ the _____ fishing _____ of Danshui. The origins behind these foods tell stories of fish villagers' _____ way of life regarding not wasting any food. Iron egg is a way to _____ the eggs ____ re-cooking and re-serving leftover eggs. Fried fish cracker is also a way ____ preserve _____ fish caught ____ the river of Danshui at a time when there was no _____ system. The story behind A-Gei is a cook's _____ ____ leftover scrap food. Iron eggs are made ____ simmering hard-boiled eggs ____ soy sauce and spices, then drying and _____ the _____ for several days. Because of the long cooking time, iron eggs are black or brownish-black and their texture is rubbery and tough. The _____ love the chewy experience ____ enjoying an iron egg. Quail eggs are the traditional type ____ egg used to make iron eggs, so the resulting snack is much smaller than a _____ chicken egg. Danshui was not always the laid-back _____ town ____ the _____ edge of Taipei, but once a focal point ____ Spanish _____ ____ the 1600s and then a key ____ Japan's colony ____ Taiwan during the first half of the 1900s.

　　鐵蛋、魚酥、阿給這些美味都是原產於淡水北部的漁村。這些美食故事的背後都在訴說著早期漁村生活不想浪費任何食物的哲學。鐵蛋是一種以再煮過，或儲備剩蛋的方式來保存蛋，魚酥也是在彼時沒有冰箱的年代，為了保存從淡水河中所捕獲的漁獲而衍生的。阿給的由來是為了不想浪費賣剩下的食材所研發的獨特小吃。鐵蛋的作法是用醬油及五香配方的滷料煮過後，再風乾，此道程序要重覆幾天才算完成。因為長時間的滷煮，鐵蛋呈黑或黑褐色，口感有彈性且硬。當地人喜歡鐵蛋的嚼勁。傳統的鐵蛋是用鵪鶉蛋，這樣做出來的鐵蛋會比一般的雞蛋小很多。早期的淡水並非像現在給人的印象是台北北部的悠閒觀光小鎮，17 世紀時西班牙曾把這裡當殖民地，在 20 世紀上半葉時，日本人把這裡當成殖民台灣的一個關鍵的地方。

屏東－胡椒蝦

▶▶ 影子跟讀「短獨白」練習　🎧 MP3 029

此篇為「**影子跟讀短獨白練習**」，規劃了由聽「**短獨白**」的shadowing練習，強化聽力專注力和掌握各個考點，現在就一起動身，開始聽「**短獨白**」！

Pingtung Pepper Shrimp
屏東－胡椒蝦

In many tropical, coastal areas of the world, shrimp is a staple food. Cultivating shrimp in small agricultural settings goes back to at least the 15th century in southeast Asia. Taiwan was an early adopter of fish farming on an industrial scale in the southern part of the island and quickly became one of the largest suppliers of exported shrimp. Sadly, the industry and the environment suffered great losses due to unsustainable practices during the 1980s. Since shrimp are relatively easy to grow and need only six months to mature from an egg to an adult shrimp, it's not surprising that shrimp is an ingredient in many traditional dishes in Taiwan. Taiwanese believe that shrimp are the sweetest when cooked in the shell. Among the dishes you may encounter in Taiwan are shrimp ball soup, shrimp in braised cabbage or stir-fried noodles, and pepper shrimp. Pepper shrimp is a relatively simple dish, made by soaking the whole unpeeled shrimp in rice wine, lightly breading it to deep fry it and then tossing in a pan for a quick stir fry with oil, garlic, ginger, and other spices. The shrimp is then arranged beautifully on a plate to be shared.

在世界許多熱帶沿海地區，蝦是一種主食。在東南亞小型的蝦養殖可以追溯到至少 15 世紀。台灣是最早在南部以產業規模做蝦養殖，並迅速成為出口蝦的最大供應商之一。不幸的是，在 80 年代期間的產業和環境，因為不當做法而遭受巨大損失。由於蝦是相對容易生長，由蝦卵到成蝦的成熟只需要六個月的成長期，所以在台灣許多傳統菜餚把蝦當作食材並不奇怪。台灣人認為，帶殼煮蝦最能煮出蝦的甜味。在台灣會常看到的蝦料理有蝦丸湯、麻油蝦、炒麵加蝦和胡椒蝦。胡椒蝦是很簡單的一道菜，把未去皮的蝦浸泡在米酒裡，輕輕裹上麵包屑後炸到金黃，撈起後在鍋裡加油和大蒜、生薑等香料快速翻炒就是一道簡單的胡椒蝦。出菜時，胡椒蝦漂亮地被鋪排在盤子上。

屏東－胡椒蝦

▶▶ 影子跟讀「短獨白填空」練習　🎧 MP3 029

除了前面的「影子跟讀短獨白練習」，現在試著在聽完對話後，完成下列填空練習，從中強化生活場景中常見的字彙以及拼字能力，答案的話請參照前面的獨白！

Pingtung Pepper Shrimp
屏東－胡椒蝦

____ many _____, coastal areas ____ the world, shrimp is a _____ food. Cultivating shrimp ____ small _____ settings goes back ____ at least the 15th century ____ southeast Asia. Taiwan was an early adopter of fish farming ____ an _____ scale in the southern part ____ the island and quickly became one of the largest suppliers of _____ shrimp. Sadly, the industry and the _____ suffered great losses due ____ _____ practices during the 1980s. Since shrimp are _____ easy ____ grow and need only six months ____ mature from an egg ____ an adult shrimp, it's not _____ that shrimp is an ingredient ____ many traditional dishes in Taiwan. Taiwanese believe that shrimp are the _____ when cooked ____ the shell.

Among the dishes you may encounter in Taiwan are shrimp ball soup, shrimp in braised _____ or stir-fried noodles, and pepper shrimp. Pepper shrimp is a relatively simple dish, made ____ soaking the whole _____ shrimp ____ rice wine, lightly breading it to deep fry it and then tossing ____ a pan for a quick stir fry ____ oil, garlic, ginger, and other spices. The shrimp is then _____ _____ on a plate to be _____.

在世界許多熱帶沿海地區，蝦是一種主食。在東南亞小型的蝦養殖可以追溯到至少 15 世紀。台灣是最早在南部以產業規模做蝦養殖，並迅速成為出口蝦的最大供應商之一。不幸的是，在 80 年代期間的產業和環境，因為不當做法而遭受巨大損失。由於蝦是相對容易生長，由蝦卵到成蝦的成熟只需要六個月的成長期，所以在台灣許多傳統菜餚把蝦當作食材並不奇怪。台灣人認為，帶殼煮蝦最能煮出蝦的甜味。在台灣會常看到的蝦料理有蝦丸湯、麻油蝦、炒麵加蝦和胡椒蝦。胡椒蝦是很簡單的一道菜，把未去皮的蝦浸泡在米酒裡，輕輕裹上麵包屑後炸到金黃，撈起後在鍋裡加油和大蒜、生薑等香料快速翻炒就是一道簡單的胡椒蝦。出菜時，胡椒蝦漂亮地被鋪排在盤子上。

UNIT ❸⓪

桃園－餡餅

▶ 影子跟讀「短獨白」練習　🎧 MP3 030

此篇為**「影子跟讀短獨白練習」**，規劃了由聽**「短獨白」**的shadowing練習，強化聽力專注力和掌握各個考點，現在就一起動身，開始聽**「短獨白」**！

Taoyuan Chinese Meat Pie
桃園－餡餅

Chinese meat pie is a simple, tasty snack of dough, filled with pork or beef and vegetables: onions or green onion, etc. Also in the meat mixture are traditional spices and flavors: soy sauce, ginger, garlic, eggs, sesame oil, pepper, salt, and sometimes monosodium glutamate. After the cook makes the simple wheat dough, he adds raw beef mixture, wraps dough around beef and pan fries 3-4 minutes per side. The result is a lovely, compact, round packet that is crispy on the top and bottom, soft on the sides, and really juicy on the inside. Common Chinese meat pies you can buy in Taiwan are a round shape, about 10 cm in diameter. Many foods from China come with a myth about how the food originated. In the case of Chinese Meat Pie, there are stories about an emperor who disguised himself in order to sample the rustic, local fare. He thought the pies were so delicious, and so much better than what he was served at the palace. He even commemorated the flavor with a hastily scribed poem.

　　餡餅是一種很簡單好吃的小吃，基本上是麵團裡包入豬肉餡或牛肉餡，加入蔬菜洋蔥或蔥等。另外在肉裡也會加入傳統的調料和香料：醬油、薑、蒜頭、雞蛋、香油、鹽，有時也會加味精。麵團做好後就可包入肉餡，然後兩邊各煎 3-4 分鐘即可。這樣就做出了小巧、紮實，上下表皮都酥脆，內餡柔軟多汁的圓餡餅。台灣攤販所賣的餡餅通常是一個 10 公分大小的圓形。很多中國食品的起源都有點神話般。就餡餅來說，有一個皇帝把自己喬裝就為了要品嚐當地的美食。他覺得餡餅很好吃，而且比任何他在皇殿裡所端上來的食物好吃多了。他甚至還匆匆的自己寫下一首詩來回味這個味道。

桃園－餡餅

▶ 影子跟讀「短獨白填空」練習 🎧 MP3 030

除了前面的**「影子跟讀短獨白練習」**，現在試著在聽完對話後，完成下列填空練習，從中強化生活場景中常見的字彙以及拼字能力，答案的話請參照前面的獨白！

Taoyuan Chinese Meat Pie
桃園－餡餅

Chinese meat pie is a simple, tasty _____ of dough, filled ____ pork or beef and vegetables: onions or green onion, etc. Also in the meat mixture are traditional spices and _____: soy sauce, ginger, garlic, eggs, _____ oil, pepper, salt, and sometimes monosodium glutamate. After the cook makes the simple wheat _____, he adds raw beef mixture, wraps dough around beef and pan fries 3-4 _____ per side. The result is a lovely, compact, round packet that is _____ ___ the top and bottom, soft ___ the sides, and really _____ on the inside. Common Chinese meat pies you can buy in Taiwan are a round shape, about 10 cm ____ diameter. Many foods from China come ____ a myth about how the food originated. ____ the case of

Chinese Meat Pie, there are stories about an _____ who _____ himself in order ___ sample the _____, local fare. He thought the pies were so delicious, and so much better than what he was served ___ the palace. He even _____ the flavor ___ a _____ scribed poem.

　　餡餅是一種很簡單好吃的小吃，基本上是麵團裡包入豬肉餡或牛肉餡，加入蔬菜洋蔥或蔥等。另外在肉裡也會加入傳統的調料和香料：醬油、薑、蒜頭、雞蛋、香油、鹽，有時也會加味精。麵團做好後就可包入肉餡，然後兩邊各煎 3-4 分鐘即可。這樣就做出了小巧、紮實，上下表皮都酥脆，內餡柔軟多汁的圓餡餅。台灣攤販所賣的餡餅通常是一個 10 公分大小的圓形。很多中國食品的起源都有點神話般。就餡餅來說，有一個皇帝把自己喬裝就為了要品嚐當地的美食。他覺得餡餅很好吃，而且比任何他在皇殿裡所端上來的食物好吃多了。他甚至還匆匆的自己寫下一首詩來回味這個味道。

UNIT ③①

南投－傳統口味營養三明治

▶▶ 影子跟讀「短獨白」練習　🎧 MP3 031

　　此篇為「**影子跟讀短獨白練習**」，規劃了由聽「**短獨白**」的shadowing練習，強化聽力專注力和掌握各個考點，現在就一起動身，開始聽「**短獨白**」！

Nantou-Taiwanese Old Style Sandwich
南投－傳統口味營養三明治

　　Taiwanese old style or nutritious sandwich uses a warm and crispy deep fried doughnut-type bread, sliced and filled with tomatoes and cucumbers, ham or sausage, slices of braised hardboiled egg and Taiwanese sweet mayonnaise. The origins of this sandwich are unknown, and even the mayonnaise may seem out of place from a western point of view. In fact, mayonnaise is the second most popular condiment in nearby Japan – second only to the ubiquitous soy sauce. Mayonnaise was probably introduced to East Asia from Europe some time during the 19th century. Now, mayonnaise has grown to such a high position in Japan that there is a mayonnaise museum called Mayo Terrace. Mayonnaise is so popular in Taiwan and Japan that American restaurant chains like Pizza Hut put mayonnaise on top of pizza in those countries. While this may sound bizarre to western tastes, globalization of food is not a new thing. Even in the 13th century, Marco Polo, the famous Italian explorer, is part of a legend in which he carries noodles from China back home to Italy. However, Italy strongly pro-tests against the idea that China invented noodles and notes that there is no archeological evidence to support the idea.

　　台灣古早味營養三明治是用炸過類似甜甜圈麵團的麵包，切片後加了番茄和黃瓜、火腿或香腸、滷蛋以及台式甜味美奶滋。這種三明治的起源無可考，西方人更想不到會有台式美奶滋這種醬料。事實上，美奶滋在日本是第二個最流行的調味品，僅次於無處不有的醬油。美奶滋可能在 19 世紀由歐洲傳入東亞。現在，美奶滋已經在日本有很崇高的地位，甚至有美乃滋展示館。美乃滋在台灣和日本非常受歡迎，美國的連鎖餐廳像必勝客會把美乃滋加在比薩餅上面。這對西方人來說聽起來匪夷所思，但食物的全球化不是最近才有的。甚至在 13 世紀，有關義大利著名的探險家馬可波羅有一個傳說，他把來自中國的麵條帶回老家義大利。然而，義大利對於中國發明麵條的說法是強烈抗議，表明沒有考古證據。

南投－傳統口味營養三明治

▶▶ 影子跟讀「短獨白填空」練習 🎧 MP3 031

除了前面的**「影子跟讀短獨白練習」**，現在試著在聽完對話後，完成下列填空練習，從中強化生活場景中常見的字彙以及拼字能力，答案的話請參照前面的獨白！

Nantou-Taiwanese Old Style Sandwich
南投－傳統口味營養三明治

Taiwanese old style or _____ sandwich uses a warm and crispy deep fried doughnut-type bread, sliced and filled ___ tomatoes and cucumbers, ham or _____, slices ___ braised hardboiled egg and Taiwanese sweet mayonnaise. The origins ___ this sandwich are _____, and even the mayonnaise may seem out of place from a _____ point of view. In fact, mayonnaise is the second most popular condiment ___ nearby Japan – second only ___ the _____ soy sauce. Mayonnaise was probably _____ ___ East Asia ___ Europe some time during the 19th century. Now, mayonnaise has grown ___ such a high _____ in Japan that there is a mayonnaise _____ called Mayo Terrace. Mayonnaise is so _____ in Taiwan and Japan that American restaurant chains like Pizza Hut put mayonnaise ___ top of pizza ___ those countries. While this may sound _____ ___ western tastes, _____ of food is not a new thing. Even in the 13th century, Marco Polo, the famous Italian explorer, is part ___ a _____ in which he carries noodles ___ China back home to Italy. However, Italy strongly protests against the idea that China _____ noodles and notes that there is no _____ _____ ___ support the idea.

　　台灣古早味營養三明治是用炸過類似甜甜圈麵團的麵包，切片後加了番茄和黃瓜、火腿或香腸、滷蛋以及台式甜味美奶滋。這種三明治的起源無可考，西方人更想不到會有台式美奶滋這種醬料。事實上，美奶滋在日本是第二個最流行的調味品，僅次於無處不有的醬油。美奶滋可能在 19 世紀由歐洲傳入東亞。現在，美奶滋已經在日本有很崇高的地位，甚至有美乃滋展示館。美乃滋在台灣和日本非常受歡迎，美國的連鎖餐廳像必勝客會把美乃滋加在比薩餅上面。這對西方人來說聽起來匪夷所思，但食物的全球化不是最近才有的。甚至在 13 世紀，有關義大利著名的探險家馬可波羅有一個傳說，他把來自中國的麵條帶回老家義大利。然而，義大利對於中國發明麵條的說法是強烈抗議，表明沒有考古證據。

南投－意麵

▶▶ 影子跟讀「短獨白」練習　🎧 MP3 032

　　此篇為「影子跟讀短獨白練習」，規劃了由聽「短獨白」的shadowing練習，強化聽力專注力和掌握各個考點，現在就一起動身，開始聽「短獨白」！

Nantou Noodles (Yi Mian)
南投－意麵

　　Nantou, Taiwan's only landlocked county is famous for its yi mian. Some noodle makers sun dry yi mian in a big, flat bamboo basket. Dry yi mian can be kept longer. They look similar to what western consumers know as Ramen noodles. The noodle dough is unique because it traditionally includes duck egg whites and soda water. Ducks were a main staple food in agricultural Taiwan. Duck yolks are soaked in salt for different dishes, leaving the whites as unneeded leftovers. Adding duck egg whites to yi mian could be just a way to use all the leftover duck egg whites. The soda water helps the noodles retain their spongy texture. Nantou County in Taiwan is 83% mountainous with 41 peaks reaching over 3,000 meters (9,800 feet) high. Beautiful inland lakes and ponds, like Sun Moon Lake, are popular tourist destinations. Nantou is also home to a 1500+ acre amusement park and cultural history living museum called Formosan Aboriginal Culture Village. The park celebrates eleven aboriginal tribes by recreating their villages and staging traditional performances for park attendees. Among the tribes featured is the smallest of Taiwan's recognized tribes, the Thao, who still make their home around Sun Moon Lake in Nantou.

南投，台灣唯一處於內陸的地方，以意麵最有名。這細扁的麵條通常都加在麵湯中。有些意麵也會在大竹籬上日曬至乾燥以利保存。乾意麵可以保存更久，意麵看起來很類似西方消費者所知道的速食麵。意麵的麵團跟一般做麵的麵團來説是比較獨特，因為意麵的麵團用的是鴨蛋蛋白和蘇打水。鴨子在以前的農業台灣算是主食。鴨蛋黃被醃製後用在不同的料理，剩下的鴨蛋白很可能是因此廢物利用拿來做意麵。蘇打水有助於麵條保留其 QQ 的口感。南投縣內有台灣83％的山地，有 41 個山峰達到 3000 多公尺（9800 英尺）。這裡有美麗的內陸湖泊和池塘，像日月潭就是熱門的旅遊地。南投也有一個有1500 英畝大的九族文化村，這是結合遊樂園和文化歷史生活館的觀光地。透過重建他們的村莊和傳統表演，九族文化村裡保留有11 個原住民的傳統。其中很有特色的部落邵族是台灣官方承認最小的部落，他們的世代祖先都住在南投日月潭。

南投－意麵

▶▶影子跟讀「短獨白填空」練習　🎧 MP3 032

　　除了前面的「**影子跟讀短獨白練習**」，現在試著在聽完對話後，完成下列填空練習，從中強化生活場景中常見的字彙以及拼字能力，答案的話請參照前面的獨白！

Nantou Noodles (Yi Mian)
南投－意麵

　　Nantou, Taiwan's only _____ county is famous ___ its yi mian. Some noodle makers sun dry yi mian in a big, flat bamboo _____. Dry yi mian can be kept longer. They look similar ___ what western consumers know as Ramen noodles. The noodle dough is _____ because it _____ includes duck egg whites and soda water. Ducks were a main _____ food ___ agricultural Taiwan. Duck yolks are soaked ___ salt ___ different dishes, leaving the whites ___ _____ leftovers. Adding duck egg whites to yi mian could be just a way to use all the leftover duck egg whites. The soda water helps the noodles _____ their spongy texture. Nantou County in Taiwan is 83% mountainous ___ 41 peaks reaching ___ 3,000 meters (9,800 feet) high. Beautiful inland lakes and ponds, like Sun Moon Lake, are _____ tourist _____. Nantou is also home ___ a 1500+ acre _____ park and cultural history living museum called Formosan Aboriginal Culture Village. The park _____ eleven aboriginal tribes by _____ their villages and staging traditional _____ ___ park attendees. Among the tribes _____ is the smallest of Taiwan's _____ tribes, the Thao, who still make their _____ around Sun Moon Lake ___ Nantou.

　　南投，台灣唯一處於內陸的地方，以意麵最有名。這細扁的麵條通常都加在麵湯中。有些意麵也會在大竹籬上日曬至乾燥以利保存。乾意麵可以保存更久，意麵看起來很類似西方消費者所知道的速食麵。意麵的麵團跟一般做麵的麵團來説是比較獨特，因為意麵的麵團用的是鴨蛋蛋白和蘇打水。鴨子在以前的農業台灣算是主食。鴨蛋黃被醃製後用在不同的料理，剩下的鴨蛋白很可能是因此廢物利用拿來做意麵。蘇打水有助於麵條保留其 QQ 的口感。南投縣內有台灣83%的山地，有 41 個山峰達到 3000 多公尺（9800 英尺）。這裡有美麗的內陸湖泊和池塘，像日月潭就是熱門的旅遊地。南投也有一個有1500 英畝大的九族文化村，這是結合遊樂園和文化歷史生活館的觀光地。透過重建他們的村莊和傳統表演，九族文化村裡保留有11 個原住民的傳統。其中很有特色的部落邵族是台灣官方承認最小的部落，他們的世代祖先都住在南投日月潭。

- 精選**26**個常見主題，短獨白雖短但納入更多解題巧思和詳盡解析，有效輔助各類型的考生自學並養成一定的聽力思維能力。除此之外，也能運用音檔，反覆演練搭配影子跟讀練習，強化「回想」聽到內容的能力，一舉獲取聽力佳績。

Part

2

短獨白獨立
演練和詳解

Unit *1*

寵物店廣告：毛小孩最佳洗髮精和護髮液

🔍 Instructions

❶ 請播放音檔聽下列對話，並完成試題。 🎧 MP3 033

1. **What products is this advertisement selling?**

    (A) toiletries for sensitive skin

    (B) toiletries for animal companions

    (C) shampoos made of organic ingredients

    (D) Skin infection treatment cream

2. **Who might be most likely interested in these products?**

    (A) people who have sensitive skin

    (B) people who have fur kids

    (C) people who have skin infection

    (D) people who walk their dogs regularly

3. **What will happen in the shop this week?**

    (A) a discount on shampoos only

    (B) giveaways

    (C) an annual sale

    (D) free pet grooming

聽力原文和對話

Questions 1-3 refer to the following advertisement

If you're looking for a shampoo and conditioner for your pets, Best Pet is the one for you. We used to diversify our products to different pets, pets, such as raccoons and rabbits, but now only focus on cats and dogs. With our products, you don't have to worry about the skin infection of your pets any more. We highly recommend you to visit our shop this week, since we will be having our annual sale. For the first one hundred customers, we're offering a special meal for you and your pets.

問題1-3請參閱下列廣告

如果你在替你的寵物尋找洗髮精和護髮液，倍斯特寵物公司是你的選擇。我們過去對於不同寵物有多樣化服務，例如像是浣熊和兔子這類的寵物，但我們現在僅將重心放在貓咪和狗身上。有我們的產品，你不用擔心你的寵物會再有皮膚感染。我們強烈推薦您這週拜訪我們的店，因為有年度銷售。對於前一百個顧客，我們會提供您和您的寵物一份特別餐。

答案：1. B 2. B 3.C

 選項中譯和解析

1. **此廣告賣什麼產品？**

   (A) 敏感性肌膚的洗護品。

   (B) 動物的洗護品。

   (C) 有機成分的洗髮精。

   (D) 皮膚感染修護霜。

2. 關於這些產品，誰最可能感興趣？

(A) 敏感性肌膚者。

(B) 有毛皮孩子的人。

(C) 皮膚感染的人。

(D) 規律地遛狗的人。

3. 本星期店裡將舉辦什麼活動？

(A) 只有洗髮精打折。

(B) 贈品活動。

(C) 年度拍賣。

(D) 免費寵物美容。

1.

· 此題屬於單字題，由pet 和toiletries 判斷出答案。寵物除了pet一字，現在也常以animal companions，companion animals，fur kids等稱呼。**正確選項(B)** 將pet換成animal companions，測試考生對類似字的理解。廣告一開始就說替寵物尋找洗髮精和護髮液，(A)及(C)是陷阱選項。雖然(A)... sensitive skin和(C) ...organic ingredients有可能是寵物盥洗用品的訴求，但廣告都未提及。另外，(D) skin infection treatment cream是針對皮膚感染的修護霜，和一般洗護品不同，因此也可刪除。單字：toiletry 身體及頭髮的洗護產品。另一快速解題技巧是：最佳選項一定要密切呼應主題，而只有(B)提到animal companions這一主題字。

2.

· 此題屬於推測題，要考生根據產品細節，推測出對產品最有興趣的人。此題型類似的問法有: Who might be the target consumers for these products? 。interested in，對...感興趣。本題題目是誰感興趣，由 第一題可知道產品是關於寵物類。選項(B)有毛小孩和(D)經常遛狗的人皆有可能，以主題切題度而言，**選項(B)更符合**。

3.

・此題是細節題。需要先理解片語 annual sale的意思，是年度拍賣。四個選項中，選項(A) a discount on shampoos only，比較有可能產生混淆，問題是only一字。廣告並沒有明確指出只有洗髮精有折扣，所以(A)不能選。選項(B) giveaways及(D) pet grooming則未提到。注意(D) pet grooming指寵物美容，雖然有pet一字，但廣告沒提及美容服務。考生要小心不要犯下過度延伸詮釋主題的思考錯誤。

Unit 2
玩具公司廣告：填充玩偶，孩子最佳良伴

Instructions

❶ 請播放音檔聽下列對話，並完成試題。 🎧 MP3 034

4. **Which of the following is NOT one of the functions of stuffed animals?**

   (A) helping kids to make friends

   (B) giving kids pleasure

   (C) keeping kids company

   (D) helping autistic kids

5. **What can be inferred about fidget toys based on this advertisement?**

   (A) They can stop children from fidgeting right away.

   (B) Fidget toys sell very well in America.

   (C) Stuffed animals are the most popular among fidget toys.

   (D) They serve soothing functions.

6. **What does the term "role play" imply?**

   (A) playing with stuffed animals

   (B) pretending to be an animal

   (C) Being a role model for children

   (D) pretending to be another person

聽力原文和對話

Questions 4-6 refer to the following advertisement

Are you looking for stuffed animals for you kids? Best Toy Company has earned its reputation not by providing the durable and eye-catching toys, but by providing chemical-free toys. Best Toy Company has tons of fidget toys, including stuffed animals. Stuffed animals have lots of functions. They give kids pleasure if they're playing the role play. They keep the kids company so that they won't feel so lonely. For kids with autism, this is especially a great thing for them, since they can have a one-on-one talk with stuffed animals. Hugging stuffed animals gives them positive energies.

問題4-6請參閱下列廣告

你在替你的小孩找尋填充玩偶嗎？倍斯特玩具公司不是以提供耐用和誘人的玩具聞名，而是以無化學物質的玩具聞名，倍斯特玩具公司有許多舒壓玩具，包含填充動物玩具。填充動物玩具有許多功能。它給予孩子們樂趣，如果他們玩角色扮演。他們讓小孩有伴所以小孩們不會感到寂寞。對自閉症小孩而言，這是特別棒的事，因為他們可以與填充玩偶有一對一的談話。與填充玩偶擁抱給予他們正向的能量。

答案：4. A 5. D 6. D

選項中譯和解析

4. 下列選項何者不是填充玩偶的功能之一？

(A) 幫助孩子交友。

(B) 給予孩子樂趣。

(C) 陪伴孩子。

(D) 幫助自閉症的小孩。

5. 根據此廣告，關於舒壓玩具，我們能推測出什麼？

    (A) 它們能阻止孩子坐立不安。

    (B) 舒壓玩具在美國賣得很好。

    (C) 填充玩偶是舒壓玩具中最受歡迎的。

    (D) 它們提供安撫功能。

6. 「角色扮演」這個詞的含意為何？

    (A) 玩填充動物。

    (B) 假裝自己是動物。

    (C) 成為兒童榜樣。

    (D) 假裝成其他人。

4.

· 此題屬於細節題，廣告中的內容幾乎和本題有關聯，因此必須全部看完，才能融會貫通。廣告中有提到pleasure（樂趣），keep the kids company（陪伴孩子），kids with autism（自閉症小孩）等等，kids with autism換句話說是autistic kids。但並未提到可以幫助孩子交友，因此**答案為(A)** helping kids to make friends。

5.

· 讀題時先定位關鍵字是重要的單字技巧，可以讓解題速度變快，並且能夠歸納。此題是推測題。從Stuffed animals have lots of functions. 之後的敘述，如pleasure... so that they won't feel so lonely...gives them positive energies等線索字，得知這些功能都是對小孩產生正面影響，對照選項，最明確和正面影響有關的只有**選項(D)** They serve soothing functions. 考生也需具備足夠單字量，知道soothing是安撫的意思。才能將以上線索字和soothing做出聯想。

6.

- 選項(A)及(B)都用了play，animal，是陷阱選項。(C) role model是模範生，榜樣。注意role是多重意義字。必須理解role model片語的意思，而不能單從role一字就驟然決定(D)是答案。role play 本身是角色扮演。四個選項中，一一分析。(A) playing with stuffed animals（和填充玩具玩）此play是指玩耍，意思不同。(B) pretending to be an animal（假裝自己是動物）語意不同。(C) being a role model for children（成為兒童榜樣）跟角色扮演無關。(D) pretending to be another person（假裝成為其他人）答案符合。

Unit 3

渡假勝地廣告：堪稱最人性化人工馬服務，浪漫不減分

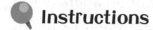

Instructions

❶ 請播放音檔聽下列對話，並完成試題。 MP3 035

7. What is this advertisement mainly about?

(A) lodging in Best Resort

(B) horseback riding classes

(C) horse-drawn carriage service

(D) riding artificial horses

8. Why does the speaker say, "it's totally humane"?

(A) The horses have lots of rest.

(B) Customers feel more at ease with artificial horses.

(C) Artificial horses are used instead of real horses.

(D) The horses receive very humane treatment.

9. When can customers use the service for free?

(A) during lunch hours

(B) on Valentine's Day

(C) in the evening

(D) on Christmas

聽力原文和對話

Questions 7-9 refer to the following advertisement

Are you looking for a fresh and romantic way of starting your day while traveling? Best Resort is having a horse-drawn carriage service for anyone who comes to our place. You won't feel like it's inhuman because it's totally humane. We actually use artificial horses to mimic the performance of the real horses. Artificial horses are covered with real horse skin. We're offering the service for free during lunch hours. It'll be charged 120% at the romantic evening and 180% on Valentine's Day.

問題7-9請參閱下列廣告

你在找尋新鮮且浪漫的方式展開你在旅行期間的日子嗎？倍斯特渡假勝地有馬車服務，提供給任何來到這的遊客。你不會感到不人道，因為很人道。我們實際上使用了人工馬去模仿真實馬的表現。人工馬會覆蓋上真實馬的真皮。我們於中午時刻提供免費服務。在浪漫傍晚會收取120%的費用，在情人節則是180%的費用。

答案：7. C 8. C 9. A

選項中譯和解析

7. 這個廣告主要和何者有關？

(A) 入住倍斯特渡假村。

(B) 騎馬課。

(C) 馬車交通服務。

(D) 騎乘人工馬。

8. 為何敘述者說「很人道」？

(A) 馬匹有很多休息時間。

(B) 客戶坐人工馬比較自在。

(C) 使用人工馬代替真馬。

(D) 馬匹受到非常人道的待遇。

9. 客人在何時可以免費使用此服務？

(A) 午餐時間。

(B) 情人節。

(C) 傍晚。

(D) 聖誕節。

7.

・此題屬於情境題，題目大意詢問廣告主題。廣告中提到度假村，馬車服務和人工馬，但未提及horseback riding classes（騎馬課），選項(B)可先刪除。從廣告中重點都在馬車服務上，如馬匹用人工馬，費用如何收取，因此推知**答案為(C)** 馬車交通服務。

8.

・考點關鍵字humane之後，馬上解釋humane的原因。「為何敘述者說很人道？」，鎖定humane後面那一句， We actually use artificial horses to mimic the performance of the real horses.（我們實際上使用的人工馬去模仿真實馬的表現。），因此**答案選(C)**。事實上，考生只要理解artificial是「人工的」意思，馬上可刪除(A) The horses have lots of rest.及(D) The horses receive very humane treatment。因為(A)，(D)都是指真馬獲得的待遇。而(B) Customers feel more at ease with artificial horses也可刪除，因為humane一字在此短講是針對人類以外的動物，但(B)強調的是顧客的感覺。

9.

- 此題是時間題目。通常在廣告後方可以找到答案。這題則是多加其他時間，增加困難度。倒數幾句提到：We're offering the service for free during lunch hours.（我們於中午時刻提供免費服務。）It'll be charged 120% at the romantic evening and 180% on Valentine's Day.（在浪漫傍晚會收取120%的費用，在情人節則是180%的費用。）選項中提到情人節和傍晚就是混淆功能。

Unit 4
動物園廣告：提供更多人和動物互動體驗、廚藝競賽

❶ 請播放音檔聽下列對話，並完成試題。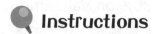 MP3 036

10. Which of the following is NOT mentioned as one of the interactions with animals?

(A) taking photos with them

(B) handling cotton candy to racoons

(C) preparing food for them

(D) grooming them

11. How much does a visitor have to pay for interacting with animals?

(A) the admission fee

(B) 5 dollars

(C) zero

(D) 10 dollars

12. Which animal is NOT mentioned?

(A) pandas

(B) koalas

(C) racoons

(D) monkeys

聽力原文和對話

Questions 10-12 refer to the following advertisement

Are you feeling a little bit tired of going to the zoo? Best Zoo is offering a great one-on-one interaction between visitors and animals. You can get close to the animals without any fees. You are able to take photos with animals, such as koalas and pandas. Have an actual contact with them, such as handing cotton candy to raccoons, while filming how they end up ruining it. You also get to prepare food for them in the Zoo kitchen. In the afternoon, we're having a contest of prepared foods by attendees. Of course, animals will be the judge to decide which is more delicious.

問題10-12請參閱下列廣告

對於去動物園，你會感到有點疲憊嗎？倍斯特動物園將提供參觀者和動物一對一的互動。你能夠與動物近距離接觸卻不用花費任何費用。你能與像是無尾熊和貓熊這樣的動物拍照。實際與他們接觸，例如遞棉花糖給浣熊，而攝影他們如何毀了棉花糖。你可以在動物園廚房準備食物給牠們。在下午，我們會有替參加者準備好的食材做為競賽。當然，動物會是評審以決定哪道料理比較美味。

答案：10. D 11. C 12. D

 選項中譯和解析

10. 關於動物一對一的互動，不包括下列哪個選項？

(A) 與牠們拍照。

(B) 遞棉花糖給浣熊。

(C) 為牠們準備食物。

(D) 梳理牠們。

11. 參觀者需要花多少錢才能和動物互動？

    (A) 入場費。

    (B) 5元。

    (C) 免費。

    (D) 10元。

12. 對話中沒被提到哪種動物？

    (A) 熊貓。

    (B) 無尾熊。

    (C) 浣熊。

    (D) 猴子。

10.

· 聽到對話，馬上鎖定**Best Zoo is offering a great one-on-one interaction between visitors and animals...**。not mentioned （沒提到、不包括），找出廣告中沒提到的部分，注意題目是「沒有」，考生很容易看到答案見獵心喜，而粗心犯錯。

· 此題屬於細節題，必須看過完整廣告才能判斷，再加上是否定，因此更加困難。廣告中提到，可以和動物互動的內容如下：You can get close to the animals without any fees... You are able to take photos with animals... handing cotton candy to raccoons... prepare food for them，因此答案並不包括梳理牠們，因此**選項(D)正確**。

11.

· 本題詢問價格。**how much**，多少錢，**visitor**，參觀者。詢問價格通常是比較簡易的題型，屬於問與答。第三句提到: without any fee

（不需要費用），就是免費之意。

- 讀題時先定位關鍵字是重要的解題技巧，如本題是how much，先從數字著手，另外的答案有可能是free（免費）或是without any fees（不用付費）。有可能以不同型式出現。選項(A)admission fee（入場費），許多地方都需要入場費，因此選項(A)用入場費，是個陷阱。考生務必讀完全部選項，再進行作答。

12.

- **首先判斷此題屬於細節題，掃描四個選項的答案，再進行下一步判斷。** 選項皆是動物，從廣告中的敘述，有提到貓熊，無尾熊和浣熊，並未提到選項(D)猴子。

- 細節題的選項通常同類相比。以本題為例，都是動物。從廣告敘述中，得知提到以下幾種動物：You are able to take photos with animals, such as koalas and pandas...such as handing cotton candy to raccoons...，因此可推知廣告中並無提到猴子。

Unit **5**

糖果公司廣告：萬聖節收服頑皮孩子就靠這款棒棒糖

🔍 Instructions

❶ 請播放音檔聽下列對話，並完成試題。🎧 MP3 037

13. What occasion does the advertisement target at?
(A) Thanksgiving
(B) Halloween
(C) Easter
(D) Christmas

14. What is the product particularly designed for greedy children?
(A) a huge piece of candy
(B) a colorful lollipop
(C) a giant chocolate bar
(D) a big bag

15. Why does the advertisement mention "win-win"?

(A) People who celebrate Halloween want to compete for the winner title for the best outfit.
(B) The child who gets the most candies wins the game on Halloween.

(C) Both chocolates and candies are children's favorite on Halloween.

(D) Both the people who give candies and those who receive them will feel glad.

聽力原文和對話

Questions 13-15 refer to the following advertisement

Still can't figure out how to be a great contributor to the Halloween gala? Come to Best Candy. We have a dazzling array of candies and chocolates. Totally suits your needs, if kids are coming to your house for "trick or treat". Plus, this year we have a giant lollipop, specially designed for the naughty kids or greedy kids. A giant lollipop is just enough, totally filling their bags. You won't have a feeling from looking at their faces that they're not satisfied or you're being too stingy. Win-win.

問題13-15請參閱下列廣告

仍不知道要如何在萬聖節慶當最棒的貢獻者嗎？來倍斯特糖果公司。我們有一系列令人暈眩的糖果和巧克力。完全能滿足你的需求，如果小孩到你們家「不給糖就搗蛋」。再者，今年我們有大型的棒棒糖，特別為頑皮的孩子或貪心的孩子所量身訂作的。小孩的裝糖袋剛好夠裝大型棒棒糖。你不用有種看著他們的臉龐卻感到他們不滿足的神情或是覺得你太過於小氣。雙贏。

答案：13. B 14. A 15. D

 選項中譯和解析

13. 此廣告的主題是何者？

(A) 感恩節。

(B) 萬聖節。

(C) 復活節。

(D) 聖誕節。

14. 何種是專門為貪心的孩子所設計的產品？

(A) 大型的棒棒糖。

(B) 五顏六色的棒棒糖。

(C) 大型的巧克力棒。

(D) 一個大袋子。

15. 為何廣告提到 "win-win"（雙贏）？

(A) 人們慶祝萬聖節想爭取最佳裝扮的冠軍頭銜。

(B) 得到最多醣果的孩子在萬聖節比賽中獲勝。

(C) 萬聖節時，巧克力和糖果是兒童的最愛。

(D) 給糖果的人和得到糖果的人都會很高興。

13.

· 聽到對話，馬上鎖定Still can't figure out how to be a great contributor to the Halloween gala?... 重點單字Halloween 萬聖節。根據第一句：仍不知道要如何在萬聖節慶當最棒的貢獻者嗎？可推知答案為(B)Halloween。

· 此題屬於情境題，題目大意詢問文章是和哪方面有關。因為廣告第一句就提到萬聖節，之後內容也是敘述關於萬聖節的一二事，如："trick or treat"（不給糖就搗蛋）因此得知答案為(C)Halloween（萬聖節）。

14.

· 首先判斷此題屬於細節題，product （產品）和greedy kids（貪心的

小孩）是重點。**先找出greedy kids，通常之後會補充說明。**greedy kids 後面接：A giant lollipop is just enough...此產品即為專門為貪心的孩子所設計。

- 細節題的選項會以同性質的答案出現，增加判斷難度。四個選項的答案，都跟甜食有關，如: (A) a huge piece of candy（大型的棒棒糖）(B) a colorful lollipop（五顏六色的棒棒糖）(C) a giant chocolate bar（大型的巧克力棒）(D) a big bag（一個大袋子）。

15.

- **看到題目直接鎖定在win-win，win-win是「雙贏」的意思。**win-win是正面之意。由廣告中找出正面的答案，再考慮細節敘述：You won't have a feeling ... that they're not satisfied or you're being too stingy。推測出給貪心的孩子大型棒棒糖，自己也會開心，故推知**答案為(D)**。

- 此題是推測題。需要先理解片語win-win的意思，再搜尋其造成雙贏的句子。因此，照之前教過的技巧，在此單字前後搜尋：You won't have a feeling from looking at their faces that they're not satisfied or you're being too stingy.（你不用有種看著他們的臉龐卻感到他們不滿足的神情或是覺得你太過於小氣。）正確選項(D)glad有高興之意。而be satisfied 是指「滿意」，都是正面情緒。選項(A) compete 是陷阱。選項(B) win the game（獲勝），和雙贏無關，透過單字win，來混淆考生。

Unit 6

超市公告：超良心酪農場，牛奶出問題不避責

Instructions

❶ 請播放音檔聽下列對話，並完成試題。 🎧 MP3 038

16. Where might this announcement be made?

(A) in a bookstore

(B) in a call center

(C) in a supermarket

(D) on a dairy farm

17. What is the announcement about?

(A) product recall

(B) the benefit of drinking milk

(C) the manufacturing process of milk

(D) where to buy milk

18. What is the problem with ABC milk?

(A) The manufacturing process of ABC milk went wrong.

(B) The speaker does not like the taste of ABC milk.

(C) The manufacture and expiration dates are not correct.

(D) ABC milk cannot be returned at the checkout.

聽力原文和對話

Questions 16-18 refer to the following announcement

Attention shoppers. We'd like you to know that there's been an oversight about ABC milk. We just got the phone call from ABC Diary, informing us that the manufacture date and expiration date are wrong. For those of you who have ABC milk, please return it at the supermarket checkout. For those who have purchased it, we will be having a news release with major media, so consumers are able to return the expired milk. Consumers are able to get their money back or in exchange for the same size of the purchased milk. We do hope you enjoy your afternoon shopping.

問題16-18請參閱下列公告

購物者注意了。我想讓你們知道關於ABC牛奶有了些疏忽。我剛與ABC酪農公司通話，製造日期和過期日都是錯誤的。對於那些手中有ABC牛奶的買家，請在超市結帳台退回商品。對於已購買者，我們將會在主要媒體有新聞發佈，所以消費者可以知道那些過期牛奶的退還日期。消費者也可拿回退款或更換相等容量的牛奶商品。希望你們都能享受這個下午的購物。

答案：16. C 17. A 18. C

 選項中譯和解析

16. 此公告可能會在哪裡發布？

   (A) 在書店裡。

   (B) 在客服中心。

   (C) 在超市。

   (D) 在酪農公司。

17. 公告內容是關於哪方面？

(A) 產品回收。

(B) 喝牛奶的好處。

(C) 牛奶的製造過程。

(D) 買牛奶的地方。

18. ABC牛奶出了什麼問題？

(A) ABC牛奶的製造過程有問題。

(B) 敘述者不喜歡ABC牛奶的味道。

(C) 製造日期和過期日不對。

(D) ABC牛奶不能在結帳櫃檯退貨。

16.

· 看到題目，目光直接鎖定在**We just got the phone call from ABC Diary ...**。根據ABC Diary，milk ，馬上刪掉(A) a bookstore及(B) a call center。又根據attention shopper（購物者注意了），推知在商店裡，因此(D)a daily farm 不符合目前場所。因此 選項(C) 超市最適合。

· 此題屬於情境題，題目大意詢問地點或是出處。本題由ABC Milk 推知 (C) in a supermarket和 (D) on a dairy farm皆有關聯，不過，透過 enjoy your afternoon shopping，則可推知超市更恰當。

17.

· 四個選項都提到**milk**，根據公告中提到製造日期有誤，可以推知產品有問題。從公告中，Consumers are able to get their money back or in exchange for the same size of the purchased milk. 推知**選項 (A)** 產品回收是正確答案。

- 此題屬於情境題，詢問公告的主題為何。讀題時先定位關鍵字很重要。milk（牛奶），return（退貨），checkout（結帳台）等等，都是本公告重要關鍵。

18.

- **公告提到：製造日期和過期日有誤，可以退貨，或是更換箱等容量的商品。** 首先判斷此題屬於細節題，掃描公告中的重點原因：the manufacture date and expiration date are wrong（製造日期和過期日都是錯誤的），因此可推知答案是(C)。

- What's the problem...? 是常見題目。通常此類型題目，無法迅速判斷，必須歸納其他點，才能得出結論。「ABC牛奶出了什麼問題？」，我們可以分析四個選項，究竟陷阱在哪裡。(A) ABC牛奶的製造過程有問題。沒特別說明這項。(B) 談話者不喜歡ABC牛奶的味道。沒提到。(C) 製造日期和過期日不對。公告第二行提到。(D) ABC牛奶不能在結帳櫃檯退貨。是錯的，可以退貨或更換牛奶。

Unit **7**
超市公告：書展之沒咖啡真的不行

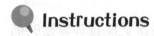

Instructions

❶ 請播放音檔聽下列對話，並完成試題。 MP3 039

19. How can a consumer get a coupon?

(A) by going to the Book Fair

(B) by purchasing 300 dollars worth of products at Best supermarket

(C) by buying books worthy of 550 dollars

(D) by buying coffee and biscuits

20. What is happening on B1?

(A) a Book Fair

(B) Coffee giveaway

(C) the opening of a supermarket

(D) the opening of a bookstore

21. What can consumers exchange with the coupons?

(A) cakes and coffee

(B) a free book

(C) a ticket to a lecture

(D) cookies and coffee

聽力原文和對話

Questions 19-21 refer to the following announcement

Attention shoppers. Since we are having a Book Fair on B1, we have collaborated with several publishers to give consumers who have purchased over 500 dollars at Best supermarket or bought books worthy of 550 dollars a coupon. You get to use the coupon at our coffee shop to exchange for cookies and a cup of coffee. All coupons will expire on Dec. 12. Bring those biscuits with you while enjoying the lecture of a major author at the Book Fair. The lecture is about physics and earth science. You certainly need the coffee.

問題19-21請參閱下列公告

購物者注意了。因為我們在地下室一樓有書展，我們與其他出版商有合作，給予在倍斯特超市消費超過500元或購書價值550元者優惠卷。你可以在我們的咖啡店使用此優惠卷換餅乾和一杯咖啡。所有的優惠卷都會於12月12日過期。可以帶著這些餅乾一邊享用一邊到書展聽主要作者演講。這個演講是關於物理和地球科學。你確實需要咖啡。

答案：19. C 20. A 21. D

 選項中譯和解析

19. 購物者要如何才能得到優惠券？

(A) 去書展。

(B) 在倍斯特超市消費300元。

(C) 購買550元的書籍。

(D) 購買咖啡和餅乾。

20. 地下一樓有什麼活動嗎？

(A) 書展。

(B) 咖啡贈品。

(C) 超市開張。

(D) 書店開張。

21. 購物者能用優惠券兌換何物呢？

(A) 蛋糕和咖啡。

(B) 免費書籍。

(C) 演講門票。

(D) 餅乾和咖啡。

19.

· 聽到對話，馬上鎖定 **give consumers who have purchased over 500 dollars at Best supermarket or bought books worthy of 550 dollars a coupon...**。有兩種方式，第一種是在超市購物，第二種是在書局購物，因此重點馬上鎖定此兩處，當然，購買金額分別為500元和550元，也是重點。

· 此題屬於細節題，通常問與答之間，前後可找到線索或答案。先定位關鍵字coupon（優惠券），其後補充說明為(1)bought books worthy of 550 dollars (2) purchased over 500 dollars at Best supermarket。purchase=buy，相當於之意。在超市購買500元，在書店購買550元都是方法之一。選項(B)在超市購買三百元，是陷阱答案，請粗心的考生入甕。

20.

· **What is happening** 是問發生何事，或是活動。定位關鍵字，

basement（地下室），再進行解題。

· 讀題時關鍵字，是非常重要的解題技巧。本題屬於開門見山。短講第一句提到：Since we are having a Book Fair on B1...（因為我們在地下一樓有書展），Book Fair（書展），giveaways（贈品活動），都是常見單字。

21.

· **exchange** （交換，兌換），**先定位關鍵字coupon，可推知兌換何物**。cookies，coffee，lecture在廣告中都有提及，尤其咖啡出現兩次，容易混淆判斷力。根據You get to use the coupon at our coffee shop to exchange for cookies and a cup of coffee，**馬上選(D)**。

· 細節題的選項描述會以類似詞或是片語出現在選項中，有時觀念不正確，或是理解度不夠，很容易判斷錯誤。「購物者能用優惠券兌換何物呢？」的題目須定位選項描述的關鍵字，同時掃描內文是否有類似字。關鍵字常是表達條件的名詞，例如(A) cakes and coffee (D)cookies and coffee 這兩個答案類似，然而廣告中提到的是cookie和coffee，因此選項(A)是個陷阱。

Unit **8**
智慧型手機公司內部談話：電子平台拓銷售

Instructions

❶ 請播放音檔聽下列對話，並完成試題。 🎧 MP3 040

22. What do most shareholders feel about Q2 and Q3?

(A) optimistic

(B) pessimistic

(C) excited

(D) thrilled

23. How has this company been promoting their smartphones?

(A) on Facebook

(B) via bestsellers and magazines

(C) on Twitter

(D) on newspapers

24. Which of the following might the company do next?

(A) doing research on digital platforms

(B) promoting their products on magazine covers

(C) abandoning smartphone productions

(D) working with a new P.R. company

聽力原文和對話

Questions 22-24 refer to the following talk

Let me begin today's sales meeting by announcing some feedback from our shareholders. 8 out of 10 shareholders are not optimistic about Q2 and Q3 sales. We need to come up with other ways to promote smartphone sales. Our research team has written a report on whether or not we should continue promoting our smartphones through magazines and bestsellers. It brings little profit for us since most consumers receive information on other digital platforms. We might consider other alternatives, such as Facebook, Twitter, and Instagram.

問題22-24請參閱下列談話

讓我為今天的銷售會議做個開頭，藉由公佈一些我們股東的回饋。10位股東中有8位對於第二季和第三季的銷售感到不樂觀。我們需要想出其他方法來促銷智慧型手機。我們的研究團隊已經寫了一份報告，關於我們是否該透過我們的雜誌和暢銷書繼續促銷智慧型手機。這替我們帶來很少的利潤，因為大部分的顧客是由其他電子平台收到資訊。我們可能要考慮其他替代方案，例如臉書、推特和Instagram。

答案：22. B 23. B 24. A

 選項中譯和解析

22. 大多數股東對**Q2**和**Q3**抱持什麼看法？

(A) 樂觀的。

(B) 悲觀的。

(C) 興奮的。

(D) 激動的。

23. 這家公司如何推廣自家的智慧型手機？

(A) 在臉書上。

(B) 透過暢銷書和雜誌。

(C) 在推特上。

(D) 在報紙上。

24. 公司下一步可能會做什麼呢？

(A) 在數位平台上進行研究。

(B) 在雜誌封面宣傳產品。

(C) 放棄製造智慧型手機。

(D) 和新的P.R.公司合作。

22.

· 聽到對話，馬上鎖定**8 out of 10 shareholders are not optimistic about Q2 and Q3 sales...** 十個中有八個的寫法為: **8 out of 10**。根據feel <感覺>，得知第一句就提出10位股東中有8位對於第二季和第三季銷售感到不樂觀(not optimistic)。因此，選項(B)悲觀的，和是不樂觀的類似單字，**答案選(B)**。

· 此題屬於單字題，題目中出現的單字，選項中以類似字呈現。第一句最後一個幾個字：not optimistic about Q2 and Q3 sales，not optimistic about，對...感到不樂觀。pessimistic 是指「悲觀」，因此語意最接近，故選(B) pessimistic。

23.

· 首先判斷此題屬於細節題，**how** 是如何，常考的方式是詢問對方健康狀態，用何種方法，或是搭乘何種交通工具。how的片語有:how long 多久，how often 多久一次。會議中提到： We need to come up with other ways to promote smartphone sales. 之後説明：continue promoting our smartphones through magazines and bestsellers，因此得知目前的推銷方式是**(B) via bestsellers and magazines**。

- 細節題的選項描述會以類似詞在文章中出現。細節題須先注意描述裡的關鍵字。例如：magazines雜誌、Facebook臉書、Twitter推特， and Instagram這幾種都是會議中提到的宣傳方式。重點是文章的中間提到：whether or not we should continue promoting our smartphones through magazines and bestsellers，表示對於目前的行銷方式有疑問，想進行改變。

24.

- **看到題目直接鎖定在We might consider other alternatives... 這句話的含意。alternative是「替代」的意思。**掃描替代雜誌行銷的類似詞，定位在最後一句的Facebook，Twitter等等平台，可以推知下一步即將進行跟此有關之事，會進行研究，看是否有利宣傳。

- 此題是推測題。需要先理解目前公司的宣傳方式，由於不滿意，推知想改變。此題和宣傳有關，分析以下選項的錯誤原因為何：(B) promoting their products on magazine covers是目前的宣傳，所以錯誤 (C) abandoning smartphone productions目前仍製造手機，未放棄。(D) working with a new P.R. company沒提過，因此建議不選。

Unit 9

公司談話：三十週年慶之這次沒魚可吃

Instructions

❶ 請播放音檔聽下列對話，並完成試題。 MP3 041

25. What is Linda in charge of?

(A) warehouse and distribution

(B) catering service

(C) barbecue equipment

(D) making beverages

26. What will Ken do according to the speaker?

(A) He will give everyone the direction to Best Park.

(B) He will prepare and send the beverages and barbecue materials.

(C) He will order foods and beverages from outside.

(D) He will drive his co-workers to Best Park.

27. Which of the following is NOT TRUE about the barbecue?

(A) The barbecue materials come from the company products.

(B) It will be held in a park.

(C) Fish will be provided.

(D) It will be held on the company's 30th anniversary.

聽力原文和對話

Questions 25-27 refer to the following talk

Hello everyone, my name is Linda. I'm in charge of the company warehouse and distribution. You all know tomorrow is our annual barbecue, and it's our 30th anniversary. This year, we are not ordering foods and beverages from outside. I was told that we will use our company products at the barbecue tomorrow. I will have Ken, who is our supermarket chain manager, prepare meat, beverages, wine and other related stuff, and ship them to Best Park. However, this year we won't be having fish. It's sort of in short supply, just wanted you to know that.

問題25-27請參閱下列談話

各位您好，我的名字是琳達。我負責公司倉庫和配送。你們都知道明天會是我們的年度烤肉，而且這是我們30周年紀念日。今年我們不會再從外面訂購食物和飲料了。我被告知我們明天烤肉會用公司產品。我會請肯，我們的超市連鎖經理準備肉品、飲品、酒類和其他相關的物品，然後運送至倍斯特公園。然而，今年我們不會有魚。只是想要你們知道，牠有點短缺。

答案：25. A 26. B 27 C

 選項中譯和解析

25. 琳達負責哪方面？

(A) 倉庫和配送。

(B) 餐飲服務。

(C) 烤肉設備。

(D) 製作飲料。

26. 根據說話者，肯將被分配做什麼事？

(A) 他將指引大家到倍斯特公園。

(B) 他將準備運送飲料和烤肉材料。

(C) 他會從外面訂購食物和飲料。

(D) 他會開車送同事到倍斯特公園。

27. 關於烤肉，下列選項何者有誤？

(A) 烤肉材料來自公司產品。

(B) 將在公園舉辦。

(C) 將供應魚類。

(D) 將在公司成立30週年之際舉辦。

25.

· 聽到對話，馬上鎖定**my name is Linda. I'm in charge of the company warehouse and distribution...**。 根據自我介紹，馬上抓住後面的重點，是倉庫和配送。

· 此題屬於細節題，在Linda的自我介紹開頭馬上有交代她負責的是warehouse and distribution。be in　charge of 是指「負責...」是常見片語。考生請掌握這個片語，非常實用。charge還可當<索費>之意，是很常見的單字。warehouse（倉庫），distribution（配送）。

26.

· 從**Ken**這個名字，定位重點句。最後兩句説明: I will have Ken... prepare meat, beverages, wine and other related stuff，因此Ken負責飲料和肉類等方面的運送。

· 讀題時先定位重點人事物，人名是解題關鍵字。此題是細節題。肯負責的工作是準備肉類，飲料，酒類和相關物品，因此推知是beverages and barbecue materials，因為meat 是屬於烤肉的重要物品，故**答案為(B)** He will prepare and send the beverages and barbecue materials.他將準備運送飲料和烤肉材料。

27.

- 首先判斷此題屬於細節題，掃描(A)的關鍵from the company products，(B) held in a park，(C) Fish... (D) held on the company's 30th anniversary.。其中魚類表示不供應，因此**答案為(C)** Fish will be provided.。鎖定重點句：this year we won't be having fish.（今年我們不會有魚）。

- 選出正確或錯誤選項的題目，通常範圍比較大，描述會分布在文章各處。「下列何者為真或錯」的細節題須先定位選項描述裡的關鍵字，同時掃描文章裡是出現。本題沒有陷阱，因此判斷時可以很清楚。再加上答案出現在文章中，請考生把握。be held 是「舉辦」，舉辦派對或是活動之意。

Unit *10*

公司談話：新人剛做幾天就被叫去法務部門，被嚇得不要不要的

Instructions

❶ 請播放音檔聽下列對話，並完成試題。 🎧 MP3 042

28. Why does the speaker ask these people to go to the Legal Department?

(A) to seek legal consultation

(B) to talk to the new lawyer

(C) to go under a legal investigation

(D) to get their bonuses

29. What does the man mean by saying, "you all have pretty well settled in here"?

(A) You look pretty.

(B) You make this place pretty.

(C) You adjust to this place well.

(D) This place does not look pretty.

30. Who might be the speaker?

(A) a supervisor

(B) a lawyer

(C) an attorney

(D) an accountant

聽力原文和對話

Questions 28-30 refer to the following talk

Hello everyone. How's everything going around here? It seems that you all have pretty well settled in here. All of you are smiling. But here is other news. You all need to go to the Legal Department right now. Shocked and amazed? Don't worry it's your signing bonuses. I've accountants ready for all signing bonuses. You'll see that it's in your envelope with your names on the cover of the envelope. I do need you to double check the money before you leave the Legal Department. After signing on the computer screen, we do need your fingerprints as well. That's all.

問題28-30請參閱下列談話

各位你好。這裡的每件事都還好吧？似乎你們都已經適應了。你們都在微笑。但是現在要說的卻是另一件事情。你們現在都需要到法務部門。感到震驚且驚訝嗎？別擔心這是你們的簽約獎金。我有請會計師們將所有簽約金準備好。你可以看到它在你們的信封裡，有你們的名字在每個信封上。我需要你們離開法務部門前再確認下金額。在電腦螢幕上簽名後，我們也需要你們的指紋。大概是這樣。

答案：28. D 29. C 30. A

選項中譯和解析

28. 發言者為何要求這些人去法律部門？

(A) 尋求法律諮詢。

(B) 與新律師對話。

(C) 進行法律調查。

(D) 獲得簽約金。

29. 男子表示"**you all have pretty well settled in here**"，其含意為何？

(A) 你們看起來很漂亮。

(B) 你們讓此地變美。

(C) 你們很適應這個地方。

(D) 這個地方看起來不太漂亮。

30. 發言者的身分可能為何？？

(A) 主管。

(B) 律師。

(C) 代理律師。

(D) 會計師。

28.

· 聽到對話，馬上鎖定**You all need to go to the Legal Department right now ...**。根據bonus（獎金），可以推知是好事，到法務部門應該是不是負面的緣因。signing bonus 是簽約金。

· 此題屬於細節題。why用來詢問原因，因此從文章中，找出真正原因為何。此類型題目，難以猜測，必須先對整段文意理解。因為提到Legal Department right（法務部），通常的答案都和律師有關。因此，很容易選錯。本題在法務部後，馬上說明原因：it's your signing bonuses. I've accountants ready for all signing bonuses.（這是你們的簽約獎金。我有請會計師們將所有簽約金準備好了。）

29.

· 首先判斷此題考片語。看到題目，直接鎖定**pretty settle**，是指「相當適應」。pretty 在此是副詞，指「相當，非常」修飾settle。四個選

項中，除了答案(C)，其他三個選項均出現pretty，此為關鍵字，讓題目增加難度。

- 此題考點較複雜，測試pretty當形容詞和副詞時的意思，也測試settle，適應的類似詞，adjust的意思。請看看四個選項。(A) You look pretty. pretty當形容詞，漂亮。(B) You make this place pretty. pretty是形容詞，漂亮。(C) You adjust to this place well. 適應。(D) This place does not look pretty. pretty形容詞，漂亮。

30.

- **who是詢問某人關係，職稱，或身分。因此，通常這種題目不會直接表明，需從文章中的敘述，聽到蛛絲馬跡。**直接鎖定在After signing on the computer screen, we do need your fingerprints as well. 在電腦螢幕上簽名後，我們也需要你們的指紋。That's all.「大概是這樣」。從以上的線索，推測此人身分應該是主管或上司。

- 此題是細節題。需要從整篇文章中歸納出來，才能推測出身分。文章中他提出：You all need to go to the Legal Department right now.; Don't worry it's your signing bonuses. I've accountants ready for all signing bonuses. I do need you to double check the money before you leave the Legal Department. 根據這幾句話判斷，此人有一定地位，比起律師，主管機率更大。

Unit 11

新聞報導：颱風來真的不是做科學專題的好時候

Instructions

1. 請播放音檔聽下列對話，並完成試題。 MP3 043

31. Why does the speaker say, "For those who are at this sandy beach, you probably need to leave"?

(A) because the beach is not clean

(B) because the beach is closed by the government

(C) because a typhoon is approaching the beach

(D) because it's harmful to one's health if one stays at a sandy place

32. Which of the following is most likely the reason that the speaker says, "I guess I've got another excuse to buy a new one"?

(A) She wants to buy a new swimming suit.

(B) Her umbrella was broken.

(C) She forgot to bring her umbrella.

(D) Her raincoat was broken.

33. Which of the following is most likely happening as the speaker speaks?

(A) They are having torrential rain.

(B) Many people are swimming in the ocean.

(C) Umbrellas are on sale.

(D) Raincoats are in high demand.

聽力原文和對話

Questions 31-33 refer to the following news report

I don't understand why we're having an early typhoon in March. As you can see, with the typhoon coming soon, it's pretty windy out there. My umbrella is...oops...I guess I've got another excuse to buy a new one. It's really pouring here. I really need to get my raincoat. For those who are at the sandy beach, you probably need to leave, since most residents are evacuating according to our early report. It really is not the time to do your science project. For the safety's sake, stay indoors probably in the basement, and this is Jane at Best beach. Now back to our news anchor Cindy Chen.

問題31-33請參閱下列新聞報導

我不知道為什麼我們在三月會有早颱。你可以看到，隨著颱風逼近，這裡風超大。我的雨傘...糟了...我想我有理由可以買隻新的了。這裡真的傾盆大雨。我真的需要拿我的雨衣了。對於在沙灘的你們，可能需要離開了，因為根據我們稍早的報導，大部分的居民正在撤離了。這真的不是做科學專題的時刻。由於安全的考量，待在室內，盡可能待在像地下室，這是簡在倍斯特海灘的播報。現在把新聞還給新聞主播辛蒂‧陳。

答案：31. C 32. B 33. A

 選項中譯和解析

31. 新聞報導說「對於在沙灘的你們，可能需要離開了」，是什麼原因？

 (A) 因為沙灘不乾淨。

(B) 因為沙灘被政府關閉。

(C) 因為颱風正逼近沙灘。

(D) 因為如果人待在沙地上，對身體有害。

32. 談話者說「我想我有理由可以買把新的了」，下列那個選項是最有可能的原因？

(A) 她想買件新的泳衣。

(B) 她的雨傘壞了。

(C) 她忘了帶傘。

(D) 她的雨衣破了。

33. 下列選項何者最有可能發生在談話者發言時？

(A) 他們遭受暴雨侵襲。

(B) 很多人在海裡游泳。

(C) 雨傘正在特價。

(D) 雨衣需求量很大。

31.

- 聽到對話，馬上鎖定**As you can see, with typhoon coming soon, it's pretty windy out there. ...**。根據typhoon is coming（颱風來了），以及風很大，推知不適合戶外運動，會有危險性，故推知you probably need to leave是因為颱風接近的關係。

- 此題屬於推測題，題目會透過暗示，讓考生推測出答案。題目：For those who are at this sandy beach, you probably need to leave？who是關係代名詞，those是指在沙灘的那些人。前面提到，with typhoon coming soon（隨著颱風逼近），因此希望那些人離開沙灘。

32.

- 從**My umbrella is...oops**，短短幾個字，可以推測出答案。**oops有糟糕之意，因此推測出雨傘負面的結果。**從第三句My umbrella is...oops，後面接I guess I've got another excuse to buy a new one（我想我有理由可以買把新的了）這句話推知雨傘可能無法使用，壞掉機率比較大。

- 讀題時先定位關鍵字詞是重要的解題技巧，因為關鍵字後常有解題線索，如**oops就是解題重點。**選項中(B) Her umbrella was broken.(D) Her raincoat was broken. 兩個類似考法，不過由於提到umbrella，因此得知答案是(B) Her umbrella was broken. broken在此是壞了，不是破掉。

33.

- **首先判斷此題屬於細節及推測題，發言者說颱風逼近，風很大，希望大家遠離海灘，根據此段話推測，大雨最有可能，再找出選項中表達大雨的單字或片語。**It's really pouring here.是下大雨之意。torrential rain是類似詞，故**正確選項是(A)**。

- 推測題的答案，通常不會重複短講內一樣的單字，常以同義字替換短講的關鍵字。「下列最有可能發生」的題目，通常須要先理解細節，再以換句話說的技巧，找出選項中最接近對話細節的詞彙。另外也可用「刪去法」將可能是正確選項的範圍縮小。如： (B) Many people are swimming in the ocean.已經通知大家離開，沒人游泳。(C) Umbrellas are on sale.只提到雨傘壞了，沒提到是否特價。(D) Raincoats are in high demand.雨衣需求量沒提到。

1 短獨白「影子跟讀」和填空練習

2 短獨白獨立演練和詳解

3 短獨白模擬試題

Unit 12
新聞報導：千鈞一髮，鯨魚差點成為棕熊的餐點

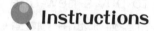 **Instructions**

❶ 請播放音檔聽下列對話，並完成試題。 MP3 044

34. Which of the following is NOT covered by the news report?

(A) a huge machine

(B) a whale

(C) water sport

(D) the video about saving a whale

35. Which of the following is the closest in meaning to "exhilarating"?

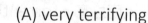

(A) very terrifying

(B) very excited

(C) very disappointing

(D) very exciting

36. What might happen this weekend?

(A) There might be a show at the department store.

(B) The saved whale might be returned to the ocean.

(C) A typhoon might hit the place.

(D) It might rain.

聽力原文和對話

Questions 34-36 refer to the following news report

I'm Mary Cheng and this is Jane Chen. First, we're going to give you an update on some exhilarating news. The whale that was found in shallow water has been saved. At least, he won't be the meal for brown bears. Let's see the video. Now back to domestic news. There is a giant automatic machine at Best Department. Wow, that certainly arouses lots of crowds. That's usually how things go. Coming up, the weather report will tell you whether we will have rainfall this weekend.

問題34-36請參閱下列新聞報導

我是瑪莉・鄭。首先我們將給你關於最令人感到興奮的新聞更新。被發現在淺水水域擱淺的鯨魚已獲救了。至少牠不會是棕熊的食物了。讓我們看下視頻。現在回到國內新聞。在倍斯特百貨公司有個巨型販售機器。哇這真的引起許多人潮。事情發展通常是這樣。接下來是，我們的天氣預測會告訴你這週是否會有降雨。

答案：34. C 35. D 36. D

選項中譯和解析

34. 關於新聞報導內容，下列何者不包括在內？

(A) 巨型機器。

(B) 鯨魚。

(C) 水上運動。

(D) 拯救鯨魚的影片。

35. 下列哪項，何者與"exhilarating"的含意最接近？

(A) 非常恐怖的。

(B) 非常興奮的。

(C) 非常失望的。

(D) 非常興奮的、刺激的。

36. 本週末將會發生何事？

(A) 百貨公司可能會有表演。

(B) 被救回的鯨魚可能會回到海洋。

(C) 可能會有颱風。

(D) 可能會降雨。

34.

- **news report（新聞報導），cover（包含）。題目為Which of the followings is NOT...，注意是否定。**根據news，找出新聞中的重點：whale，giant automatic machine，video，因此選項(C) 水上運動，並沒提到。

- 此題屬於細節題，題目大詢問新聞沒報導的部分。新聞中提The whale that was found in shallow water has been saved.（被發現在淺水水域擱淺的鯨魚已被救了）。Let's see the video. 讓我們看下視頻。There is a giant automatic machine at Best Department.在倍斯特百貨公司有個巨型販售機器。內容沒有提到水上運動。

35.

- **聽到短講，馬上鎖定First, we're going to give you an update on some exhilarating news.**。First, we're going to give you an update on some exhilarating news. 後面出現鯨魚獲救的消息，推知此新聞偏向激勵人心方面。

- 本題考單字題。可以由前後文，推知此單字的意思。exhilarating是

（令人興奮的）。題目中，選項(A)恐怖的，選項(C)失望的，可先刪除。選項(B) excited，本身有「興奮」的意思。不過通常主詞為人，表示某人感到興奮，振奮。選項(D) exciting指「有興奮的，刺激的」，通常用來形容事或物。如:the game is exciting （這場比賽很刺激）。

36.

· **聽到短講，馬上鎖定Coming up, the weather report will tell you whether we will have rainfall this weekend.**。根據時間點this weekend及rainfall，降雨，**馬上選(D)** It might rain。

· 本題考細節題。天氣預報是多益聽力的必考主題，考生只要熟悉常用的氣候現象的單字，並掃描哪個選項有類似描述，極容易得分。注意此篇先報導關於鯨魚，接著提及巨型機器的新聞，直到Coming up，接下來，這一**轉折詞**才暗示考生記者要轉換話題，除了轉折詞很重要，the weather report 也是關鍵線索字。(A)及(B)是陷阱選項，雖然whale，department store都是新聞提及的單字，但不符合題目問的時間點this weekend。(C)的typhoon颱風，全篇未提。

Unit 13

新聞報導：雨季一來，路況百出

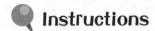 Instructions

❶ 請播放音檔聽下列對話，並完成試題。 🎧 MP3 045

37. What happened in tunnel A?

(A) Some car accidents happened.

(B) It was too foggy in tunnel A.

(C) It was heavily jammed.

(D) Some landslides occurred.

38. What are car drivers advised to do?

(A) to take the bus

(B) to take a different route

(C) to join a carpool

(D) to take the subway

39. What is wrong with the airport?

(A) It's shot down permanently.

(B) There are not enough runways to accommodate incoming flights.

(C) It's too old and needs refurbishment.

(D) It's shut down due to the weather condition.

聽力原文和對話

Questions 37-39 refer to the following news report

Morning it's the morning news. First, the important news about tunnel A. There've been several landsides happening, so it's officially closed. Car drivers are suggested to take tunnel B instead or take Road 555 through the super high way. This problem won't be fixed until weather is more stable, which according to our newsman it's gonna last until next Friday, and of course it's our rainy season. Next is also related to our transportation. Due to heavy rain and fog, the airport will be temporarily shut down for a while. For more flight information please visit our website. Front page.

問題37-39請參閱下列新聞報導

早安，這是早間新聞。首先，最重要的新聞是關於隧道A。持續有幾個山崩的狀況發生。所以隧道正式關閉了。建議開車的駕駛透過高速公路行駛隧道B或公路555號。根據我們新聞播報人員，此問題在天氣較穩定前不會修復好，且情況會持續到下週五，當然這是我們的雨季。下則報導也是有關於我們的交通運輸。由於大雨傾盆，機場會暫時關閉。更多航班資訊，請瀏覽我們的網站。首頁。

答案：37. D 38. B 39. D

 選項中譯和解析

37. 隧道A發生什麼事？

(A) 發生車禍。

(B) 隧道A內濃霧瀰漫。

(C) 塞車嚴重。

(D) 發生山崩的狀況。

38. 汽車駕駛被建議做何事？

(A) 搭公車。

(B) 開不同路線。

(C) 加入共乘。

(D) 搭地鐵。

39. 機場發生什麼事？

(A) 永久關閉。

(B) 跑道不夠安排航班。

(C) 太老舊需要翻新。

(D) 由於天氣狀況(不佳)而關閉。

37.

· 聽到對話，馬上鎖定**First, the important news about tunnel A. There's been several landsides happening,...**。根據第一句，可得知答案。tunnel是指隧道，本題的核心單字。landside是指山崩。

· 此題屬於開門見山題，題目的答案通常在文章中的第一二句。看到 tunnel A，後面句子會補充說明此發生之 事。landside（山崩），由於山崩，所以決定closed（關閉），因此**答案為(D)**Some landslides occurred.發生山崩的狀況。

38.

· 從**advise**（建議），來判斷答案。新聞中有提到：**Car drivers are suggested to take tunnel B instead or take Road 555...**（建議開車的駕駛透過高速公路行駛隧道B或公路555號...）。advise的同義字是suggest，雖然新聞中沒提到advise，但由suggest來判斷建議事項。

- 讀題時先定位關鍵字詞是重要的解題技巧，因為關鍵字後常有解題線索，如take tunnel B instead就是解題重點。此題是細節題。Car drivers are suggested: (1) take tunnel B instead (2) take Road 555 through super high way. 建議走其他隧道，以及開到高速公路，雖然沒直接說搭不同路線，然而可以判斷出來**答案為(B)**。

39.

- **首先判斷主題是airport，找出新聞中和機場相關的事件。**倒數第二句提到：Due to heavy rain and fog, the airport will be temporarily shut down for a while. 因此推知**答案為(D)** 由於天氣狀況（不佳）而關閉。due to 是指由於，for a while是指一段時間。
- 細節題的選項描述會以不同句型或單字將意思敘述重述。新聞中提到：Due to heavy rain and fog...因此機場暫時關閉。due to，由於，後面接原因。heavy rain and fog指「傾盆大雨和霧」。選項中未出現此單字。因此找出最接近的原因是the weather（天氣）問題。

Unit 14

航空公司公告：班次大亂，好險有補償

Instructions

❶ 請播放音檔聽下列對話，並完成試題。 MP3 046

40. What is the problem with flight CX1098 from Frankfurt to Holland?

(A) It is cancelled.

(B) It is delayed.

(C) It is under maintenance.

(D) It is overbooked.

41. What happened to CV2687 and CW1098?

(A) They are overbooked.

(B) They are delayed.

(C) They are cancelled.

(D) They are under maintenance.

42. Why is the word "coupons" mentioned?

(A) It is mentioned as a promotion strategy.

(B) It is mentioned because the airline is generous.

(C) It is mentioned as a compensation to consumers.

(D) It is mentioned because consumers asked for them.

聽力原文和對話

Questions 40-42 refer to the following announcement

Attention please. Due to some mechanical problems, flight CX1098 from Frankfurt to Holland has been cancelled. Again...flight CX1098 from Frankfurt to Holland has been cancelled. Also, there seems to be some problems with the left wings of CV2687 and CW1098, so they're delayed. There's going to be another announcement for whether or not CX1098 will be able to depart tomorrow morning, and now it's our final boarding call for CX2687. For the overbooked problems of CV1098, we're going to compensate you by giving coupons for a 50% discount. For safety concerns, please wait patiently. We sincerely apologize for any inconvenience caused.

問題40-42請參閱下列公告

請注意。由於一些機械問題，從法蘭克福到荷蘭的CX1098班機已經取消。重複...從法蘭克福到荷蘭的CX1098班機已經取消。而且CV2687和CW1098飛機左翼有些問題。所以他們延遲了。對於CX1098在明早是否能起飛將會有另外的公告。現在是我們對CX2687的最後登機呼叫。對於CV1098超賣的問題，我們將補償顧客5折優惠卷。由於安全的考量，請耐心等待。我們誠摯地對於任何引起的不便感到抱歉。

答案：40. A 41. B 42. C

 選項中譯和解析

40. 從法蘭克福到荷蘭的CX1098班機出了什麼問題？

(A) 飛機被取消了。

(B) 飛機誤點了。

(C) 飛機正在維修。

(D) 飛機超賣。

41. CV2687和CW1098航班有什麼問題？

(A) 它們超賣。

(B) 它們誤點了。

(C) 它們被取消了。

(D) 它們正在維修。

42. 為何會提到「優惠券」這個單字？

(A) 被提到因為宣傳策略。

(B) 被提及是因為航空公司很大方。

(C) 被提及是因為對消費者進行補償。

(D) 被提到是因為消費者要求。

40.

· 聽到對話，馬上鎖定**flight CX1098 from Frankfurt to Holland has been cancelled...**。根據what's the problem可知詢問班機出現某些問題，因此根據後面文字敘述，可推知**答案為(A)** It is cancelled.

· 此題屬於細節題，題目詢問CX1098班機出了什麼問題。牽涉到數字的題目，考生須眼耳並用，以數字當定位字，同時掃描選項，答案常出現在數字之後的細節。flight CX1098 from Frankfurt to Holland has been cancelled...從法蘭克福到荷蘭的CX1098班機已經被取消，動詞時態是現在完成式，再搭配被動語態have/has been +過去分詞，已經被...。另外，從A處到B處的片語: from A to B。

41.

· 由what happened得知是細節題，和第一道題目What is the problem，問法類似。**聽到對話，馬上鎖定there seems to be some problems with the left wings of CV2687 and CW1098, so**

they're delayed...（CV2687和CW1098飛機左翼有些問題。所以他們延遲了）。

- 本題關鍵字為delay（延遲，誤點）。公告中提到兩架飛機因為某些原因而誤點。此題沒有陷阱，可直接判斷。選項中的細節題須先定選項描述裡的關鍵字。(A) They are overbooked. 超賣是班機CV1098的問題。(B) They are delayed. 公告中有提到。(C) They are cancelled. 取消班機是另外一架。(D) They are under maintenance. 並未提到此狀況。

42.

- **看到題目目光直接鎖定在coupons，coupons是「優惠券」的意思。** 掃描coupon出現的原因。答案通常就在此單字的前後，會加以補充敘述。因此，聽到關鍵字，馬上注意前後文。

- 此題是細節題。公告中提到： For the overbooked problems of CV1098, we're going to compensate you by giving coupons for a 50% discount. （對於CV1098超賣的問題，我們將補償5折優惠卷）。compensate是（補償）之意。compensate Sb. by ... ，用...補償某人。

Unit 15
航空公司公告：邁向最佳航空公司，巧妙化解班次突然取消的問題

Instructions

❶ 請播放音檔聽下列對話，並完成試題。 MP3 047

43. What will passengers taking CZ1088 probably do after the announcement?

(A) receive a compensation

(B) talk to the ground crew

(C) wait for the plane to be repaired

(D) see the bulletin board

44. How does the airline solve the problem with CZ1088?

(A) by giving passengers coupons

(B) by arranging a new flight

(C) by giving each passenger 50 dollars

(D) by refunding

45. Which of the following is TRUE regarding flight CZ1089?

(A) It's from Dubai to Taiwan.

(B) It's an indirect flight.

(C) Passengers taking CZ1089 will be compensated.

(D) It is going to land in 20 minutes.

聽力原文和對話

Questions 43-45 refer to the following announcement
Passengers taking CZ1088 from Taiwan to Dubai are cancelled. Passengers please contact our ground crew as soon as you can. They'll arrange another flight CZ1089, also from Taiwan to Dubai. The difference is that it's a direct flight, so you won't have to take a transfer through HK. There won't be any compensation. Since it's a direct flight, it'll take less time to arrive at Dubai Airport. Please be ready, CZ1089 is about to land in twenty minutes. For other flight information, please see our bulletin board.

問題43-45請參閱下列公告
搭乘CZ1088從杜拜到台灣的班機取消了。乘客請盡早聯繫我們的地勤人員。他們將安排另一個班機CZ1089，也是從台灣到杜拜。差別在於這是直航航班，所以你不用在香港轉機。將不會有任何補償，且既然這是直航航班，會花較少時間就能抵達杜拜機場。請準備好CZ1089會於20分鐘左右降落。關於更多班機資訊請看我們的公告欄。

答案：43. B 44. B 45. D

 選項中譯和解析

43. 聽完通知後，搭乘**CZ1088**班機的乘客可能會做什麼？

　　(A) 獲得賠償。

　　(B) 跟地勤人員說話。

　　(C) 等待飛機維修。

　　(D) 去看公告欄。

44. 航空公司如何解決**CZ1088**班機的問題？

　　(A) 給旅客優惠券。

(B) 安排新航班。

(C) 給每位乘客50元。

(D) 退款。

45. 關於CZ1089航班，下列敘述何者為真？

(A) 從杜拜飛到台灣。

(B) 轉機。

(C) 乘坐CZ1089的乘客將獲得賠償。

(D) 將在20分鐘內降落。

43.

· 聽到短講，馬上鎖定**Passengers please contact out ground crew as soon as you can....**。根據公告，由於班機取消，於是告知與地勤人員聯絡。故乘客下一個步可能會和地勤人員談話。

· 此題是細節題。公告一開始就說明原因，因此找到cancelled（取消），從前後文，可以得知蛛絲馬跡。讀題時先定位關鍵字是重要的解題技巧，和某人說話時，除了talk，還有contact（聯繫），discuss（討論）和communicate（溝通），這些單字都是可能選項。

44.

· 從**how**，推知詢問「方法，身分，感覺」等等問題。在此是詢問解決方式。又從第三句的They'll arrange another flight CZ1089, also from Taiwan to Dubai. 他們將安排另一個班機CZ1089，也是從台灣到杜拜。，因此得知是安排另外一架飛機。

· 此題需要先理解solve the problem的意思，再搜尋其解決方式。公告內文多，然而定位關鍵片語，答案呼之欲出。文中提到:They'll arrange another flight CZ1089, also from Taiwan to Dubai.和選項

(B) by arranging a new flight（安排新航班） 意思相符，因此**答案為 (B)**。本題選項均有可能發生，因此無法直接用題目判斷，請小心。

45.

- 看到題目目光直接鎖定在 **Which of the followings is TRUE**，是「下列敘述何者為真」的意思。**regarding**是「對於、關於」之意。首先找到CZ1089航班，根據前後文，可理解出它的敘述有哪幾項，再進行下一步判斷。

- 細節題的選項描述會以類似詞或不同句型將短講敘述重述。「下列何者為真或錯」的細節題須先定位到每個選項描述裡的關鍵字，同時搜尋短講裡裡是否有類似關鍵字的單字。關於CZ1089航班，公告中指出：CZ1089 is about to land in twenty minutes，因此推知**答案為(D)** It is going to land in 20 minutes.。

Unit 16

體育場公告：娛樂性「親吻鏡頭」，人人都有機會

🔍 Instructions

❶ 請播放音檔聽下列對話，並完成試題。 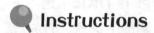 MP3 048

46. Where might this announcement be heard?

(A) on a sports field

(B) in an aquarium

(C) in a shopping mall

(D) in a restaurant

47. Which of the following is the closest in meaning to "intrigued"?

(A) very scared

(B) very excited

(C) very interested

(D) very attractive

48. Which of the following is NOT mentioned?

(A) hot dogs

(B) diet soda

(C) hamburgers

(D) cokes

聽力原文和對話

Questions 46-48 refer to the following announcement

Welcome to Best City Field. It's a clear, sunny morning. Our hot dogs are just as fresh as you might think, and it's "buy one get one free". Our diet soda and coke are also on discount. In addition to foods and beverages, we are having a whole new scoreboard, with the Kiss Cam in the middle. Don't be afraid of showing some love to your loved one. Here I mean, not just among couples. Kissing your kids can also be shown on the big screen. Anyone that makes our photographers intrigued, you'll see your face up there.

問題46-48請參閱下列公告

歡迎來到倍斯特體育場。這是無雲且陽光普照的早晨。我們的熱狗就像你所能想到那樣新鮮，而且它是「買一送一」。我們的健怡蘇打和可樂也在折扣中。除了食物和飲品，我們也有一整個新的計分板，有親吻鏡頭在中間。別害怕對自己喜愛的人展示些愛。對此我指的是不只是夫妻間。親吻你的小孩也可能被展示到大螢幕上喔。任何人使得攝影師感到興趣者，你都會在那看到你的臉龐在上面喔。

答案：46. A 47. C 48. C

 選項中譯和解析

46. 哪裡可以看到這個公告？

(A) 在運動場。

(B) 在水族館。

(C) 在購物中心。

(D) 在餐廳。

47. 下列哪個選項最接近「興趣」一字？

(A) 非常害怕的。

(B) 非常興奮的。

(C) 非常感興趣的。

(D) 非常有吸引力的。

48. 下列選項何者沒提到？

(A) 熱狗。

(B) 健怡蘇打。

(C) 漢堡。

(D) 可樂。

46.

· 聽到對話，馬上鎖定**Welcome to Best City Field. It's a clear, sunny morning..**。根據field，可推知是田野，或是球場。因此**選項 (A) on a sports field**適合。

· 此題屬於開門見山題，公告第一句，通常會先聲明場地的名稱。休閒地點除了sports field，還有swimming pool游泳池、court球場、playing ground操場等等，都是常見的地方。

47.

· **本題考單字題，直接詢問單字的意義。**單字intrigued本身的意思是很感興趣。選項(C)very interested <非常感興趣>，常見片語: be interested in ...，對......感興趣的，其他選項語意不合。

· 讀題時先定位關鍵字是重要的解題技巧，如本題單字題，如果考生本身不瞭解此單字，可以從前後文來判斷出意思。此題可從後文或句子判斷出意思。Anyone that makes our photographers intrigued, you'll see your face up there.如果臉被看到上面，表示他吸引了攝影師的注意，讓其感興趣，因此推知**答案為選項(C) very interested**。

48.

- **首先判斷此題屬於細節題，掃描選項的單字，有印象後，可從公告中推知答案。**第三句提到hot dogs，diet soda，cokes，直到公告結束，並沒有提到漢堡，因此**答案為(C)hamburgers漢堡**。

- 細節題的選項常列出屬性一樣的名詞。「下列何找沒被提及」這種題目必較費時，因為可能分布在每個句子當中。Our hot dogs are just as fresh...我們的熱狗就像你所能想到那樣新鮮Our diet soda and coke are also on discount.我們的健怡蘇打和可樂也在折扣中。，公告中提了幾項食物和飲料，但並沒有hamburger。

Unit 17
錄製訊息：前往新加坡進行公司收購

Instructions

❶ 請播放音檔聽下列對話，並完成試題。 🎧 MP3 049

49. Why does the speaker want the colleagues to cover up his duty?

(A) He needs to take a sick leave.

(B) He needs to go abroad to find another investor.

(C) He will take a personal leave.

(D) He will be on a business trip abroad.

50. Which of the following is NOT mentioned by the speaker?

(A) inviting investors

(B) a list of investors

(C) a project

(D) having lunch with investors

51. When will the company driver pick investors up?

(A) Dec. 1st

(B) Dec. 9th

(C) Dec. 5th

(D) Dec. 2nd

聽力原文和對話

Questions 49-51 refer to the following recorded message

Dear fellow colleagues, since I'll be at Singapore for company acquisition from Dec. 1st to Dec. 9th, I'm recording messages for you to cover up my duty while I'm in Singapore. I need you to find another investor for our project. I have a list of investors on my desk, and their contact information of course. Invite them to our hotel annual meeting and have dinners with them all. Be sure to give them the wonderful treatment. The boss has granted us to use the company limo. You can have our driver pick them up at Dec. 5th, 2025, 2 p.m. Thanks.

問題49-51請參閱下列錄製訊息

我親愛的同事們，既然我在12月1日到12月9日會到新加坡進行公司收購。我錄製了訊息，讓你們能於我在新加坡時，完成我的工作。我需要你們找另一位我們專案的投資者。我已經列出了投資者清單，當然還有他們的聯繫資訊。邀請他們到我們旅館參加年度會議並與他們共進晚餐。承諾給他們美好的待遇。老闆已經允許我們使用公司豪華車。你可以用我們的司機在2025年12月5日下午兩點接送他們。謝謝。

答案：49. D 50. D 51. C

選項中譯和解析

49. 為何敘述者（敘述者）希望同事幫忙做他／她的工作？

(A) 他需請病假。

(B) 他需出國尋找另一名投資者。

(C) 他將休假。

(D) 他將到國外出差。

50. 下列選項，何者敘述者未提到？

(A) 邀請投資者。

(B) 投資者名單。

(C) 一個專案。

(D) 與投資者共進午餐。

51. 公司司機何時會去接送投資者？

(A) 12月1日。

(B) 12月9日。

(C) 12月5日。

(D) 12月2日。

49.

· 聽到對話，馬上鎖定since I'll be at Singapore for company acquisition from Dec. 1st to Dec. 9th, I'm recording messages for you to cover up my duty...。根據第一行提到此人要到新加坡出差，因此需要同事幫忙：cover up my duty。duty是「責任，職責」。

· 此題屬於因果題，詢問原因或是結果。因為此人要在新加坡for company acquisition（進行公司收購），這是公事，因此**選項(D)** business trip（出差）比較適合。其他請假說法如下：take a sick leave 病假，take a personal leave休假、事假。

50.

· **首先判斷此題屬於細節題。先歸納出留言的幾個重點，再進行判斷。此類考法比較全面性，相對難度較高。**留言簡單包括幾項，其中一項是和投資者共進晚餐，不是午餐：have dinners with all.。此為陷阱題，

請小心作答。

- 細節題的選項描述會以類似詞或不同句型將文章敘述重述。「下列何者為不包括」的細節題，需快速整理全文。我們將所需項目簡單化：company acquisition ，cover up my duty，find another investor for our new project. ，I have a list of investors ，have dinners with an investor，因此選項(D) having lunch with investors有誤。

-

51.

- **看到題目目光直接鎖定在when和pick up，pick up是「接送某人」的意思。**掃描when可能出現的答案。留言中出現的日期有三項，前兩項是出差日期，最後一項是接送日期： Dec. 5th, 2025，故答案為**(C)** Dec. 5th。

- 此題是考時間。通常時間有年月日，日期或是幾點。選項中除了選項(D)，其他均有出現。(A) Dec. 1st → 出差日 (B) Dec. 9th → 回國日 (C) Dec. 5th → 接送投資者(D) Dec. 2nd → 在新加坡出差。

錄製訊息：助理就是要認命些，接貓、衣物送洗樣樣要做

🔍 Instructions

❶ 請播放音檔聽下列對話，並完成試題。 🎧 MP3 050

52. To whom is the message addressed to?

(A) the speaker's assistant

(B) the speaker's friend

(C) the speaker's boss

(D) the speaker's child

53. Why does the cat need to be dressed up?

(A) The speaker will arrange a photoshoot for the cat.

(B) The speaker will take the cat to a party.

(C) The speaker just wants to make his/her cat look gorgeous.

(D) The speaker will take the cat to a masquerade.

54. Which of the following is NOT included in the tasks assigned by the speaker?

(A) grooming her pet

(B) moving her car

(C) picking up her pet

(D) sending her clothes to dry cleaning

聽力原文和對話

Questions 52-54 refer to the following recorded message
My dear assistant, I do need you to pick up my cat at Best Pet at 3 p.m., and have our house maid dress him up. I'll be taking him to my friend's party tonight, and I forgot to tell you my car is still at C lot. My friends gave me a ride to the company, so I don't have time to move it to A lot. Please do that before I finish my meeting at 2:30 p.m. Send my clothes to dry cleaning at 3:30 p.m, since they only accept clothes before 4 p.m.

問題52-54請參閱下列錄製的訊息
我親愛的助理，我需要你在下午三點時到倍斯特寵物店接我的貓咪，然後叫我的傭人將牠打扮好。晚上我會帶牠到我朋友的派對，還有我忘了告訴你我的車還在C停車場。我的朋友載我到公司了，所以要請你將車移到A停車場。請在我下午兩點半會議結束前完成這些。將我的衣物在下午3點30送洗，因為在他們只在下午四點前受理衣物。

答案：52. A 53. B 54. A

 選項中譯和解析

52. 這封訊息是給誰呢？

　　(A) 留言者的助理。

　　(B) 留言者的朋友。

　　(C) 留言者的老闆。

　　(D) 留言者的小孩。

53. 貓咪為何需要打扮？

　　(A) 留言者將為貓安排照片拍攝。

　　(B) 留言者將帶貓帶到派對上。

(C) 留言者只是想讓他／她的貓看起來亮眼。

(D) 留言者將帶貓到化裝舞會。

54. 留言者指定的任務中，下列選項何者不包括？

(A) 梳理她的寵物。

(B) 移動她的車。

(C) 接送她的寵物。

(D) 把她的衣服送去乾洗。

52.

· 聽到對話，馬上鎖定**My dear assistant, I do need you to pick up my cat at Best Pet at 3 p.m....**。根據訊息一開始的收件者是： Dear my assistant（親愛的助理），推知**答案為(A)留言者的助理**。

· 此題屬於開門見山題，題目通常在第一句出現，抓到技巧後，考生可以節省很多時間搜尋。assistant是「助理」，boss 是「老闆」。即使開頭未說明給誰，訊息中交代的事情，亦可推知叮囑給助理或秘書的工作。

53.

· **be dressed up 是「被打扮」之意。本題why 開頭，詢問原因，因此先定位關鍵字cat和dress up**。又從第三句I'll be taking him to my friend's party tonight...晚上我會帶它到我朋友的派對。推知原因。him是指cat，因為要去派對，所以需要打扮。

· 讀題時先定位關鍵字是重要的解題技巧，因為關鍵字前後常有解題線索，例如本題: pick up my cat at Best Pet at 3 p.m., and have our house maid dress him up. I'll be taking him to my friend's party tonight。have Sb.+原型動詞，要某人去做某事情。have在此片語是

使役動詞，常表達命令，這句have our house maid dress him up是祈使句。

54.

- **首先判斷此題屬於細節題，掃描關鍵字task（任務），從留言中找出幾項交代事項。** 將留言中線索字以更精簡的方式重述： pick up my cat... dress him up ... move it to A lot... Send my clothes to dry cleaning。所以**正確選項是(A) grooming his/her pet**。

- 細節題的選項描述會以類似詞或不同句型將文章敘述重述。「下列何者沒被提及」的細節題，每個選項描述裡的關鍵字，同時掃描文章裡是否有類似的關鍵字。(A) grooming his/her pet 訊息中沒提到。(B) moving his/her car → 移車到A停車場。(C) picking up his/her pet 第一句提到。(D) sending his/her clothes to dry cleaning 三點半前送洗。

Unit 19
公司談話：工會大勝，牙齒保健納入保險

Instructions

1. 請播放音檔聽下列對話，並完成試題。 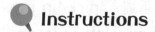 MP3 051

55. What does the speaker mean by saying, "sorry to cut your afternoon short"?

(A) sorry that no afternoon tea will be served

(B) sorry to interrupt your afternoon

(C) sorry that you cannot order pizza this afternoon

(D) sorry that the afternoon break will shortened

56. What does the triumph refer to in this talk?

(A) free pizza and chicken wings

(B) dental insurance

(C) free biscuits

(D) longer afternoon break

57. Where might this talk be given?

(A) in a dentist's clinic

(B) in a cafeteria

(C) in a company

(D) in an insurance company

聽力原文和對話

Questions 55-57 refer to the following talk

Good afternoon, sorry to cut your afternoon short, but I do have good news to tell you. It's not that we're gonna order pizzas and chicken wings or get free biscuits and cakes from our manufacturers. This is actually another triumph for our employees. The Labor Union has convinced the board to include dental in our insurance. That means starting next Monday, you can do your dental for free. It's covered. Even I can't wait to do the teeth whitening myself. So congratulations guys.

問題55-57請參閱下列廣告

下午好，抱歉打斷你們下午，但是我有幾個好消息要告訴你們。不是關於我們要訂購比薩和雞翅或從製造商那裡拿到免費的餅乾和蛋糕。實際上這是關於員工的另一個勝利。工會已經說服董事會將牙齒保健納入保險。這意謂著下週一，你可以免費做牙齒。費用包含在內了。甚至我都等不及要替自己做個牙齒美白了。所以恭喜各位。

答案：55. B 56. B 57. C

選項中譯和解析

55. 發言者說「抱歉打斷你們下午」，意思為何？

(A) 抱歉沒有下午茶。

(B) 抱歉打斷你們的下午。

(C) 抱歉今天下午你不能點披薩。

(D) 抱歉午休會縮短。

56. 發言者所指的勝利是指什麼？

(A) 免費披薩和雞翅。

(B) 牙齒保險。

(C) 免費餅乾。

(D) 午休時間較長。

57. 這段發言的可能地點在哪裡？

(A) 在牙科診所。

(B) 在自助餐廳。

(C) 在某家公司。

(D) 在保險公司。

55.

· 聽到對話，馬上鎖定**sorry to cut your afternoon short, but I do have good news to tell you. ...**。根據sorry to cut your afternoon short，後面接的子句：but I do have good news to tell you...表示中斷對方的下午的時間。cut 有「切斷、打斷」之意。

· 此題屬於釋義題，題目通常用俚語或片語來出題。因為(B) interrupt有「打斷」之意，因此推知此答案較為接近。選項(A)抱歉沒有下午茶，談話中並未提到。選項(D) shortened （縮短），是因為short 這個字，容易造成考生認為意思接近。Sorry to + V....，很抱歉做出...動作。

56.

· 首先判斷此題屬於細節題，搜尋**triumph**出現的位置。**triumph**（勝利），但此談話在辦公室，和戰爭無關，因此，透過**triumph** 前後文來判斷出所指為何。從第二句This is actually another triumph for our employees.，another是另外項目，還有另外一項勝利，關注後面提到的：include dental in our insurance（牙齒保健納入保險）。

- 讀題時先定位關鍵字是重要的解題技巧，本談話的關鍵字是：include dental in our insurance（牙齒保健納入保險）。此題是細節題。先鎖定triumph這個單字，下一句馬上聽到答案：This is actually another triumph for our employees. The Labor Union has convinced the board to include dental to our insurance. 相關單字：Labor Union（工會），insurance（保險）。

57.

- **首先判斷此題屬推測題。將談話所有內容，找出重要關鍵，推測出真正適合的答案。**這裡有個小陷阱是dental（牙齒保健）和do the teeth whitening（牙齒美白）。乍聽之下，第一個反應是選牙科診所，因為內容都圍繞牙齒方面。然而，仔細思考，納入保險只是公司的福利，並非一定是牙醫診所。

- 細節題的選項描述會以出現在對話中的類似詞，當成選項，造成混淆效果，增加難度。首先，先來理解四個選項：(A) in a dentist's clinic（在牙科診所）→ 提到牙齒保健問題，但無直接關聯。(B) in a cafeteria（在自助餐廳）→ 談話提到餅乾、蛋糕和雞翅，但和餐廳無直接關係。(C) in a company（在某家公司）→ 提到工會和保險，可能性最大。(D) in an insurance company（在保險公司）→雖然提到insurance，但和保險公司無直接關係。

公司談話：食品檢查不合格率高，員工們繃緊神經

 Instructions

❶ 請播放音檔聽下列對話，並完成試題。 MP3 052

58. How does the speaker feel about the result of the examination by the Food and Drug Administration?

(A) glad

(B) interested

(C) disappointed

(D) encouraged

59. What might the speaker do next?

(A) call Food and Drug Administration

(B) spray pesticide in all of the shops

(C) survey the company's shops

(D) read the examination result again

60. What kind of company does the speaker most likely work for?

(A) a restaurant franchise

(B) a tea shop

(C) a hostel

(D) a school cafeteria

聽力原文和對話

Questions 58-60 refer to the following talk

Good morning everyone. I just got a call from Food and Drug Administration. 26 out of 60 shops did not pass the examination. We're a company dedicated to producing high-quality and healthy foods to our customer. I don't see why this is happening. Cockroaches are rampant in several shops, and some major ingredients are expired. Totally unacceptable. I wanna you prepare all forms here because I'm going to check with your guys per shop today. Grab your documents and meet me in the hall, right now.

問題58-60請參閱下列談話

各位午安。我剛收到食物藥品管理局的來電。60間店有26間沒有通過檢驗。我們是間致力於產出高品質和健康食品給我們顧客的公司。我不知道為什麼有這種事會發生。蟑螂蔓延在幾間店裡，而且有些主要的原料成分是過期的。這真的令人無法接受。我想要你們在此準備所有的表格，因為我今天要到每間店與你們逐一檢視。現在拿著你們的文件到大廳等我。

答案：58. C 59. C 60. A

 選項中譯和解析

58. 說話者對食物藥品管理局審查的結果，反應如何？

(A) 高興的。

(B) 興趣的。

(C) 失望的。

(D) 鼓舞的。

59. 說話者接下來會做什麼？

    (A) 致電美國食品藥物管理局。

    (B) 在所有店裡噴灑殺蟲劑。

    (C) 檢查公司的商店。

    (D) 再次閱讀審查結果。

60. 說話者最有可能在哪間公司任職？

    (A) 連鎖店。

    (B) 茶店。

    (C) 旅館。

    (D) 學校自助餐廳。

58.

· 聽到對話，馬上鎖定**26 out of 60 shops did not pass the examination ...以及I don't see why this is happening...**。根據I don't see why this is happening. 由這麼多店檢驗沒通過，推知心情不佳，刪去(A)及(B)。談話者對於沒通過檢驗比例之高，產生疑惑和沮喪。因此(C) disappointed最適合。

· 此題屬於推理題，題目大意是由於檢驗結果，26間沒通過： 26 out of 60 shops，根據結果來推測說話者感受。談話中有句提到：Totally unacceptable.（無法令人接受）。由於太多商店沒通過檢測，因此可推知說話者，無法接受，甚至disappointed（失望的）。glad，interested和encouraged 都是正面之意，和本題不符合，故答案**選(C)**。

59.

· 首先判斷此題屬於細節題，掃描(A)call Food and Drug

Administration，致電美國食品藥物管理局(B) spray pesticide（噴灑殺蟲劑），(C) survey 檢測，(D) read the examination result（閱讀審查結果）。線索字以更精簡的方式重述：prepare all forms 準備所有的表格，check with your guys per shop today因為我今天要到每間店逐一與你們檢視。由此句得知說話者要檢查商店，所以正確選項是(C) survey the company's shops。

- 推測題的選項，通常都是歸納出談話中的結論。「說話者接下來會做什麼」發言中可能直接或者間接表達出答案為何，通常會先敘述其他事項，最後提出結論。如本題，說話者表達了檢驗結果、失望的感覺、蟑螂蔓延，等等問題。然而，他接下來做什麼，是依據這些問題而產生。因此推知：survey the company's shops。

60.

- **看到題目直接鎖定在work for，work for是「任職」的意思。**掃描說話者闡述的幾個重點如下：由60間店有26間沒有通過檢驗，到每一間店去檢視，推知應該是連鎖餐廳或加盟餐廳，所以**答案選(A)**。

- 此題是推測題。需要由幾個聽力訊息的整合後作出推斷，最後選出最佳答案。 (B) a tea shop→提到致力於產出高品質和健康食品，因此茶飲店比較不恰當。(C) a hostel→ 這是餐廳，提到產出高品質和健康食品。(D) a school cafeteria →乍看之下，此答案也有機會。 請看最後一句：Grab your documents and meet me at the hall, right now.（ 現在拿著你們的文件到大廳等我。）前面提到要去每間店檢視，因此相較之下，**(A)連鎖餐廳更加正確**。

1 短獨白「影子跟讀」和填空練習

2 短獨白獨立演練和詳解

3 短獨白模擬試題

Unit 21
錄製 line 訊息：員工被挖角，大老闆的反擊

Instructions

❶ 請播放音檔聽下列對話，並完成試題。 MP3 053

61. Which of the following is the closest in meaning to "steal" as in "to steal our Marketing Director"?

(A) to hide

(B) to fire

(C) to flatter

(D) to recruit

62. What is the purpose of this talk?

(A) to give directions about what Bob should do

(B) to prevent an important employee from flying to L.A.

(C) to ask Tina to arrange flights and a hotel

(D) to prevent an important employee from being hired by another company

63. What will Bob probably do after this talk?

(A) to ask Tina to arrange flights and boarding

(B) to take over the Marketing Directors' job

(C) to take over the duty of his co-workers who will fly to L.A.

(D) to seal a contract

聽力原文和對話

Questions 61-63 refer to the following recorded line message

I heard that Best TV is trying to steal our Marketing Director. They are offering twice the pay. They're scheduling a lunch meeting with him, probably talking about other benefits. I want you to fly to L.A. and convince him to stay before he signs the contract. As a CEO, I won't let this happen. Shareholders are gonna be so pissed if they find out our Marketing Director is being poached. Talk to my assistant, Tina, she will arrange flights and a hotel for you. I'll have Bob do your work while you are not here.

問題61-63請參閱下列錄製的line訊息

我聽説倍斯特電視試圖要獵取我們的行銷總監。他們提供了兩倍的薪資。他們安排了與他的午餐會議，可能要談論其他的福利。我要你飛往洛杉磯且在他簽約前説服他留下。身為CEO，我不會讓這種事發生。股東們會很生氣如果他們發現我們的行銷總監被獵走。跟我們的助理Tina説下，她會替你安排班機和旅館。我會要求Bob在你離開這段時間完成你的工作。

答案：61. D 62. D 63. C

 選項中譯和解析

61. 以下哪一項與「獵取我們的行銷總監」中的「獵取」最接近？

(A) 偷竊。

(B) 炒魷魚。

(C) 奉承。

(D) 招聘。

62. 訊息的目的為何？

(A) 指導Bob應該做什麼。

(B) 防止重要員工飛往洛杉磯。

(C) 要求Tina安排班機和旅館。

(D) 防止重要員工被其他公司任用。

63. 看完訊息後，**Bob**可能會做什麼？

(A) 要求Tina安排班機和登機。

(B) 交接行銷總監的工作。

(C) 和將飛往洛杉磯同事的交接工作。

(D) 簽訂合約。

61.

· 聽到對話，馬上鎖定**Best TV is trying to seal our Marketing Director. ...**。根據They are offering twice the pay. Talking about other benefits. 這兩句，推知和提供工作有關，seal本身有適合獵取之意，在此為獵人頭，因此**答案為(D) recruit**（雇用、招聘）。

· 此題屬於單字題，由談話中的大意，來推測出單字的含意。有些單字意思很多元，不同地方，可能含意相差甚遠。本題的seal，有「密封、獵取、海豹、確認、蓋章」之意。不過如果將此單字用在工作上面，則有招聘其他家公司的優秀領袖之意。

62.

· 本題考主旨，無法從一個句子中判斷出答案，必須融會貫通整個談話內容，答題時才不會游移不定。幾個重點單字，需要理解，助於答題。seal our Marketing Director，offer...（提供...薪資），benefit（員工福利），sign the contract（簽約），由這幾個重要單字，推知本

文主旨和防止行銷總監跳槽，故答案選(D)。

- 主旨題目是基本考題。題目常見寫法為: main pint，purpose，theme等等。此題是推測題。必須全文看過，才能理解答案為何。請見選項的盲點。 (B) to prevent an important employee from flying to L.A.不是防止員工飛洛杉磯，而是要求對方去洛杉磯勸總監留下。(C) to ask Tina to arrange flights and a hotel這不是主旨。(D) to prevent an important employee from being hired by another company 是CEO安排。這麼多事情，就是要防止總監被挖角，故**答案為(D)**。

63.

- 首先判斷此題屬於推測題，**CEO要求某人去阻止行銷總監簽約，因此談話結束後，此人有可能去完成任務。**此人不是Bob，這是小小的設計，第一個想法會將Bob帶入，而做出錯誤的判斷。此人將和Bob交接工作，將飛往LA。

- 推測題看似簡單，容易掉落陷阱。「Bob可能會做什麼？」這裡的Bob並非CEO傳訊息的人，因此看看四個選項，來進行篩選答案。 (A) to ask Tina to arrange flights and boarding→這和Bob無關。(B) to take over the Marketing Directors' job → 錯，CEO希望行銷總監不要離職。(C) to take over the duty of his co-workers who will fly to L.A. →正確，他是職務代理人。(D) to seal a contract→錯誤，只是透過contract來引導考生。

Unit 22
電影公司公告：看電影順道玩玩挖寶遊戲、電腦遊戲

Instructions

❶ 請播放音檔聽下列對話，並完成試題。 🎧 MP3 054

64. Where might you hear this announcement?

(A) in a zoo

(B) at a movie premiere

(C) at a cinema

(D) in a school

65. How will people gain the opportunity to join the treasure hunt?

(A) by hugging the cartoon characters

(B) by posting photos of themselves and the cartoon characters on Facebook

(C) by leaving nice comments about the movies on Facebook

(D) by posting their selfies taken in front of the theater on Facebook

66. How can a person get a stuffed animal?

(A) by playing a computer game

(B) by buying the ticket to see Zootopia

(C) by leaving comments on Facebook about Zootopia

(D) by playing with the cartoon characters at the entrance

聽力原文和對話

Questions 64-66 refer to the following announcement

Welcome to Best Cinema. We have cartoon characters at the entrance. Some of you probably have noticed that. Taking a photo with them after watching the film and posting photos on Facebook will get you the chance to join the treasure hunt with us. You'll be getting three free tickets of your choice. If you don't get anything, don't feel discouraged yet. If you match all cartoon characters of Zootopia through the computer screen, and get all of them correct, you will get a stuffed animal of your choice.

問題64-66請參閱下列公告

歡迎到倍斯特電影。我們在入口有卡通人物。你們有些人可能已經注意到了。在觀看電影後與他們拍張照且上傳到臉書將讓你有機會與我們一同參加尋寶。你會得到你所想看的電影的三張免費票卷。如果你沒有得到任何東西，也別為此感到失望。如果你透過電腦螢幕配對動物方城市的所有卡通角色，且全部答對，你將獲得你喜愛的填充玩偶。

答案：64. B 65. B 66. A

 選項中譯和解析

64. 在哪裡能看到此廣告？

(A) 在動物園裡。

(B) 在電影首映會。

(C) 在戲院。

(D) 在學校。

65. 人們如何能獲得參與尋寶的機會？

(A) 透過擁抱漫畫人物。

(B) 在臉書張貼自己和卡通人物照。

(C) 在臉書留下好評。

(D) 在臉書上張貼電影院前拍的照片。

66. 如何才能得到填充娃娃？

(A) 玩電腦遊戲。

(B) 透過買票看動物方城市。

(C) 在臉書評論動物方城市。

(D) 在門口和卡通人物玩。

64.

· 聽到對話，馬上鎖定**Welcome to Best Cinema .We have cartoon characters at the entrance...**。根據cinema（電影院、戲院），可得知答案跟電影院有關。選項中有兩個電影院選項：(B) at a movie premiere在電影首映會，(C) at a cinema在電影院必須從細節中，推知何者最為適合。

· 此題屬於情境題，題目大意詢問對話在哪種媒體或地方出現。因為一開始說：Welcome to Best Cinema. 推知可能電影院聽到此對話。再經過其他公告內容，可以得知更確切的答案。如：我們在入口有卡通人物。Taking a photo with them after watching the film and posting photos on Facebook will get you the chance to join the treasure hunt with us.這些可推測出是電影首映會。

65.

- **how** 是詢問用「方法，工具，交通，和感受」等等。本題是考用何種方法，因此由**join the treasure hunt**（尋寶機會）前後子句，可以得知方法。又從第二句的得知Taking a photo with them after watching the film and posting photos on Facebook will get you the chance...（在觀看電影後與他們拍張照且上傳到臉書將讓你有機會...）。**讀題時定位重要的疑問詞是解題技巧之一**。w-的疑問詞有：who（誰），how（如何），where（哪裡），when（何時），what（什麼）。

- 此題是細節題，先找出關鍵字。本題關鍵字是join the treasure hunt，因此找出這個片語，再即使不瞭解意思，從前後文來判斷，亦可以判斷出答案。

66.

- 首先判斷此題屬於細節題，公告中敘述許多活動。定位關鍵字**stuffed animal**（填充玩偶）。最後一句If you match all cartoon characters of Zootopia through the computer screen就明白地告知聽眾利用computer可獲得玩偶。

- 此細節題需要稍微以換句話說的技巧，推測最佳選項。最後一句If you match all cartoon characters of Zootopia through the computer screen換言之，就是某種電腦遊戲，所以選 **(A)** by playing a computer game。注意(C) by leaving comments on Facebook about Zootopia和(D) by playing with the cartoon characters at the entrance是陷阱選項，雖然有提及Facebook和cartoon characters，但和獲得填充玩偶都沒有直接的因果關係。

Unit 23

電視節目公告：獎金雙倍讓人躍躍欲試

🔍 Instructions

❶ 請播放音檔聽下列對話，並完成試題。 🎧 MP3 055

67. How will the candidates be selected to participate in the race?

(A) by submitting their videos and resumes

(B) by proving that they are 20 years old

(C) by submitting their diplomas

(D) by cooperating with others

68. What does the speaker mean by "we're gonna pair you at random"?

(A) We are going to pay you.

(B) The candidates will be picked randomly.

(C) We are going to assign a partner to you by chance.

(D) We're going to pair you with the person you like.

69. How much was last year's award?

(A) 2 million dollars

(B) 1 million dollars

(C) 20 million dollars

(D) 3 million dollars

聽力原文和對話

Questions 67-69 refer to the following recorded footage

Best Race is going to pick our candidates for the next season. All candidates have to submit their resumes and videos to our website before July 3rd, 2018, and the age limit is 20. You should be at least 20 years old to apply. For this season, we're gonna pair you at random, so this really tests your ability to cooperate with another person in order to win. I highly recommend chosen candidates stay positive during the entire race. For this season, the winner will get an award of two million dollars, twice that of last year's. Are you ready?

問題67-69請參閱下列錄製的影片片段

倍斯特競賽要替下季選角。所有候選人必須在2018年7月3日之前遞交他們的履歷和視頻，而且年齡限制是20歲。你應該要至少滿20歲才符合申請資格。對於這季，我們會隨意配對參賽者，所以這真的考驗你與其他人合作而獲勝的能力。對於這季，贏家會獲得200萬元的獎金，比去年多兩倍。你準備好了嗎？

答案：67. A. 68. C 69 B

 選項中譯和解析

67. 候選人如何才能被選中參加比賽？

(A) 遞交他們的視頻和履歷。

(B) 證明他們滿20歲。

(C) 遞交畢業證書。

(D) 與他人合作。

68. 廣告中的談話者說「我們會隨意配對參賽者」，其含意為何？

(A) 我們要付錢給你。

(B) 候選人將被隨機挑選。

(C) 我們將隨意指派夥伴給你。

(D) 我們要把你和喜歡的人配對。

69. 去年的獎金有多少？

(A) 200萬元。

(B) 100萬元。

(C) 2000萬元。

(D) 300萬元。

67.

· 聽到對話，馬上鎖定**All candidates have to submit their resumes and videos to our website...**（遞交他們的履歷和視頻）。根據candidate，找出被選中參賽資格是submitting their videos and resumes，因此**答案為(A)** by submitting their videos and resumes。

· 此題是詢問管道和方式。此種問與答的模式，是獲取分數的好機會。candidate（候選人），submit（遞交），resume（履歷表）。這些重點單字，在多益考題中很常見，請熟背。

68.

· 看到題目目光直接鎖定在**pair you at random**，**pair you at random 是「隨意配對參賽者」的意思**。掃描pair you at random的類似詞，pair在此是動詞，指「配對」，random「 隨意」，因此推知並非和自己選擇的人當夥伴，而是隨意配對，故**答案為(C)**。

- 此題是細節題。需要先理解動詞片語pair you at random的意思，再搜尋其類似詞。cooperate with another person 是指「與其他合作」，這也是隨機配對的用意之一。本題答案選項，容易混淆，請小心。(A) We are going to pay you. → pay是付錢，和pair 沒有關係。(B) The candidates will be picked randomly. → 是隨意配對。(C) We are going to assign a partner to you by chance. → by chance 是重要片語。(D) We're going to pair you with the person you like. → 不能自己選擇。

69.

- 首先判斷此題屬於細節題，掃描**award**（獎金，獎項）的關鍵字。**How much**，多少錢。注意是問去年的獎金，因此還要從今年的獎金推測答案。短講快結束時提到，今年的獎金是去年的兩倍，今年是two million dollars，兩百萬元。因此推知答案為**(B)one million dollars**。

- 本題乍看之下是細節題型，但因為講者沒有明講去年的獎金，所以仍需要運用推測能力，才不會落入陷阱。(A) 2 million dollars就是陷阱選項。本公告到數第二句提到：今年獎金是two million dollars，是去年的兩倍，因此去年是一百萬。twice as last year's 是指「去年獎金的兩倍」，請注意此細節。

Unit 24

醫院公告：A型跟AB型血之情況大逆轉

Instructions

❶ 請播放音檔聽下列對話，並完成試題。 🎧 MP3 056

70. What is the purpose of the announcement?

(A) introducing the benefit of blood donation

(B) talking about a collision on the highway

(C) asking people to donate blood

(D) describing the process of blood donation

71. What does the sentence, "people with type A are so accident prone", imply?

(A) People with type A are prone to depression.

(B) People with type A blood get involved in accidents often.

(C) People with type A are usually careless.

(D) Blood types have nothing to do with car accidents.

72. Why does the speaker say "We're gonna need type AB donors"?

(A) A hospital just announced that type AB blood is running out.

(B) He thinks type AB blood is rare.

(C) Everyone who is injured in the collision has type AB blood.

(D) Some serious car crashes might cause the demand of type AB blood.

聽力原文和對話

Questions 70-72 refer to the following announcement
On behalf of Best Memorial Center, I'd like you to know there's gonna be a blood donation booth outside our building from 9 a.m. to 6 p.m. We're totally running out of blood. We're in desperate need of type A blood donors. Type B and type O are also below the norm. I don't think we should joke about it that's why people with type A are so accident prone, whereas people with type AB are in the paradise. Oh my phone just vibrated...there's a series of collisions on the highway. We're gonna need type AB donors.

問題70-72請參閱下列公告
代表倍斯特紀念中心，我想讓你了解在早上九點到下午六點，將有捐血站在我們的建築物外頭。我們幾乎用光了血量。我們迫切地需要A型血的捐贈者。B型血和O型血也在標準值下。我不認為我們應該要拿這個來開玩笑，為什麼A型血這麼易於受到意外傷害，而AB型血的卻活在天堂。噢我的手機震動了...在高速公路上發生連環車禍。我們需要AB型的血液捐贈者。

答案：70. C 71. B 72. D

選項中譯和解析

70. 此公告的目為何？

(A) 介紹捐血的好處。

(B) 談論高速公路上的連環車禍。

(C) 要求人們捐血。

(D) 描述捐血的過程。

71. 句子「**A型血這麼易於受到意外傷害**」是什麼意思？

(A) A型的人容易憂鬱。

(B) A型的人經常遇到傷害。

(C) A型的人通常很粗心的。

(D) 血型與車禍無關。

72. 發言人為何說「**我們迫切地需要A型血的捐贈者**」？

(A) 醫院剛剛宣布AB型血即將用光。

(B) 他認為AB型血是罕見的。

(C) 車禍受傷的每個人都是AB型血。

(D) 一些連環車禍。我們需要AB型的血液捐贈者。

70.

· 聽到對話，馬上鎖定**there's gonna be a blood donation booth outside ... We're totally running out of blood...**。根據run out of blood 得知用光血量，因此推知需要眾人捐血。廣告一開始提到: 早上九點到下午六點，將有捐血站在我們的建築物外頭。答案非常清楚。

· 此題屬於主旨題，題目大意詢問目的或是主旨為何。將廣告簡化出幾個單字，加強理解。如：a blood donation booth，running out of blood， type A blood donors， need type AB donors ...等等。

71.

· 聽到對話，馬上鎖定**I don't think we should joke about it that why people with type A are so accident prone...**。從句子描述

中，發現A型的人容易受到意外傷害。accident意外，是重點單字，有此推知答案(B) People with type A blood get involved in accidents often.正確。

- 本題的細節題，廣告中說到各血型的特點，以及血庫嚴重不足的情況。accident prone 容易遇到意外傷害。accident 本身有意外之意。選項(A)depression（憂鬱），選項(B)意外(C)粗心，選項(D)車禍。

72.

- 首先判斷此題屬於細節題，掃描(A)的關鍵字提到AB型，和A型不同。選項(B)AB型沒提到是否罕見。選項是(C)關於車禍都是AB型的人，不見得，**選項(D)** 一些連環車禍。我們需要AB型的血液捐贈者，則在公告的最後一句提到。

- 找出need type AB donors原因，請注意本句的前後子句。「我們迫切地需要A型血的捐贈者」的原因，請見最後一句：there's a series of collisions on the highway. We're gonna need type AB donors. 因為發生連環車禍的因素，才會有大量需求。

Unit 25
電影工作室公告：解壓有道，讓員工玩玩水晶球、算個塔羅牌也無妨

Instructions

❶ 請播放音檔聽下列對話，並完成試題。 🎧 MP3 057

73. According to the speaker, which of the following topics are the sessions about?
   (A) astronomy
   (B) making crystal balls
   (C) fortune telling
   (D) health problems

74. Why does the speaker say, "I benefited from that"?
   (A) Studying astrology allowed him to find out his health problems.
   (B) The palm reading gave him a chance to find out his health problems.
   (C) He made some money from palm reading.
   (D) Reading tarot cards has many benefits.

75. Which of the following is the closest in meaning to the phrase, "drag you down there", as in "It's really not my business to tell you to come to afternoon sessions, and drag you down there"?

(A) make you come down to the basement

(B) The sessions really drag.

(C) drag something out of you

(D) make you go somewhere you might not want to go

聽力原文和對話

Questions 73-75 refer to the following talk

I know you probably work overtime lately, rewriting stories. It's really not my business to tell you to come to the afternoon sessions, and drag you down there. They include knowing astrology, crystal ball learning, palm reading, and tarot cards. Definitely, don't get so obsessed with those things, but it won't cause a harm to get to know them. Last year, I did the palm reading and I found out my health problems. I benefited from that. Reading tarot cards allows you to get to know your career path or your relationship problems, and it's free.

問題73-75請參閱下列談話

我知道你們近期都加班，改寫故事。告知你們要來下午的會議和把你們拖到這來不在我的職務範圍。他們包括了了解星相、讀水晶球、看手相和塔羅牌。沒有必要那麼沉迷那些東西，但了解下其實也無傷大雅。去年我透過讀手相發現自己的健康問題。我從中獲益。解讀塔羅牌能讓你了解你的職涯走向或感情問題，而且是免費的。

答案：73. C　74. B　75. D

選項中譯和解析

73. 根據談話者敘述，下列哪些話題和會議有關？

(A) 天文學。

(B) 製作水晶球。

(C) 算命。

(D) 健康問題。

74. 談話者說「我從中受益」，其含意為何？

(A) 學習占星術使他能找出自己的健康問題。

(B) 看手相讓他有機會找出他的健康問題。

(C) 他從看手相中賺了一些錢。

(D) 閱讀塔羅牌有很多好處。

75. 在「告知你們要來下午的會議和把你們拖到這來不在我的職務範圍。」句子中，下列哪個選項和片語「把你們拖到這來」意思最接近？

(A) 讓你到地下室。

(B) 會議真的拖延。

(C) 迫使你交代某事。

(D) 讓你去可能不想去的地方。

73.

· 根據第三句，會議和星相、水晶球、塔羅牌有關，綜合以上，可推知為算命(fortune telling)。

· 此題是屬於單字理解部分。一個句子有許多類似的技能，很容易因此搞混了其中的意思，請考生小心。注意這題的topics是指會議主題，不是

詢問整篇短講的主題。考生要小心不要將此題和整篇主題題型搞混。首先定位題目的關鍵字sessions，會議。關鍵字在第二句出現，下一句就交代會議內容：They include knowing astrology, crystal ball learning, palm reading, and tarot cards.統整這句細節，都是算命方式，**故選(C) fortune telling**。

74.

· 理解題通常需要很多資料，或許無法直接得知答案。palm reading 是指「手相」，說話者提到看手相時，發現了健康問題。這點讓他從中受益。health problem（健康問題）。選項(A)不是占星數，是手相。**選項(B)正確**，選項(C)沒提到金錢部分，選項(D)跟受益沒有直接關連。

75.

· take one down there 只把某人拖到他們不想去之處，這是屬於不情願的行為，因此**答案是(D)**。選項(B)的drag是拖延之意，是屬於混淆作用。

· 此題是單字題。需要先理解動詞片語drag you down there的意思。四個選項各自意思不盡相同。(A) make you come down to the basement讓你到地下室(B) The sessions really drag.會議真的拖延。(C) drag something out of you 迫使你交代某事(D) make you go somewhere you might not want to go 讓你去可能不想去的地方此四個選項，**選項(D)**和此片語意思最接近。

Unit 26

公司公告：幾個分公司裁撤，打道回洛杉磯總部

Instructions

❶ 請播放音檔聽下列對話，並完成試題。 MP3 058

76. What does "a brutal battle" refer to in this announcement?

(A) bidding on a shopping website

(B) fighting with co-workers

(C) the takeover bid

(D) the takeover of the HR department

77. What does the new owner want?

(A) moving to L.A.

(B) building a new headquarters

(C) reading every worker's resume

(D) reducing human power cost

78. Which of the following is the closest in meaning to the phrase, "dust off your resume"?

(A) renew your resume

(B) print out your resume

(C) send your resume

(D) check your resume

聽力原文和對話

Questions 76-78 refer to the following announcement

This morning the takeover bid was just as crazy. It was a brutal battle. Unfortunately, we lost. Several branch offices are gonna get cut. Apparently, the new owner wants to reduce the cost of human power. We won't get the exact information until HR managers contact me. I don't even know whether I will keep my position. Oh, HR managers are here. It seems that our jobs are safe, but we all need to move to the L.A. headquarters. For those who can't move to the headquarters, you probably have to dust off your resume to see where your parachute is.

問題76-78請參閱下列公告

今天早上收購競標如往常一樣瘋狂。競爭嚴峻。不幸的是，我們輸了。幾個分公司會被裁撤。顯然地，新的雇主想要減少人事成本。我們直到人事部經理們告知我時，才得知確切的消息。我甚至不知道為什麼我的職務未更動。噢人事部經理來了。似乎我們的工作都受到保障，但是我們都需要搬至洛杉磯總部。對於那些不能搬至總部者，你可能需要更新履歷看自己下個落腳處在哪了。

答案：76. C 77. D 78. A

 選項中譯和解析

76. 此公告中「競爭嚴峻」是指什麼？

(A) 在購物網站上競標。

(B) 與同事打架。

(C) 收購競標。

(D) 收購人力資源部。

77. 新的雇主想要什麼呢？

(A) 搬到洛杉磯。

(B) 成立新總部。

(C) 看每個員工的履歷。

(D) 減少人事成本。

78. 下列選項，何者的意思與「更新履歷」最接近？

(A) 更新你的履歷。

(B) 列印你的履歷。

(C) 寄出你的履歷。

(D) 檢查你的履歷。

76.

· 聽到對話，馬上鎖定第一句**This morning the takeover bid was just as crazy**。It was a brutal battle，競爭嚴峻，延續第一句，可推測It指的是第一句的takeover bid。

· 此題屬於推測題，題目考點的brutal battle和字面意思不同，不是指真的戰役，考生須具備代名詞的文法觀念，及熟悉bid這個單字有「競標」之意，才能推測出brutal battle的深層意思。是比較難的推測題。brutal指「嚴峻的、殘酷的」。從第一句得知： takeover bid.... It was a brutal battle，因此可以推知在此指的是the takeover bid（收購競標）。

77.

· **What 是詢問什麼，題目越短，必須吸收的可能更多。** 從第五句： the new owner wants to reduce the cost of human power. 這是前因後果，因為收購競標失利，造成公司裁撤，因此需要減少人力成本。

· 讀題時先找出關鍵字:want（想要）和what（何者）。原因有很多，

如： we lost. Several branch offices are gonna get cut. Apparently, the new owner wants to reduce the cost of human power. 由於競標失利，造成後續的損失，因此減少成本是可以推測得知的答案。

78.

· **聽到對話，馬上鎖定have to dust your resume to see where your parachute is...**。dust one's resume 是更新履歷之意。由於減少人力成本，加上要搬到洛杉磯總部，因此有人無法前往的，就會被裁員。此時，更新履歷是最重要之事。

· 單字題以不同字彙檢測考生同義轉換能力。考生平常準備的單字充足與否，此時就能見真章。重點一一解析，答案豁然開朗。where your parachute is是指「何處是落角處」，換句話說，亦即下一分工作在哪間公司。dust off one's resume是「更新某人履歷」，renew 也有更新之意，因此**選項(A)**renew your resume為正確答案。

- 包含一整回的試題演練，適應此長度的短獨白考題，漸進式攻略新多益短獨白練習，並於練習後參照中英對照的原文段落和試題，確實理解文意，最後搭配解析觀看確實理解各考點，於考場中取得高分。

Part

3

短獨白模擬試題

聽力模擬試題

▶ **PART 4** 🎧 MP3 059

Directions: In this part, you will listen to several talks by one or two speakers. These talks will not be printed and will only be spoken one time. For each talk, you will be asked to answer three questions. Select the best response and mark the corresponding letter (A), (B), (C), (D) on your answer sheet.

---

71. **Who most likely are the listeners?**
    (A) policemen
    (B) photographers
    (C) department employees
    (D) audiences

---

72. **According to the reporter, which cannot be found on the ground?**
    (A) unfinished burgers
    (B) French fries
    (C) precious metal
    (D) coke

---

73. **Why does the woman say, "not so tough are you"?**
    (A) to demonstrate the spirit of the reporter
    (B) to get the applause for tackling down the criminal
    (C) to respond in a mocking, humorous way
    (D) to show other criminals that they need to be tougher

74.What is the purpose of this camp?
(A) tackle rattlers in the wild
(B) get the water by traveling long distance
(C) appreciate things and know about environmental conservation
(D) prepare more cotton candy

75.Why does the woman say, "I really shouldn't have fallen on deaf ears"?
(A) because it is the lesson she now learns
(B) because she has a hearing problem and she doesn't want to admit it
(C) because she never thought knowledge could be useful and someone told her before
(D) because her phone doesn't work

76.Which of the following can be the cure for dealing with the rattler?
(A) cotton candy
(B) raccoons
(C) rats
(D) rabbits

77.Which of the following items was received by the monkey?
(A) bagels
(B) banana
(C) cookies
(D) peach

78.Which of the following is not what the reporter jokes to throw at the python?
(A) bananas
(B) cookies
(C) sandwiches

(D) peach

---

79. **Which of the following will be used to grieve the monkey?**
    (A) sandwiches
    (B) peach
    (C) cookies
    (D) bananas

---

80. **Where most likely is the news report taking place?**
    (A) on a ship
    (B) on a canoe
    (C) on a cruise
    (D) on a raft

---

81. **Why does the man say, "I just never saw it coming"?**
    (A) because he didn't see the torrent
    (B) because he wasn't experienced to see the torrent
    (C) because he didn't expect it to show up
    (D) because he didn't have a cloth to change

---

82. **Which of the following do not pose any danger to them?**
    (A) pythons
    (B) crocodiles
    (C) torrents
    (D) tuna sandwiches

---

83. **What will be provided to the octopus?**
    (A) a crab
    (B) the flounder
    (C) a clam
    (D) a lobster

---

84. **Which of the following is the activity that the octopus most desires to do?**

(A) solve a difficult puzzle
(B) use instruments
(C) use magical coloration
(D) endless crabs to eat

85. What is the essence of the octopus?
(A) aggressive
(B) greedy
(C) dazzling
(D) pleasurable

Best Aquarium/profile of the octopus (Adam)	
description	food
least enjoyed	Pacific eels
one of the favorites	Pacific huge clams
most enjoyed	Australia large crab
relative enjoyed	Boston lobsters

86. Look at the graph. What is Adam's most favorite food?
(A) Pacific eels
(B) Pacific huge clams
(C) Australia large crabs
(D) Boston lobsters

87. What is not mentioned about the lobster?
(A) it is larger than the octopus
(B) it has no clue that the octopus is nearby
(C) it's kind enough to let the reporter not see what's cruel
(D) its body is fastened by the tentacles of the octopus

88. What can be inferred from the fate of the lobster?
(A) escaped

(B) injured
(C) alive
(D) dead

Rescue	
animals	**fees**
Barnacle geese	US 20
Camels	US 290
Horses	US 250
Wolves	US 240
Note: barnacle geese will be not used as vehicles	

89.Why does the local villager mention barnacle geese?
(A) to applaud the sanctity of the cliff
(B) to downplay the negative feelings of the news report
(C) to entertain news reporters
(D) to satirize the foolish behavior

90.What could be the means of transportation to carry the survivors?
(A) automobiles
(B) ladders
(C) airplanes
(D) creatures

91.Look at the graph. Which of the following animal transportation will cost the least money?
(A) barnacle geese
(B) horses
(C) wolves
(D) camels

92.Who most likely are the listeners?
(A) trainers who are about to start the session
(B) customers sitting on the row of evacuation seats
(C) guests sitting on the economy seats
(D) flight attendants at the training school

93.What is the purpose of mentioning the swap list?
(A) to entertain the students
(B) to make students sleepy
(C) to make students vigilant
(D) to meet the demand of the students

94.What is the topic of the talk?
(A) how to avoid smell the heavy jet fuel
(B) how to use the swap list
(C) how to stay awake
(D) continuation of the training lessons

95.What is the requirement of this assignment?
(A) 500 words
(B) it depends
(C) no longer than 1000 words
(D) 2000 words

96.Where most likely is the talk given?
(A) in a classroom
(B) at the gallery
(C) at the museum
(D) at the swimming pool

97.Why does the speaker find the last painting odd?
(A) it was painted by a famous painter
(B) it has worms on the woodpecker

(C) because the shape of the apple

(D) because how the leg is perceived

Descriptions	Time
DWI/citizens	8:39 A.M.
DWI/mayor	9:45 A.M.
Train derailed	10:20 A.M.
Restaurant fire	11:35 A.M.
Note: DWI = driving while intoxicated	

98. According to the speaker, what will the donation money be used for?

(A) the film companies

(B) the prize

(C) the ceremony

(D) academic achievement

99. According to the talk, who will not be attending the event?

(A) the CEO

(B) the mayor

(C) the senator

(D) the governor

 100. Look at the graph. When did the mayor get involved in a car accident?

(A) 8:39 A.M.

(B) 9:45 A.M.

(C) 10:20 A.M.

(D) 11:35 A.M.

模擬試題 解析

 PART 4

聽力原文與中譯

Questions 71-73 refer to the following news report

This is reporter...Cindy Lin...I'm here at Best Mall...one of the largest malls in the area...in a few minutes...this place is gonna be treated as the crime scene...let's take a quick look....on the second floor...apparently there were gun shot residues and blood on the scene...it's assumed that there were some struggles and the gun went off...and on the fifth floor...pearls and silver necklaces randomly scattered on the floor...and...unfinished burgers...from BFC...and French fries from Best burger king......we have no idea...wait...someone is screaming for help...I think it's best that we find a place to hide...our photographer is still shooting...of course we can't give them our cameras...it's the company's assets...and my smartphone...that's my personal property...I think that leaves me with no choice...I have no choice but to knock him with my microphone...not so tough are you?

問題71-73請參閱下列新聞報導

這是倍斯特記者...辛蒂·林...我現在位在倍斯特購物中心...在這地區中其中之一的大型購物中心...在幾分鐘內...這個地方就會被視為是犯罪現場...讓我們很快看一下...在二樓...顯然在現場有槍擊的殘餘物和血液...可以假定出現場有些掙扎，且槍枝走火了...在五樓...珍珠和銀飾項鍊隨意散落在地面上...還有...吃剩的漢堡...BFC的...還有倍斯特漢堡王的薯條...我們沒有任何想法...等下...有人發出求救之喊...我想我們最好要找個地方躲藏...我們的攝影師仍在拍攝...當然我們不能將我們的相機交給歹徒...這是公司的資產...還有我的智慧型手機...這是我的個人財產...我想這樣我沒有選擇的餘地...我不得不以我的麥克風擊倒他...看來你也沒有多麼強悍？

71. Who most likely are the listeners? (A) policemen (B) photographers (C) department employees (D) **audiences**	71. 新聞報導的聽者最可能是誰? (A) 警察 (B) 攝影師 (C) 部門員工 (D) **觀眾**
72. According to the reporter, which cannot be found on the ground? (A) unfinished burgers (B) French fries (C) precious metal (D) **coke**	72. 根據新聞記者所述,在地面可能會發現什麼? (A) 剩餘的漢堡 (B) 薯條 (C) 珍貴金屬 (D) **可樂**
73. Why does the woman say, "not so tough are you"? (A) to demonstrate the spirit of the reporter (B) to get the applause for tackling down the criminal (C) **to respond in a mocking, humorous way** (D) to show other criminals that they need to be tougher	73. 為什麼女子提及「not so tough are you」? (A) 展示新聞記者的精神 (B) 為了獲取擊倒罪犯的喝采 (C) **以嘲諷幽默的方式回應** (D) 向其他罪犯展示,他們要更難對付才是
答案:71. D 72. D 73. C	

解析

- **第71題**，這題最有可能的聽眾是電視機前的觀眾，所以要**選D**。
- **第72題**，這題是詢問細節的部份，precious metal指的是silver，所以要小心別誤選C，這樣一來排除了ABC是文章中有提到的部分，答案為**選項D**。
- **第73題**，最後一題稍難，不過可以推想下女子會講這句話的口吻，其他三個選項均不正確，僅有C較符合，女子在不得已的情況下拿了麥克風擊倒可能攻擊自己和攝影師等的歹徒，才講這句，沒想到一擊就倒，意謂著連她這樣的記者都能擊倒對方，帶有點嘲諷且以幽默的方式看到這起事件，故**答案為C**。

聽力原文與中譯

Questions 74-76 refer to the following news report

This is reporter...Cindy Lin...I'm here at Desert Camp...a meaningful activity for kids to learn the awareness of our environment and conservation...often things we take for granted...here you have to walk long miles to get to the water you need...wait...what do you mean rattlers? Some students are pointing to me that there are several rattlers gathering near the place where we camp...are they venomous?...I'm gonna use my phone...but unfortunately...there are no signals...oh boy...that reminds me of a teacher in our biology class...I really shouldn't have fallen on deaf ears...oh my god...there are plenty of snakes...throw them...some rats...no rabbits...fine...I'm calling backups...once I am in the van...they are dead to me...we always have a few raccoons on our car...whoever takes down a few rattlesnakes will get more cotton candy...go...

問題74-76請參閱下列新聞報導

這是倍斯特記者…辛蒂‧林…我現在位在沙漠露營區…一個對於孩童們學習我們環境和保育意識有意義的活動…通常我們所認為理所當然的事情…在此你要長途跋涉才能獲取你所需的水源…等等…你所指的有響尾蛇是什麼意思？有些學生向我指著，有幾條響尾蛇在我們露營的地方聚集著…牠們是有毒的嗎？…我來用我的手機看看…但是不幸的是…沒有訊號…噢！我暈…這讓我想到我們生物課的一位老師…我當時真的不該充耳不聞…我的天啊…這有許多蛇…丟牠們…丟些老鼠…不，丟些兔子…好吧…我來叫援軍…一旦我到了箱型貨車處…他們對我來說就如同死掉了一般…我們總是會帶幾隻浣熊在我們車上…誰擊倒幾隻響尾蛇的會拿到更多的棉花糖…快去吧！

試題中譯與解析	
74. What is the purpose of this camp? (A) tackle rattlers in the wild (B) get the water by traveling long distance (C) **appreciate things and know about environmental conservation** (D) prepare more cotton candy	74.此次露營的目的是什麼？ (A) 在野外應付響尾蛇 (B) 長途跋涉取水 (C) **珍惜事物且了解環境保育** (D) 準備更多的棉花糖
75. Why does the woman say, "I really shouldn't have fallen on deaf ears"? (A) because it is the lesson she now learns (B) because she has a hearing problem and she doesn't want to admit it (C) **because she never thought knowledge could be useful and someone told her before** (D) because her phone doesn't work	75.為什麼女子提及「I really shouldn't have fallen on deaf ears」？ (A) 因為這是她現在所學的一課 (B) 因為她有聽力問題且她不想承認此事 (C) **因為她從未想過知識會那麼有用且之前有人告訴過她** (D) 因為她的電話沒有反應

| 76. Which of the following can be the cure for dealing with the rattler?
(A) cotton candy
(B) **raccoons**
(C) rats
(D) rabbits | 76. 下列哪一項能成為對付響尾蛇的良方呢?
(A) 棉花糖
(B) **浣熊**
(C) 老鼠
(D) 兔子 |

答案:74. C 75. C 76. B

解析

- **第74題**,這題是詢問目的,當中提及響尾蛇但制伏牠並非camp的目的,汲取水源也是事實的細節描述,不是目的,答案其實是一開始講到的環境意識和保育,所以答案為**選項C**。

- **第75題**,女子提到不該充耳不聞,最有可能的原因是,她想起生物課老師提過但當時自己不以為意,而在手機沒訊號無法查詢下,有感於當初自己沒留心,而自己未曾想到這個知識將來自己會用到且這麼重要,所以最可能的答案為**選項C**。

- **第76題**,這題很明顯答案會是浣熊,雖然女子有提到要丟些老鼠和兔子,但都並非擊倒響尾蛇的治療之方。

Questions 77-79 refer to the following news report

This is reporter...Jason Thornes....taking this trail isn't that hard...the air is incredibly fresh...quite soothing...and I'm bringing some bananas to feed those monkeys...wow they are not afraid of human contact...but they are intimidated by python contact...kidding...it's not that a python will suddenly appear and attack the monkeys...however, there are alarm bells...I'm gonna keep my composure...perhaps they are trying to scare me off...oh no...the python zeros in on the monkey...run...no fight back....apparently it can't fight back...I can't throw some bananas to the python can I, that would be so unfair...perhaps some sandwiches and bagels...or my cookies...kidding...but I really have to go...local inhabitants are taking me upstream to a more safer place...I'm gonna leave my peach here as a mourning for the monkey which took my banana a few minutes ago...

問題77-79請參閱下列新聞報導

這是記者...傑森‧索恩...跋涉這樣的小徑並不是太難...空氣相當的新鮮...相當撫慰人心...我帶了一些香蕉來餵那些猴子...哇！牠們不太懼怕跟人接觸...但是牠們懼怕巨蟒接觸...開玩笑的...又不是突然之間就會有條巨蟒出現然後攻擊猴子...然而，還是有警戒呼叫存在...我正保持鎮定...或許牠們試圖嚇跑我...喔...不好了...巨蟒對準了猴子...跑啊...別回擊...顯然，猴子無法回擊...我不該向巨蟒丟些香蕉，是嗎？...這樣就會很不公平...或許丟些三明治和貝果啊...或是我的餅乾...開玩笑的啦！...但是我真的要走啦...當地居民正帶我往上游走去更安全的地方...我正將我的桃子遺留在現場...哀悼那隻幾分鐘前拿我香蕉的猴子...。

77. Which of the following items was received by the monkey? (A) bagels (B) **banana** (C) cookies (D) peach	77. 下列哪個物品是猴子拿走的？ (A) 貝果 (B) **香蕉** (C) 餅乾 (D) 桃子

78. Which of the following is not what the reporter jokes to throw at the python? (A) bananas (B) cookies (C) sandwiches (D) **peach**	78. 下列哪個項目不是新聞記者開玩笑說要丟巨蟒的？ (A) 香蕉 (B) 餅乾 (C) 三明治 (D) **桃子**
79. Which of the following will be used to grieve the monkey? (A) sandwiches (B) **peach** (C) cookies (D) bananas	79. 下列哪個項目用於哀悼猴子呢？ (A) 三明治 (B) **桃子** (C) 餅乾 (D) 香蕉

答案：77. B 78. D 79. B

解析

- 第**77**題，這題要注意結尾提到猴子的部分as a mourning for the monkey which took my banana，所以知道猴子有跟他拿香蕉，故答案為**選項B**。
- 第**78**題，他有開玩笑要向巨蟒丟東西，而沒提到的就是peach，故答案為**選項D**。
- 第**79**題，最後提到的是I'm gonna leave my peach here as a mourning for the monkey，所以答案還是peach，答案為**選項B**。

1
短獨白「影子跟讀」和填空練習

2
短獨白獨立演練和詳解

3
短獨白模擬試題

Questions 80-82 refer to the following news report

This is reporter...Jason Thornes....continue our trip...the river is not as violent as most experts deem it is...and I'm not on a ship or a canoe...but on the crafted raft...it's amazing these villagers have the wisdom that was passed on to them and can still be really useful today....the downside of the raft is....oh...a huge torrent...I just never saw it coming...I guess I'm getting soaked and never thought I would get topless sooner...I might steal the show and get the most attention...which I want to avoid...other inhabitants on the raft are informing me that there are crocodiles beneath the river...I'm trying to find a lighter...it's getting dark...and I'm hungry...so do those crocodiles...and pythons...are they interested in my tuna sandwiches...?

問題80-82請參閱下列新聞報導

這是記者...傑森‧索恩...繼續我們的旅程...這條河並不是大多數的專家所認為的那樣，那樣的猛烈，而我並非在船上或者獨木舟上...而是在精心編織的筏上...令人吃驚的是這些村民們有這樣的智慧歷代相傳給他們且到今日都還是相當有用...乘坐竹筏的缺點是...噢...有巨大激流...我從沒預料到激流會來...我想我浸溼了而且沒想到我會這麼快就上裸...我可能會搶走風頭並且得到最多的關注...這也是我所想要避免的...在竹筏上的其他居民們向我告知，在河底下有鱷魚...我正試圖找尋打火機...天色正變暗...而且我餓了...所以那些鱷魚...以及巨蟒...牠們會對於我的鮪魚三明治有興趣嗎...?

80. Where most likely is the news report taking place?	80. 這段新聞報導最有可能發生在何處？
(A) on a ship	(A) 在船上
(B) on a canoe	(B) 在獨木舟上
(C) on a cruise	(C) 在郵輪上
(D) **on a raft**	(D) **在竹筏上**

81. Why does the man say, "I just never saw it coming"? (A) because he didn't see the torrent (B) because he wasn't experienced to see the torrent **(C) because he didn't expect it to show up** (D) because he didn't have a cloth to change	81. 為何男子提及「I just never saw it coming」？ (A) 因為他沒有看到激流 (B) 因為他沒有具有經驗到能看到激流 **(C) 因為他沒有料到激流會突然出現** (D) 因為他沒有衣服可以更換
82. Which of the following do not pose any danger to them? (A) pythons (B) crocodiles (C) torrents **(D) tuna sandwiches**	82. 下列哪個項目並未對他們造成威脅？ (A) 巨蟒 (B) 鱷魚 (C) 激流 **(D) 鮪魚三明治**

答案：80. D 81. C 82. D

解析

- **第80題**，一開始有提到I'm not on a ship or a canoe...but on the crafted raft，故答案很明顯是**選項D**。
- **第81題**，這題很也容易，主要是男子沒有預料torrent的到來，故答案為**選項C**。
- **第82題**，這題也很容易，對他們的威脅中（包含野生生物和自然力量），最不可能的是三明治。

Questions 83-85 refer to the following news report

This is reporter...Cindy Lin...I'm here at Best Aquarium...I'm gonna ask some professional questions to our marine biologist...Susan...what might seem to be the most exciting thing that an octopus expects to do...solving a really hard puzzle...under the water...using tools to get what it wants...showcasing its magic...by using coloration...and make this place dazzling...or finding a shelter and outwit his opponent, the flounder....and she said...none...so what exactly is the thing octopuses aspire to do...Susan told us it's the all-you-can eat buffet of crabs...and finally I get her point...eating is still considered the most pleasurable thing to do for both animals and humans...and no exception...and Susan is handing me a large clam to feed the octopus... the camera is gonna capture its gluttonous nature and apparently...it doesn't care...

問題83-85請參閱下列新聞報導

這是記者...辛蒂·林...我現在位於倍斯特水族館...我要向我們的海洋生物學家...蘇珊詢問一些專業的問題...什麼可能是一隻章魚最期待做的事情呢？...解決一個極困難的謎...在水裡...使用工具得到其想要的東西...展示牠的魔法...藉由使用色彩變換...讓這個地方暈眩奪目般...或是找到庇護所且智勝牠的對手比目魚...而蘇珊回應...以上皆非...所以什麼事情才是章魚最期待做的事情呢？...蘇珊告訴我們答案是「免費的螃蟹自助餐吃到飽」...而我最後懂蘇珊説的了...吃東西對於動物和人們來説仍被視為是最愉悦的事情...而且毫無例外...而蘇珊遞給我一支大型蚌要餵食這隻章魚...相機正捕捉到章魚貪吃的天性而顯而易見的是...牠絲毫不在乎呢？

83. What will be provided to the octopus?	83. 會提供什麼給章魚？
(A) a crab	(A) 螃蟹
(B) the flounder	(B) 比目魚
(C) **a clam**	(C) **蚌**
(D) a lobster	(D) 龍蝦

84. Which of the following is the activity that the octopus most desires to do? (A) solve a difficult puzzle (B) use instruments (C) use magical coloration (D) **endless crabs to eat**	84. 下列哪項活動是章魚最渴望做的? (A) 解決困難的謎題 (B) 使用工具 (C) 使用魔術般的顏色變換 (D) **數之不盡的螃蟹可供食用**
85. What is the essence of the octopus? (A) aggressive (B) **greedy** (C) dazzling (D) pleasurable	85. 章魚的本性是什麼? (A) 侵略性的 (B) **貪婪的** (C) 令人感到暈眩的 (D) 令人感到愉悅的

答案:83. C 84. D 85. B

解析

- 第**83**題,由最後的Susan is handing me a large **clam** to feed the octopus,可以得知答案為**選項C**。
- 第**84**題,可以看到有的選項有同義改寫,不過很明顯可以刪除掉ABC,而 endless crabs to eat是all-you-can eat buffet of crabs的改寫,故答案為 **選項D**。
- 第**85**題,這題的話要想到nature即是essence,而章魚的貪吃本性,其中 greedy對應到gluttonous,故答案為**選項B**。

Questions 86-88 refer to the following news report

Best Aquarium/profile of the octopus (Adam)	
description	food
least enjoyed	Pacific eels
one of the favorites	Pacific huge clams
most enjoyed	Australia large crab
relative enjoyed	Boston lobsters

This is reporter...Cindy Lin...I'm still here at Aquarium...wondering whether the octopus is still remembering me...perhaps it doesn't...but perhaps it will remember me this time...I'm bringing the octopus the exceedingly large lobster...almost twice the size of the octopus' body to see if it can tackle...I'm starting to get nervous...the lobster has no idea the octopus is adjacent...and there is a underwater castle...the lobster is trying to occupy it as if the castle is his...own...but the pressing issue is the threat lurking in front of him...the tentacles of the octopus instantly attach to the lobster...it's being dragged into the lair of the octopus...I guess the end is inevitable...and I think the octopus is kind enough for not getting me seen the bloody scene...perhaps knowing that I am a female.

問題86-88請參閱下列新聞報導

倍斯特水族館 / 章魚的檔案 （亞當）	
描述	食物
最不喜愛的	太平洋鰻魚
其中一個喜愛的	太平洋大型蚌
最喜愛的	澳洲大型螃蟹
相對來說喜愛的	波士頓龍蝦

這是記者...辛蒂‧林...我現在仍在水族館...思考著章魚是否仍記住我呢...或許牠不記得了呢...但是或許牠這次會記得我呢...因為我帶給章魚一隻極大型的龍蝦...幾乎是章魚體積的兩倍大...看看牠是否能夠應付...我開始有點緊張...龍蝦對於章魚就在鄰近處絲毫沒有想法...而這裡有個水底下城堡...這隻龍蝦試圖要佔據這城堡彷彿這座城堡是牠所擁有的...但是更迫切的議題是他前方所潛藏的威脅...章魚的觸手即刻附著在龍蝦上...龍蝦被拖進章魚的巢穴裡了...我想結果是無可避免的了...而我想章魚善良到不讓我看見這血腥的場景...可能知道我是位女性。

試題中譯與解析	
86. Look at the graph. What is Adam's most favorite food? (A) Pacific eels (B) Pacific huge clams (C) **Australia large crabs** (D) Boston lobsters	86. 請參考圖表。亞當最喜愛的食物是什麼呢？ (A) 太平洋鰻魚 (B) 太平洋大型蚌 (C) **澳洲大型螃蟹** (D) 波士頓龍蝦
87. What Is not mentioned about the lobster? (A) it is larger than the octopus (B) it has no clue that the octopus is nearby (C) **it's kind enough to let the reporter not see what's cruel** (D) its body is fastened by the tentacles of the octopus	87. 關於龍蝦的敘述何者為非呢？ (A) 牠比章魚的體積還要大 (B) 牠對於章魚在附近毫無線索 (C) **牠善良到讓新聞記者不去目睹到血腥的畫面** (D) 牠的身體被章魚的觸手繫住了

| 88. What can be inferred from the fate of the lobster?
(A) escaped
(B) injured
(C) alive
(D) **dead** | 88. 從新聞報導中可以推測出龍蝦的命運為何呢?
(A) 逃跑了
(B) 受傷的
(C) 活著的
(D) **死亡了** |

答案：86. C 87. C 88. D

 解析

- **第86題**，可以從圖表中得知章魚的名稱是Adam，所以要找的是牠最喜愛的食物，試題中的most favorite food等於列表中的most enjoyed，故答案為Australia large crab，故**答案為C**。
- **第87題**，關於龍蝦的敘述何者為非，ACD均為錯誤的描述，故可以排除。而選項C是is kind enough for not getting me seen the bloody scene的改寫，故答案為**選項C**。
- **第88題**，這題是推測題，可以從敘述中向是the end is inevitable等，得知龍蝦死了，故答案為**選項D**。

聽力原文與中譯	

Questions 89-91 refer to the following news report

Rescue animals	fees
Barnacle geese	US 20
Camels	US 290
Horses	US 250
Wolves	US 240
Note: barnacle geese will be not used as vehicles	

This is news anchor Bella James...good morning...first...let's take a look at what happened at the resort yesterday...as you can see the cliff is at least 2,000 feet...and youtubers went to the extreme...trying to climb down and filmed the video...but slipped...according to the residents two people got injured and four died in the accident...a local villager told us that they are no barnacle geese...and mimicking the behavior of these creatures to get more hits just is not worthy of it...and the rescue team which arrived at the scene found it hard to rescue...cars are unable to drive on the steep road...so only animal-transport is more likely...and it's really cold out there...losing body temperatures can be detrimental according to our health experts...and stretchers and ladders will also be using to rescue them.

問題89-91請參閱下列新聞報導

救援	
動物	費用
黑雁	20 美元
駱駝	290 美元
馬匹	250 美元
狼	240 美元
註: 黑雁不會用於交通工具	

這是新聞主播貝拉‧詹姆士…早安…首先…讓我們來看下在昨天度假勝地所發生的事情…你可以看到峭壁至少有2000尺…而youtubers走極端路線…試圖要爬下來拍攝些視頻…但是滑跤了…根據當地居民…兩人受傷而有四個人死於這起事件之中…有位當地居民告訴我們他們並不是黑雁…而且模仿這些生物的行為以換取更多的點擊…關於這點是不值得的…而剛抵達的搜救團隊發現搜救是有多麼困難…車子無法駛向陡峭的道路上頭…所以僅有動物交通工具是較有可能的…而這裡真的相當冷…失去體溫的話真的會有危害，根據我們的健康專家所述…而擔架和梯子將會用於救援他們。

試題中譯與解析

89. Why does the local villager mention barnacle geese? (A) to applaud the sanctity of the cliff (B) to downplay the negative feelings of the news report (C) to entertain news reporters (D) **to satirize the foolish behavior**	89. 為什麼當地居民會提到黑雁？ (A) 盛讚峭壁的神聖性 (B) 輕描淡寫新聞報導的負面感受 (C) 娛樂新聞記者們 (D) **諷刺愚蠢的行為**

90. What could be the means of transportation to carry the survivors? (A) automobiles (B) ladders (C) airplanes (D) **creatures**	90. 什麼可能會用於搭載生還者的交通工具呢? (A) 汽車 (B) 梯子 (C) 飛機 (D) **生物**
91. Look at the graph. Which of the following animal transportation will cost the least money? (A) barnacle geese (B) horses (C) **wolves** (D) camels	91. 請參考圖表。下列哪一個動物運輸將花費最少的金錢? (A) 黑雁 (B) 馬 (C) **狼** (D) 駱駝

答案:89. D 90. D 91. C

解析

· **第89題**,這題要意會一下,而當地村民會講到黑雁的部分主要是嘲諷這樣行為其實是愚蠢的,故答案要選**選項D**。

· **第90題**,要對應到cars are unable to drive on the steep road...so only animal-transport is more likely,故可以刪除掉非動物的運送方式,也要注意animals換成了creatures,故答案為**選項D**。

· **第91題**,這題是詢問花費最少的,但是別太快選表格中對應到最少的金額,在表格下方的note有提到黑雁不會用於交通運送,僅用於救援,所以雖然黑雁是金額最低的,但仍要排除掉,故答案要選擇**選項C**。

1 短獨白「影子跟讀」和填空練習

2 短獨白獨立演練和詳解

3 短獨白模擬試題

Questions 92-94 refer to the following video

I'm your trainer...Jason Lin......this is the back of the Boeing 747...you certainly can smell the heavy jet fuel...right?...let's head inside to the economy seats...last time we talked about the manners and request each of you to practice the serving part...and this week...we are practicing the evacuation parts...this is especially important because it involves the safety of both passengers and members of the flight attendants...I saw some of you back there are feeling sleepy...being at training school can be boring sometime...I get it...but lighten up...there are a bunch of fun things ahead of you after the training...for example...you get to use the swap list to exchange the flight you don't want as long as someone is willing to make a change...I used to do that very often...

問題92-94請參閱下列視頻

我是你們的訓練師...傑森・林...這是波音747後部...你確實可以聞到濃厚的噴射機燃料...對吧？...讓我們到經濟艙裡頭...上次，我們談論到儀態和要求你們練習了關於服務的部分...而這週...我們會練習撤離的部分...這是特別重要的，因為這牽涉到乘客和機組成員的安全...我看到你們有幾個在後方有瞌睡蟲敲門了...在訓練學校有時候可能是很無趣的...我懂的...但是打起精神吧...例如，你能夠用交換名單來更換掉你不想要飛的行程，只要有人願意跟你交換...我之前就常幹這種事...。

92. Who most likely are the listeners? (A) trainers who are about to start the session (B) customers sitting on the row of evacuation seats (C) guests sitting on the economy seats (D) **flight attendants at the training school**	92. 聽眾最有可能是誰? (A) 正要開始上課的訓練師們 (B) 坐在逃生排位的乘客們 (C) 坐在經濟艙的客戶們 (D) **在訓練學校的空服員們**

93. What is the purpose of mentioning the swap list? (A) **to entertain the students** (B) to make students sleepy (C) to make students vigilant (D) to meet the demand of the students	93. 提及交換清單的目的是什麼? (A) **娛樂學生們** (B) 讓學生們感到昏昏欲睡 (C) 讓學生們有警覺性 (D) 達到學生們的需求
94. What is the topic of the talk? (A) how to avoid smell the heavy jet fuel (B) how to use the swap list (C) how to stay awake (D) **continuation of the training lessons**	94. 這個談話的主題是什麼? (A) 如何避免聞到噴射機的燃料味道 (B) 如何使用交換清單 (C) 如何保持清醒 (D) **接續的訓練課程**
答案:92. D 93. A 94. D	

解析

- **第92題**,根據聽力原文的敘述,最有可能的是空服員在訓練學校上課的內容,故答案為**選項D**。
- **第93題**,教練會提到是因為想要娛樂學生或希望他們能打起精神,所以才講些無關或較能引起他們興趣的事情,故答案要選**選項A**。
- **第94題**,這篇談話的主題是接續上次訓練課程的內容,故答案為**選項D**。

Questions 95-97 refer to the following talk

We have been to four galleries and you all have demonstrated your ability to draw...now it's time that we do the analysis of the following paintings...four to be exact...feel free to comment on them...although one of the paintings could be my work...ha...but it's ok and hand in five hundred words for each...painting...the first one is a two-headed worm crawling out the apple...it's amazingly crafted...next...a horrifying scene...only a closer look can know what's going on...the third one....is a woodpecker and its back is filled with worms...that allures other birds...and the last...a muscular guy swimming in the lake...but at some angles...the leg seems amputated...how bizarre...

問題95-97請參閱下列談話

我們去過了四間藝廊，而你們都顯示了你們的繪畫技巧了...現在是時候，我們要替接下來的繪畫作評析了...實際上確實有四個...可以隨意評論它們...儘管其中有幅繪畫可能是我所繪製的...哈...但是這是ok的，還有要提交每幅繪圖各500字的報告...第一幅是從蘋果中爬出的兩頭蟲...下一幅...是一個恐怖的場景...只有近看後才能知道發生了什麼事情...第三幅...是啄木鳥而其背後佈滿了蟲子...這吸引了其他鳥類...最後一張是...一位肌肉健壯的男子在湖中游泳...但是在某些角度...腿像是截肢般...多麼奇特呀！...。

95. What is the requirement of this assignment? (A) 500 words (B) it depends (C) no longer than 1000 words (D) **2000 words**	95. 這項作業的需求是什麼? (A) 500字 (B) 視情況而定 (C) 1000 字以內 (D) **2000字**
96. Where most likely is the talk given? (A) **in a classroom** (B) at the gallery (C) at the museum (D) at the swimming pool	96. 此篇談話最有可能發生在何處? (A) **在課堂中** (B) 在藝廊 (C) 在博物館 (D) 在泳池裡

| 97. Why does the speaker find the last painting odd?
 (A) it was painted by a famous painter
 (B) it has worms on the woodpecker
 (C) because the shape of the apple
 (D) **because how the leg is perceived** | 97. 為什麼説話者覺得最後一幅畫古怪?
 (A) 由知名畫家所繪製
 (B) 有蟲在啄木鳥上頭
 (C) 因為蘋果的形狀
 (D) **因為觀看腿的方式** |

答案:95. D 96. A 97. D

- **第95題**,這題也要小心,教授有提到要交每篇500字的分析報告,然後有四項藝術品,所以別誤選了500字的選項,500*4=2000,故答案為**選項D**。
- **第96題**,這題是詢問地點,最有可能的地方是教室內,故答案為**選項A**。
- **第97題**,最後要注意的是最後一幅畫,講者為什麼會覺得怪呢,其實主要原因是腳的觀看角度,這對應到選項D,故答案為**選項D**。

1 短獨白「影子跟讀」和填空練習

2 短獨白獨立演練和詳解

3 短獨白模擬試題

Questions 98-100 refer to the following talk

Descriptions	Time
DWI/citizens	8:39 A.M.
DWI/mayor	9:45 A.M.
Train derailed	10:20 A.M.
Restaurant fire	11:35 A.M.
Note: DWI = driving while intoxicated	

Hi...I'm the host Jeremy...this event is for father-son...and all donations will go right to our charity and use as the scholarship for either single fathers and those kids who are parentless...first is the ceremony...the governor is awarding the prize to the CEO of our charity...feel free to take pictures...then we are moving on the speech given by the senator...welcome...third...we are having tea time with several homeless kids and the meal is prepared by one of the famous chefs...and also the assistant to the mayor...but the mayor is not coming due to a drunk-driving accident...fourth...we're going to take the hot air balloon...those kids are so thrilled...and is totally sponsored by one of the largest Film companies...

問題98-100請參閱下列談話

描述	時間
DWI/市民	上午8:39
DWI/市長	上午9:45
火車出軌	上午10:20
餐廳失火	上午11:35
註: DWI = driving while intoxicated	

嗨...我是主持人傑瑞米...這個活動是替「父一子」而辦的...而且所有的捐贈都會直接匯至我們的慈善會,並且充當成單親父親的孩子或那些無父母的小孩的獎學金...首先是儀式...州長會頒贈獎品給我們慈善會的執行長...可以隨意拍照...然後我們會接續進行由議長的致詞...歡迎...第三,我們會有與無家可歸的孩子一同的茶時光,然後餐點是由其中一位名廚所準備...而她同時也是市長的助理...但市長無法到場,導因於一場酒駕意外...第四...我們會搭乘熱氣球...那些小孩都會感到無比興奮...還有這全數由其中一個大型的電影公司所資助...。

試題中譯與解析

98. According to the speaker, what will the donation money be used for? (A) the film companies (B) the prize (C) the ceremony (D) **academic achievement**	98. 根據說話者,捐贈的錢會用於什麼用途? (A) 電影公司 (B) 獎品 (C) 儀式 (D) **學術成就**
99. According to the talk, who will not be attending the event? (A) the CEO (B) **the mayor** (C) the senator (D) the governor	99. 根據此篇談話,誰不會參加這場活動? (A) 執行長 (B) **市長** (C) 議員 (D) 州長

100. Look at the graph. When did the mayor get involved in a car accident? (A) 8:39 A.M. (B) **9:45 A.M.** (C) 10:20 A.M. (D) 11:35 A.M.	100. 請參考圖表。何時市長牽涉到一場車禍事件裡頭呢? (A) 上午8點39分 (B) **上午9點45分** (C) 上午10點20分 (D) 上午11點35分

答案：98. D 99. B 100. B

解析

· **第98題**，這題可以先看到聽力原文中的all donations will go right to our charity and used as the scholarship，所以是scholarship，scholarship對應到academic achievement故答案要選**選項D**。

· **第99題**，根據談話內容，不會參加的是市長，因為酒駕意外的關係，故答案為**選項B**。

· **第100題**，這題要對應到圖表的內容，很明顯可以對應到**選項B**。

國家圖書館出版品預行編目(CIP)資料

新制多益聽力題庫：短獨白,附詳盡解析/
Amanda Chou著. -- 初版. -- 新北市：倍斯特,
2020.10　面；公分. -- (考用英語系列；027)
ISBN 978-986-98079-7-5 (平裝附光碟片)

1.多益測驗

805.1895　　　　　　　　　　109014616

考用英語系列　027

新制多益聽力題庫：短獨白，附詳盡解析（MP3）

初　　版　　2020年10月
定　　價　　新台幣420元

作　　者　　Amanda Chou
出　　版　　倍斯特出版事業有限公司
發 行 人　　周瑞德
電　　話　　886-2-8245-6905
傳　　真　　886-2-2245-6398
地　　址　　23558 新北市中和區立業路83巷7號4樓
E - m a i l　　best.books.service@gmail.com
官　　網　　www.bestbookstw.com
總 編 輯　　齊心瑀
特約編輯　　陳韋佑
封面構成　　高鍾琪
內頁構成　　菩薩蠻數位文化有限公司
印　　製　　大亞彩色印刷製版股份有限公司

港澳地區總經銷　　泛華發行代理有限公司
地　　　　址　　香港新界將軍澳工業邨駿昌街7號2樓
電　　　　話　　852-2798-2323
傳　　　　真　　852-3181-3973